## DEATH BY CHERRY COBBLER

Rounding the end of the counter I'd used the night before, the light beam caught something shiny. I stopped. I ran the light over the floor. Food. Odd; I'd watched the cleaning crew scrub. I took another step and swirled the light on the floor: more food; it was red and looked like cherries.

My cobbler! Someone or something had dumped my cobbler on the floor. Shining the light straight in front of me, I screamed and jumped back. My knees weakened, making it hard to keep my balance in my high heels. I wobbled and snatched at the air with my free hand until I found the corner of the counter to help me remain vertical.

My cobbler hadn't been dumped on the floor.

It'd been used to kill Mick . . .

# COBBLERED TO DEATH

## *Rosemarie Ross*

KENSINGTON BOOKS
www.kensingtonbooks.com

First Printing: December 2019
ISBN-13: 978-1-4967-2275-1
ISBN-10: 1-4967-2275-2

ISBN-13: 978-1-4967-2276-8 (ebook)
ISBN-10: 1-4967-2276-0 (ebook)

10 9 8 7 6 5 4 3 2 1

Printed in the United States of America

With gratitude to Julie Day and Marcine Smith for seeing my writing abilities and encouraging me to pursue them.

# CHAPTER ONE

"What a perfect place to film a friendly baking competition!" I peered out an arched window. The setting sun cast shadows across the rolling hills that backdropped wide-open space for miles. Coal Castle Resort, a mansion built by a coal magnate in the Gilded Age, sat in the valley region of Pennsylvania's Pocono Mountains.

Born and raised in Chicago, I was used to seeing concrete lined with brick and mortar rather than pristine land. All the green space gave me a sense of calm. "It's peaceful here."

"Ssh."

My producer Eric Iverson's soft warning pulled me from my thoughts, and my eyes from the window.

Index finger to his lips, he glanced around the small seating area of the resort's coffee shop, Castle Grounds, where we occupied two chairs at a table for four. Leaning closer, he whispered, "Remember, Courtney Archer is the farmer's daughter. Which means you wouldn't seem surprised by the peaceful feeling the great outdoors instills. Watch what you say, or at least check your surprised tone."

My shoulders sagged. I started to rebut when Eric held up a halting hand.

"It's in your contract to play the part."

"I know." Eric, always the good producer and friend, was only trying to protect me and my career. The truth of the matter was, it was the only part of my job I didn't like, keeping my background a secret. A secret that made me uncomfortable because it was, well, a lie. The falsehood I lived had begun to wear on me. With my thirtieth birthday in sight, I regretted conceding to this charade. Or maybe I just wanted more out of my career?

After graduation from culinary school, where I'd focused on fruit and vegetable carving, I had no luck landing a job in my chosen field, so I took the first job offer that came my way, a food demonstrator at a regional chain of grocery stores aptly called Farmers Market. Making my rounds to a different location each week, I did an hour demonstration creating easy and nutritious meals from the items in their store ad.

That is where Eric discovered me, ponytailed and clad in a red-gingham shirt and jeans. He too had recently graduated from college and was hungry to start his communications career. He talked me into filming an audition tape for a cooking show. He drew on his farming background and my current persona, dubbing the show *Cooking with the Farmer's Daughter*, and began pitching the show to various networks.

At the time, I didn't think much about the fact

that I wasn't a farmer's daughter. My father, a retired pediatrician, donates his time to Doctors Without Borders, with my mother along for the ride because it's what she does: support my dad's endeavors.

To both our delight, a national cooking network needed to fill a niche for their rural viewers and offered us the show. I was ecstatic to use my culinary degree and work in my food carvings. Eric was over the moon to be a producer. Being young and new to television programming, we agreed to all their terms, which included the farmer's daughter persona. Something I thought only included hair and wardrobe. Boy, was I wrong! The ratings blew up like a mislatched lid on a pressure cooker. Viewer correspondence indicated they believed the show's title was my background. The network ran with it, despite my protests. Thank goodness, Eric promised to help me field correspondence or viewer questions because he'd grown up on a farm.

To be clear, I love the viewers, not the lie created by my network. They insisted I close down all my personal social media sites when they received the approval ratings for our show. Most of my accounts were set to private, so I didn't leave much of a digital footprint. Nothing incriminating anyway, if anyone decided to Google my fairly common name. The network's public relations staff handled all interview questions for magazines or blogs concerning my farming background, along with managing the social media site for our show. Because I have no line of products or a cookbook to sell, there is no need for public appearances, which helped to safeguard the farm girl persona. Now, with three on-location tap-ings of my show in front of live audiences, I was ap-prehensive. And so, obviously, was Eric.

I sighed and looked around the room. An older gentleman, the only other occupant in the area, sat one table over, scouring his newspaper. "I don't think anyone heard me. Besides, would it really hurt the show if people found out I'm not a farmer's daughter? I mean, they watch it for the food and recipes, right?" I'd lowered my voice.

"Yes, it could hurt the show's ratings." Eric's index finger air-punctuated his statement, then waggled in warning. "Be careful what you say. Your show is the reason you are here." Eric and his hand quit talking as he took a sip of his coffee and scanned the room again.

The man reading the paper shifted in his chair. Leaning back, he snapped the paper erect, holding it in midair. It was obvious he was engrossed in the news, not our conversation. Why else would anyone choose to hold a paper in that position?

"True." I heaved a heavy sigh. "It's just . . ." My eyes searched Eric's.

He shrugged. "After five years, the show has grown stale for me too. But you've hooked your viewers hook, line and sinker with your catchphrase."

I gave Eric a half-hearted smile.

"Courtney, don't look so sad." He leaned forward, found my hand and squeezed it. "Having people like you is not a bad thing."

"I know. I just wish the network would let me show-case my food designing abilities."

Eric quirked a brow. "There isn't much demand

for a watermelon rind carved into the shape of a wishing well and filled with fruit flowers, or salad ingredients arranged in a beautiful kaleidoscope pattern on a working farm. Believe me, I know. It's hard work that requires hearty sustenance."

I sighed. I'd heard it all before. "I just feel pigeonholed."

"Still?" Surprise flashed in Eric's blue eyes. "Even with this wonderful opportunity? I worked hard to get your name to the right people, and this could lead to . . ."

"A spot on a show with an ensemble cast where I could actually use my skills." I smiled at Eric to let him know I did appreciate his efforts to move my career along before taking a sip of my coffee. Being offered a spot as host on a new baking competition program, *The American Baking Battle,* was a wonderful opportunity. The only drawback? The show expected me to be the farmer's daughter.

One of a couple of reasons I'd been reluctant to sign on. Reality television, with its manufactured drama, wasn't my batch of brownies. I reconsidered when I read the script. This competition program injected civility into every aspect of the show: no temper tantrums, no backstabbing and no sabotage to your fellow competitors. Instead, encouragement to all and by all was, well, encouraged.

I snickered at my own thought. A positive competition I could go for because cooking should be fun. Besides, if the first season was a hit, I'd be asked back. It would give me variety and, just maybe, I could talk the director or producer into featuring some baking using food designs and letting me demonstrate them to the contestants. Eventually, I'd like to design a knife set and write cookbooks to instruct all cooks in the art of carving food into objects.

"You're right. It is a wonderful opportunity for my career. I'm still not sure about the humor. I don't think I can pull off the corny jokes." Puns and plays on words riddled the script.

"I don't think the humor is a problem. You have a wonderful sense of humor and a great on-camera presence. You underestimate yourself."

Eric's blue eyes shone with kindness. He was a terrific friend to have in your corner. I gave him a smile and squeezed his hand to show my appreciation before breaking contact.

The rattle of a newspaper page turning filled the silence of the room.

"I wonder where everyone is?" Eric checked his watch. "Our itinerary said to report to the coffee shop for a cast meeting at seven, followed by a social mingle with the contestants at eight."

I shrugged. Eric had a skewed sense of punctuality. He arrived fifteen minutes early and felt those who showed up on time were late. "They'll be here. We're early. Besides, the mansion is huge. Maybe we're not in the right coffee shop, or everyone else got to explore their surroundings." I refrained from adding *like I wanted to*.

Coal Castle Resort was once the private home of Henry Cole. It housed his family and an impressive guest list of visitors, from dukes and duchesses to John D. Rockefeller. Four stories high, the castle boasted three turrets, one of which surrounds the bedroom in my guest suite.

The massive stone structure had taken two years to build. A garden of hybrid and imported flowers encircled the structure in a moatlike fashion. Mr. Cole made his fortune in the mining business but dabbled in inventions, holding many patents to gadgets that never found a home in American culture. His vast workshop, a mere quarter of a mile from the castle and tucked into a wooded area, would be repurposed as the set of the cooking competition.

I knew a lot about my current location. I'd done my due diligence before our arrival.

"Hello. Are y'all with the cooking show?"

The soft Southern drawl drew me from my memorized castle trivia. I turned my attention to the direction of the voice. A woman glided toward us with posture to rival any beauty contestant. Her long, blond hair waved down to her shoulders and cascaded down her back. She wore a soft denim miniskirt, a blue-plaid blouse and cowgirl boots. She'd accessorized her ensemble with a bright smile.

Shannon Collins, host of *Southern Comfort Foods*, was one of the two network stars hired to judge our show. Right now, she looked like a farmer's daughter. I did not. I'd styled my long hair into a chignon and had chosen a soft pink designer dress to accentuate my fair complexion and black hair. I'd slipped on a pair of taupe heels to add the illusion of length to my legs. Now, I wondered if I should have dressed in character.

Eric stood. "Yes, we are." He motioned for me to stand.

I complied and held out my hand for a shake.

"Nice to meet you." The words barely exited my mouth when I was wrapped into a tight hug.

"It's nice to meet you too. I've binge-watched your show for a week. I love it. Love it! Especially your catchphrase. It's so much better than mine." Shannon held me out at arm's length and rolled her eyes. "Like all Southern cooks holler out their door, 'Supper's on!' "

Her expression and admission made me smile. "Thank you. I'm glad you like my show."

"I just know we'll become fast friends. We have so much in common."

Shannon's entire face radiated hope. Although I doubted we had much in common, something about her made me want to be her friend. I flashed her a broad smile. "I hope so! I enjoy your show very much."

Pride beamed from Shannon's features. "I try very hard to make it authentic. I want to do justice to my heritage."

Shannon's words poked at my conscience. Did she know my real background? Or was my own guilt making me paranoid?

Eric cleared his throat and offered his hand to Shannon. To his surprise, Shannon greeted him in the same manner she had me. A rush of color brightened his face, and after a little stammering, he offered her a chair, which she graciously accepted.

"I'm a little early. Isn't this place a dream, and a little overwhelming?" Shannon nodded to a large stone fireplace that covered most of a wall.

"I haven't had a chance to explore it much." Before I could spew out any trivia on the Coal Castle Resort, hands clapped together.

"Hello, everyone! I'm Brenden Hall, the director and producer of the show."

I watched a trio of men approach us. With Brenden's announcement, the man at the other table must have realized this might be business. He slid back his chair but kept his nose in the paper while sidling past the group and exiting the room.

We all stood and received Brenden's handshake.

"This is Harrison Canfield, host of *At Home Gourmet*. He is Shannon's male counterpart for judging." Brenden held his hand in front of a distinguished gentleman whose head of snow-white hair put him in the silver fox category.

"And Skylar Daily, host of *Grocery Store Gambit*."

Skylar flashed an ultrawhite smile, mocked holding a microphone and filled the space with his soothing baritone. "On your mark, get set, get ready to make a hit television show."

While we all laughed at his antics, he ran his fingers over his slicked-back hair before gliding his hands down his tailored suit. I drank in his image. Brown hair, blue eyes, bright smile, designer suit and wingtips. Not only was my cohost attractive, we were cut from the same cloth in our apparel choice. I no longer felt overdressed for the evening.

Once our round of introductions and show recaps died down, Brenden handed out the list of our job duties. "Everyone needs to note that in addition to filming our show, Courtney has three live filmings of her show lined up."

"I thought we nixed any extras," a booming voice called from across the room.

Wide shoulders stretched a white T-shirt to its limits, blue jeans hugged muscular thighs as Mr.-Tall-Dark-and-Hunky stalked across the room. A shorter, stockier man trailed behind him.

My heart fluttered. Shannon's and my intakes of breath squeaked at the same time.

"Oh. My. Gravy," I whispered. My catchphrase on the show to describe something delectable bled over into my daily vocabulary.

"I'll say." Shannon squeezed my arm. "If I were single, he could frost my cake any day." Shannon and I shared a schoolgirl giggle, cementing both of our wishes to become fast friends.

"No, we didn't agree." Brenden's sharp tone drew me out of my silliness. "Courtney is filming a few episodes of her show on location," he said.

Dark brown eyes assessed Brenden. "We need an amendment to our contract if you want us to provide security outside the resort."

He was security. That explained the physique. I could go for my very own bodyguard.

"I don't think that is necessary. We are taping in one of the hotel conference rooms and busing in the audience."

What was Eric saying? I shot him a look. If this bundle of muscle wanted to protect me, who were we to argue?

The shorter man flicked his finger across a tablet. "Her fan base is mostly middle-aged women. Not much threat there."

"Exactly." Brenden threw his hands into the air. Eric nodded his agreement.

I scowled, just a little offended not only for myself and my safety but for middle-aged women in general.

Before anyone could make a rebuttal, Brenden said, "Everyone, this is Drake Nolan, former FBI and owner of Nolan Security, and his next in charge, Travis Taylor."

A series of handshakes and hellos followed. Drake's hand lingered on mine while he assessed me. Could I be sparking his interest?

He turned to Travis. "You're sure her fan base is middle-aged women?"

My hope deflated like punched-down bread dough. Not interest, business.

"Yes." Travis glanced down at the tablet. "You never know, though." Travis raised his eyes and swept his gaze across the group. "Danger lurks all around."

Drake broke our contact and turned to Travis. "And it is our business to keep everything secure. We'll have to coordinate the security detail with the hotel on days they tape her show. It may mean more manpower or an adjustment to our schedules." He jerked his head to the corner of the room.

Travis ignored my outstretched hand and followed his boss to a table.

"I wanted us to gather here so we can walk into the ballroom together. You know, a big entrance for the stars of the show." Brenden smiled and motioned for us to follow him. In the elevator to the ballroom, Brenden briefed us on what to expect tomorrow, the first day of filming. A woman holding a clipboard waited in front of the closed ballroom doors.

"Everyone, this is my personal assistant, Kinzy Hummel."

She flashed a brief smile our way.

"Are they filming?"

She nodded.

Brenden turned to us. "We will introduce you one by one. Of course, the contestants know who you are, but we may use this footage for advertising or voice-overs on the first show. Don't worry about hair, makeup or wardrobe. If the footage is used, it will be bits and bytes. No formal, individual introductions will be made. The diverse group of six male and six female contestants are to mingle with you and introduce themselves to get over any fangirl or fanboy emotions. We want everyone to act like a happy family on camera. We can't do that if we don't know and care about one another."

Once our entrances were made, I snagged a drink from a passing waiter, smiled and nodded hello to several contestants who'd locked eyes with me. Shannon, Harrison, Skylar and I had agreed to fan out in different directions. The contestants smiled and awkwardly danced from foot to foot. No one approached us.

"Enough." Brenden clapped his hands. "We are one big happy family. Mingle."

Brenden's instructions earned an eye roll from a twentysomething blond girl. When her eyes met mine, I quirked a brow. Her skin pinked. She flashed me an innocent smile that I didn't buy. She wasn't here to make nice. She was here to win. I was sure of it.

I cringed inside, thinking the worst about someone I didn't know. Maybe it was Brenden's choice of words she didn't like. Perhaps her family wasn't big or happy. Still, I felt something was amiss with this contestant and hoped to dispel the feeling when she approached me and we conversed.

Right now, she'd singled out Harrison. Unlike the other hesitant contestants, she cut a straight path to him. She paused briefly when an older gentleman, who looked familiar, caught her arm. Although his features looked pleasant while he spoke, she scowled, jerked her arm away and continued walking toward Harrison. The gentleman followed on her heels.

Hmmm . . .

I glanced around. Shannon and Skylar each had one person approach them. Most of the contestants conversed with one another. They all probably wanted one-on-one time rather than a group conversation. No one headed my way, so I worked my way through the room until I was within earshot of Harrison and his groupies. They had pushed off to the edge of the room farthest from the camera. I stopped a few feet away and pretended I was waiting for someone to approach me.

Technically, I was waiting for someone to approach me. A quick scan of the baking contestants revealed I was still the hot potato in the group; no one wanted to be caught with me.

I angled my body to look approachable to the bakers, yet able to keep an eye on the trio teetering on the edge of the gathering. All three wore fake smiles. Those smiles belied a terse conversation. I couldn't catch the words, but their hostile tones drifted my way.

I inched closer. My movement caught Harrison's eye. He waved me into the group with jerky motions.

"Courtney, have you met Tabitha Miller and . . ."

"Mick Henderson," the older gentleman interrupted Harrison.

In the instant it took him to turn my way, I recognized the back of his head. The paper reader.

"Nice to meet you." I shook Tabitha's hand before turning to Mick.

As soon as his hand enveloped mine, one corner of his mouth curled into a lopsided smirk while one brow twitched into a slight quirk.

He'd been eavesdropping, not reading the paper. He'd heard Eric's and my conversation. I was sure of it.

"It was nice to have met you." Harrison's voice held an edge. "I'll be off to mingle with the others. Best of luck to you both."

Tabitha frowned, and threw Mick a steely look. "See what you've done." She stormed after Harrison before Mick had a chance to respond.

"Is there a problem?" I asked.

Mick shrugged and smiled. "Just a friendly greeting. Maybe you're not the only person here with a secret to hide." His eyes darkened and his grin sent a chill down my spine.

I drew a deep breath. Was he an extortionist trying to blackmail a win? Were he and Tabitha in this together? Is that why they'd cornered Harrison? Surely he knew I wasn't a judge and he couldn't blackmail me into a win. Or was it something else? He wanted his own cooking show and thought if he leaked the truth about my background and the fact that I felt stymied on my current show, it would open an opportunity for him? Which seemed far-fetched because it wasn't how the networks worked, but did Mick know that?

"Hello."

My body jerked. I hadn't heard anyone approach. I turned my attention to a tall, sturdy woman. White hair curled around her face. She wore red, plastic-framed glasses that complemented her fair skin and brought out the pink in her cheeks.

"I'm Barb Tornquist, and a huge fan of your show. It takes me back to my childhood, when I lived on a farm. I too am a farmer's daughter." Her faced beamed with pride.

Mick snorted, then chuckled. I flashed him a narrow-eyed threat before turning my full attention to Barb, whose focus was on Mick, her brows drawn in confusion.

"Well, being a city boy myself, I'll have nothing to add to this conversation. I'll leave you two to talk shop." Mick patted my shoulder. As he passed by me, he angled in and whispered, "Farmer's daughter indeed. Don't worry, your secret is safe with me."

I knew it wasn't.

# CHAPTER TWO

The first day of shooting dawned bright and early. The hosts' and judges' instructions stated to report to the second floor of the workshop-turned-baking-battle set that had been converted into makeup and wardrobe, no later than six in the morning.

Not heeding Eric's warning to rise before five and arrive at the set by five thirty, it was five forty-five when I'd pulled on a yoga outfit and hurried to the lobby. I'd studied the hotel exit map and knew the coffee shop had a door leading to a path that wound its way to the workshop. The wide, stone path was deserted. I glanced around for Harrison, Shannon or Skylar. No one in sight.

Odd, because I was on time. I'd hoped I'd run into one of my coworkers for the morning walk. I needed a distraction. Mick's actions troubled my mind. Last night, I'd considered every angle I could think of on why he'd eavesdrop on Eric's and my conversation, which he did under the guise of reading the paper, or anyone else involved in the show's conversation either. All angles pointed to blackmail to win the competition.

It was a possibility his overhearing my and Eric's conversation might have been a lucky coincidence. Unlike his terse conversation with Harrison, which had had a personal tone. Did Mick feel Harrison owed him something? Or did he know damaging information about him? I had a strong feeling there was a threat involved in that conversation. Which made sense, because Harrison was a judge, and civil show or not, all competitors wanted to win the contest and the prize. I wasn't a judge, so he'd have nothing to gain by spilling my secret. However, if he told the right people that Eric and I thought *Cooking with the Farmer's Daughter* was getting stale, he could hurt both our careers. I cringed at the thought.

Then again, my guilt over my background misconception and being bored with the show that started my career might have me jumping to conclusions to keep my mind off my nerves at shooting the baking battle. I needed to focus on today and the show. I pushed my musings aside.

The weekly episodes for my cooking show were shot once a month in a two-day time frame. Although I lived in the city where my show was filmed, I wouldn't have to, because I only needed to be on set for one week each month. The remaining weeks were spent planning the month's episode themes and recipes, which I did via email and Skype from my home office. I also used the time to practice the recipes in our agreed upon menu. We no longer rehearsed because the set never changed, and we'd blocked and marked all the camera angles. If I stood on the tape mark on the floor, didn't flub my lines or drop the food, filming went fast.

To save expense for the baking battle, Brenden had crew members stand in for the cohosts and judges to block and mark the camera angles. I'd been told my tape was green, Shannon's pink, Skylar's blue and Harrison's plain. The show was filmed on location, and to keep travel expenses at a minimum, all ten episodes would be filmed in twelve days, which included before and after interviews with the contestants, as well as extra scenes with the judges and the cohosts introducing each show. The contestants had been told the first challenges for each episode, so they could practice and hone their skills on those recipes. The second and third challenges, as time progressed, were a surprise to show their true baking skills.

I knew the filming days would be long and grueling at first because the contestants weren't used to being filmed. After the first few days and eliminations, the filming would go smoother. Until that time, I needed to remain patient and calm.

I drew a deep breath and let nature soothe me. Summer grass and fragrant flowers with a hint of barnyard tickled my nose. A definite change compared to my usual morning scents: bus exhaust or garbage on the curb. I had to admit the country air was a nice change of pace, and the serene setting complemented the civility of the show.

The path rounded before slicing through a grove of dense trees. The forest, albeit small, blocked the sun, making the air cooler and dank with the scent of moist soil. A few more steps and the workshop came into view. From this vantage point, I could see two other paths leading to the area. My path led to the back of the building. My coworkers must have chosen the paths less traveled, or maybe I had?

Stonework matching the castle crept halfway up the sides of the workshop. Large panes of windows lined the upper edge and red-tile shingles topped it off. The framework reminded me of a carriage house, a large carriage house.

The building bustled with activity. Crew hands pulled thick electrical cords to large generators. Utility terrain vehicles purred across the lawn and paths except for the one headed, full speed, straight at me.

I stopped walking and hopped into the grass along the edge of the walkway.

Travis continued his head-on path toward me. Unfazed by his second-in-charge's actions, Drake, seated on the passenger side, continued his phone conversation. He flashed a smile and a saluted wave my way. Travis stopped the four-passenger UTV mere inches away from me.

"Good morning." I smiled from ear to ear.

Travis frowned. "What are you doing on this path?"

"Reporting to work." I pointed to the workshop-turned-baking-show-set.

The corners of his lips drew down more deeply, alerting me that I'd said the wrong thing.

"Good morning, Courtney." Drake pocketed his phone. His bright features, a contrast to Travis's, made me wonder if this was a good-cop, bad-cop thing.

"Good morning." I looked past Travis and hoped neither noticed the little giggle at the end of my greeting. "Have I done something wrong?"

"This path is off-limits." Drake tapped his tablet and held it out for my viewing. "Please stay on path one or two." He traced the Google map image with his finger. "Path three is closed."

"Sorry." I drew my brows together. "I didn't see a sign."

"There isn't one," Travis snapped. "All the information was in the safety instructions left in your room. Didn't you read them?"

Um . . . obviously not. I gave my head a small shake. I didn't appreciate Travis's scolding tone.

"Well, read them. Your safety may depend upon it." His index finger pointed at my chest.

Put off by his tone and body language, I crossed my arms over my chest. "Really? Is there something going on I don't know about? I mean, you were overly concerned about our safety last night too. If someone has a stalker or something, you should tell the rest of us." My tone was edged with annoyance.

"No, nothing like that." Drake shot Travis a warning look before turning his dazzling smile on me. "Travis takes his job seriously, that's all. Please stay on path one or two. Have a great day."

Travis hit the pedal and whizzed away before I could say goodbye or, in Travis's case, good riddance.

Still annoyed, I watched them enter the trees. Even though Drake had explained, Travis seemed a little too intense about security for our show. Unless there was something Security was worried about. Our world had changed. Violent incidents happened often, and Travis was hired to keep us secure. Even though I didn't care for his bedside manner, his dedication to our safety should bring me peace of mind. Yet it didn't.

At least now, I knew why I hadn't run into anyone else on my way to hair and makeup.

Yikes!

I brought my hands to my face. I'd just conversed with Drake in my wake-up hair and face. My heart drooped. So much for trying to spark his interest.

I hurried to the building and rounded the side to the front entry. I slipped inside the heavy wooden door and stepped into a large, open room equipped with twelve kitchen workstations.

Although it was only May, the pilot show would air from late June through July, so the producers had decided on a patriotic theme. Pleated American flag bunting wrapped around the walls. Brand-new red mixers stood proudly on the blue workstation countertops.

I scanned the room locating the staircase. Once on the second floor, I entered the door marked "Makeup and Wardrobe."

"Good morning, Courtney." Shannon sat bright-eyed, sipping coffee with her blond hair twisted around large hot curlers, the pins sticking out haphazardly.

"'Morning." I took the makeup chair next to hers.

"I looked for you but must have missed you on the path." Shannon twisted her chair around to face me. "Maybe we can coordinate tomorrow."

A stylist snapped a cape around my neck.

"Good idea." It'd keep me out of trouble with Security.

"Did you grab breakfast?" Shannon popped the last bite of a slice of bacon into her mouth.

"No, I don't usually eat breakfast."

Shannon threw me a skeptical look. "Really? I thought all good country girls ate a hearty breakfast. After all, you've done several episodes on the importance of a hearty breakfast before you start your busy day."

Oops. My heartbeat drummed in my ears loud enough that I was sure Shannon could hear it too. What should I say to that? "Um . . . I meant, I don't usually eat breakfast until later in the morning."

It wasn't entirely a lie. I did eat brunch on Sundays.

"Well, you should have something." Shannon took a piece of toast slathered with peanut butter from her plate and offered it to me.

Smiling, I accepted it. "Thank you." I took a nibble, which tasted very good, so I bit off a generous mouthful.

While the stylists went to work on our hair, Shannon glanced at me out of the corner of her eye. "So, what do you think of my cojudge?"

Had she noticed the terse exchange that had taken place last night too?

Before I answered, she continued. "He's a little standoffish, don't you think? I tried to make conversation with him last night and it fell flat. I'm afraid I'm out of my league. I saw you talking to him. Did you get that vibe?" Worry was folded into her drawl.

"I only spoke with him briefly. He seemed . . ." I didn't want to say "angry" or "worried."

"Stuffy?"

I laughed. "Maybe, a little."

"I know they chose us for a contrast, fancy chef and down-home cook. I just hope it films well. You of all people know what I mean, right?"

I swallowed hard and gave her a weak smile. This was the type of conversation that made me uncomfortable. Somehow, I had to make the network understand and get this ridiculous clause out of my contract.

Lucky for me, Harrison chose this moment to enter the room.

"Good morning!"

Shannon's cheerful drawl drew his eyes to her, then me. Harrison nodded a greeting and kept walking to the chair farthest away from us. Shannon shot me a perturbed look.

I picked up the conversation. "Are you looking forward to filming today, Harrison?"

"Work is work." Harrison fished a magazine, *The Gourmet Cook*, from his attaché and stuck his nose into it.

I got the hint. Not quite the happy family the director had described. Harrison didn't plan to fraternize. Or was it something else? Something to do with Mick?

"Good morning. Sorry I'm late." A disheveled man entered the room, his palms together as if in prayer. "I overslept. Won't happen again."

He slipped into the vacant chair next to mine.

"Skylar?" I gasped.

"Who else would it be?"

I studied Skylar through the mirror. "Sorry; you look so different." His hair, free of styling product, hung over his ears. His bangs pushed to the side with a slight flip up. Dark stubble outlined his jaw and dotted his cheeks.

A hearty laugh boomed through the small space. "This is the real me. I don't wear my hair slicked back unless I'm on television. Nor do I shave every day. Keeps me incognito."

His words earned a glance and eye roll from Harrison. "Like you don't want the attention and admiration."

"What? No!" Skylar turned in the swivel chair to face Harrison.

With a huffed sigh, Harrison laid his magazine in his lap and took a turn looking at each of us. "Of course you do. Your small shows need the ratings bump that hosting or judging this competition show will provide. Not one of you is a trained professional. I was asked to host on reputation alone." He leveled his words with a look and lifted his magazine.

Anger surged through me. Harrison's assumption wasn't true. I'd been to culinary school. I was a trained professional. I had to purse my lips, hard, to keep from spouting off.

Skylar swiveled toward me and Shannon and mouthed, *Can you believe this guy?* The apple of his cheeks as dark as the skin of a Red Delicious.

We shook our heads. The remaining time in hair and makeup was tense to say the least.

Harrison's assessment of us wasn't true. We'd all been chosen for this show for a reason. Harrison, the most popular chef on television, owned and operated high-end restaurants in major cities across America. He knew his stuff about technical cooking. Shannon had turned being an amateur cook into a cooking empire by relying on her grandmothers' and great-grandmothers' tried-and-true recipes. Although I didn't use my technical training on my show, I did prepare wholesome meals with organic meat, veggies and fruits. Skylar had the only noncooking role. Attractive and personable, he was here to draw female viewers who were more interested in him than cooking. Once my anger simmered down, I wondered if Harrison's ego dictated his attitude toward us. Or was it something else? I'd felt a sting of fear about my career with Mick's innuendos. After witnessing the tense conversation last night, maybe Harrison was worried or scared. Something definitely was going on between him, Mick and Tabitha.

I looked at my fellow cast mates. Each of their expressions held some level of annoyance. Our first day on the show wasn't off to a good, or civilized, start.

Finally, Kinzy came and escorted us to the set. It felt nice to breathe in untempered air. I pasted a smile to my face and noted Shannon's wide smile didn't hold the usual sparkle of welcome. Neither Skylar nor Harrison attempted to look pleasant as we all trudged down the stairs.

I cringed inside. Our attitudes would probably be in direct opposition to the excitement shining from the contestants' faces, which wasn't fair to them. I assumed their nerves and hope bubbled together, giving them high spirits ready to boil over. That thought lifted my own mood. I replaced my forced smile with a genuine one. No matter what happened upstairs, I needed to maintain a positive outlook for the contestants. They felt enough pressure trying to vie for the monetary prize; they didn't need bad vibes from me or anyone else.

We were ushered to our tape marks in front of the workstations. The contestants stood behind their counters. I'd expected to see happy. I was wrong. Their dour expressions outdid Harrison's and Skylar's, especially Tabitha and Mick.

The two people who shouldn't, shared a work area. Tabitha, blond hair in a high ponytail, formed a canister blockade, making a line she expected Mick not to cross. Mick kept nudging them her way, garnering a lethal, narrow-eyed stare for his efforts.

"Stop." The word hissed through Tabitha's clenched teeth.

Mick flashed her a smug smile. "They are in my way."

"I can't work like this," Tabitha blurted out toward the director. "I want to share a workstation with someone else." She turned to Mick. "Anyone else." Then she snapped a tea towel against the countertop and paced in the aisle between the workstations.

Mick's expression morphed into innocence. Something I guessed he hadn't been in years. He held up his hands, palms out.

Exasperation pinched Brenden's features. He headed toward the workstation amid the grumblings of the other contestants about not trading places. He stopped Tabitha's pacing and talked to her in hushed tones. He didn't stop the hateful looks she cast in Mick's direction.

"Harrison, Courtney, what do you think? Should I trade spaces with someone? Maybe be in the front row for more camera time?" Mick voiced his questions loud and clear. The murmuring stopped in time for most of the contestants to see him wink our way, including Tabitha.

"That's it. This contest is rigged. He knows a judge and a cohost." Tabitha jerked her head in our direction. "I saw him talking with them last night. I'm sure they were creating a plan for him to win." She pointed at Mick. Her head swiveled to all the other contestants. "This is not fair."

Her outburst created a small roar throughout the set. I turned to Harrison, who glowered in Mick's direction.

"I don't know him." I said the words out loud, but I was not even sure Shannon or Skylar could hear me over the commotion.

A shrill whistle cut through the room and stung my ear. I turned to see Skylar, thumb and pinkie in mouth, blasting a whistle to get everyone's attention. His action versus his *GQ* appearance dripped with irony. It was effective. The roar dimmed. After another whistle, silence ensued.

Tabitha, fists to hips, stared down Brenden. "I am sure they know each other, which could result in favoritism. I want Security to do a thorough background check to see what past connections they have."

"We did background checks."

Before Brenden could finish, Tabitha interjected. "I said thorough. Not the topical ones you do for employment that show whether you're a felon or have bad credit." She cast a narrow-eyed glare toward Mick before letting it rest on Brenden. "If you don't do it, I'll contact the press."

Brenden pursed his lips. "Fine. We'll take five." He threw his hands in the air. "Someone find Drake."

I shot a look in Mick's direction. He no longer looked like an average, middle-aged man with graying hair and a thickening waistline. His curled lips and quirked brow gave him a menacing, and pleased, look.

He was up to something. I didn't know what. I did know I had no ties to him. I turned to say as much to Harrison, my words dying on my taste buds. My eyes widened. Harrison's coloring matched my kitchen walls, stark eggshell. His reaction solidified my suspicions. Harrison had something to hide. Mick knew what it was. Maybe Tabitha too. Which would explain the animosity between Mick and Tabitha. Whatever it was, it must be something big, life-changing if discovered. Harrison's apparent distress made me wonder exactly what caused this reaction. Mick and Tabitha's bickering, Mick's innuendos or the thorough background check?

# CHAPTER THREE

I didn't have time to wonder long. Harrison's body started to shake.

Afraid he was going into shock, I placed a hand on his shoulder. "Do you need to sit down?"

His eyes, round with fear, seemed to see something other than me. He managed to shake his head. "No." He cleared his throat and blinked. The action brought him back to his senses. Anger burned the fear from his eyes and blazed his cheeks with red. He brushed my hand from his shoulder and stalked to Brenden and Tabitha. "I passed the background check and have the letter from the show to prove it." Outrage edged his words.

"Well, as Tabitha said, those were for financial and felon information, not personal relationships with the contestants." The director winced. "A possible oversight on my part."

Harrison glared at Tabitha, then at Mick.

Mick flashed him a smug smile and a finger wave.

Hatred morphed onto Harrison's features. He

fisted his hands and took a step toward Mick's workstation.

I held my breath. I glanced at Shannon and Skylar. By their expressions, they shared my disbelief.

"What is going on here?" Drake entered the room in long strides. Travis jogged a little to keep up.

"They know each other." Tabitha spat out the words while pointing to the men. "I know it."

"You have proof?" Drake asked, voice calm and smooth. And dreamy.

"Well . . ." Tabitha let her arms drop to her sides. Her body language screamed resolve, yet her eyes darted from Harrison to Mick and held a flicker of emotion. Contemplation, maybe? "It just seems like it to me. We all want a fair chance at winning the prize, right?" She cranked her neck and nodded at the other contestants.

Picking up on her cue, murmured affirmations filled the air.

"What do you want me to do about this?" Drake addressed Brenden while putting himself between the two men. Harrison relaxed his hands.

Brenden's sigh cut through the room. "Recheck their backgrounds for personal connections, hometowns, schooling, former employment."

"I am not signing another background check form." Lifting his chin, Harrison walked back to the front and, to my surprise, nudged himself between me and Shannon. Now he wanted to be friends?

Drake rubbed his chin with his forefinger and thumb. "We can use the first authorization."

Shannon and I turned in unison at Harrison's gasp.

"See." Tabitha picked up on Harrison's inadvertent response. "They do know each other."

"Okay, okay." Brenden held up his hands. "Drake will start more thorough background checks. While he is doing that, we will start filming."

"How fair is that?" Tabitha blurted out. "If they are in cahoots, Mick will win for sure."

"Or you could both lose." Harrison stepped forward and addressed the group. "You all need to know that I am a professional. I will be judging you on your cooking abilities." He turned to the director. "I will be in my dressing room, talking to my agent."

Brenden's eyes widened. He started to follow Harrison, then stopped. He checked his watch. "We will delay filming for two hours. Drake, come with me."

A collective groan bounced through the room. "Thanks a lot, you two," Barb said, ripping off her apron and throwing it across the workstation.

"Hey, don't be mad at me," Tabitha yelled. "I spoke up for all of us."

"Well, who died and left you boss?" a stout man with billy goat chin whiskers asked in a heavily French-flavored accent.

If memory served, he was a Cajun barbecue cook-off winner from Louisiana. Tabitha shot him a narrow-eyed glare he met with a shrug. Before anyone else responded, Kinzy began ushering them out of the kitchenettes. "We'll all go wait in the resort lobby."

"What are we supposed to do?" Shannon drawled. "I mean, do they want us to mess up our hair, makeup and wardrobe?"

Lips pursed, Skylar raised his palms and shrugged.

"Good question." I fished my phone from my pocket,

ready to call Eric. Before I had a chance, Kinzy bustled back into the room. "Ms. Collins, you may relax
in the dressing room. Mr. Dailey and Miss Archer,
please follow me. We'll film the opening of the series."

"See you later." Shannon finger waved.

Skylar and I were led to a large firepit between the
castle and the workshop, where two cameramen and
Brenden waited. Hanging from an iron hook over a
fake fire was a black, cast-iron pot.

"What gives with the witch's cauldron? We're in
Pennsylvania, not Massachusetts." I smiled at my own
reference.

Brenden drew his brows together. "That is a Dutch
oven."

Skylar's laughter tinkled around me. "Good one,
Courtney. No wonder they hired you; you have the
same type of humor as the writers."

Brenden smiled and rolled his eyes. "For a minute
there, I thought you were serious."

I smiled and shrugged my shoulders.

After several run-throughs and lighting adjust-
ments, Brenden hollered, "Action."

Skylar, standing to my left so they could shoot his
best side, started. "Welcome to *The American Baking
Battle*, where twelve contestants will vie to win a cash
prize of twenty-five thousand dollars."

"Keeping to our colonial roots," I smiled into the
camera and waved a hand at the Dutch oven on the
hook, "the contestants must use cast-iron cookware
to prepare their challenges."

Skylar arched a brow and panned to the camera.
"An American baking battle using a Dutch oven?"

Shrugging, I kept my eyes on the camera and flashed an innocent look. "Stay with us and see if our cast irons out their culinary imperfections to take home the prize."

"Cut, perfect," Brenden yelled.

I stifled a yawn. Not only had filming started late, we'd had several technical delays. One oven and two kitchen appliances didn't work. The contestants grew restless while the crew switched out the broken items. Most of them kept to themselves except Mick. He left his station to converse with other people. I kept a tired eye on him. One time he caught me looking and mimed locking his lips and throwing away the key. Annoyance washed through me with his action. Mick was a piece of work, but smart. His antics happened off camera. When the cameras rolled, he was Mr. Congeniality. All the contestants were.

The first challenge went well. Of course, they'd known what it was and had practiced it at least once at home. Today's surprise baking challenge was chosen by Shannon: cherry cobbler infused with lavender.

I'd smiled when I heard the challenge because cherry cobbler prepared in a cast-iron fry pan was what I'd be preparing at my first on-location filming tomorrow. Now, after a fourteen-hour day, I wished I wasn't such a perfectionist about my final product. I liked to prepare the recipe a day ahead, so the end example looked mouth-watering. Plus, it helped me get my timing for how long I could spend on a certain preparation task. I wanted to make sure I could complete the recipe with as few retakes as possible. The easiest way to lose a crowd's interest was repeating the same task. Something I learned in my early demonstration days with the grocery store chain.

When the judges had tasted and critiqued the last of the cherry cobblers, Skylar and I joined them, toes on the appropriate tape mark, in the front of the room. I'd been given a slip of paper with the baker of the day award. Skylar got to send the first contestant home. It was a role we'd reverse from week to week.

I hoped we could get through this in one take. I had a cobbler to bake.

Taking my cue, I smiled at the contestants. "I get the pleasure of bestowing the baker of the day on . . ." I paused for dramatic effect, and to cover my surprise, smiled wider and said, "Mick Henderson."

Mick's grin stretched from ear to ear. He finger-shot at Harrison, then me, before turning to Tabitha. A move that could not make it more incriminating that he knew us or, in my case, knew my secret. I had no idea who this guy was or exactly what he thought he stood to gain knowing my secret. The weariness of the day and knowing more work awaited me, I decided I'd confront Mick the first chance I got.

I panned the rest of the group. Polite smiles, clapping and a few congratulations were shouted. To Tabitha's credit, she moved close enough to pat Mick on the back. He lifted his arm to draw her into a side hug. She sidestepped to skirt his embrace.

Skylar cleared his throat and, in an apologetic tone, announced the baker who'd head home, "Larry Kennedy."

Crestfallen described the features and body language

of Larry, a bakery owner from Colorado who specialized in brownies. The young man slumped worse than a failed soufflé. His bottom lip trembled as the rest of his peers gathered around him for hugs and support.

After a minute or two, Brenden yelled, "Cut." The group's show of support stopped. Most returned to their workstations and removed their aprons.

Not Tabitha. A pan banged against the countertop. "What has your security detail found out?" She jerked her head in Mick's direction while stomping toward Brenden. "It is obvious by his win and reaction he knows these two." She waved an arm in Harrison's and my direction.

Brenden held up his palms as if Tabitha was robbing him. "Drake is handling it. I must trust the judges that his cobbler tasted the best today. There are two judges. Miss Archer didn't even sample the dishes."

"My secret is almond flavoring over vanilla." Mick used a taunting tone and hovered close to Tabitha. "It pairs well with lavender."

Tabitha's ponytail sliced through the air as she whirled around to face Mick. Her eyes narrowed. Her jaw clenched. "Don't mess with me." The threat hissed through her closed teeth.

Anger hooded Mick's eyes.

Brenden snapped his fingers and pointed. Travis hurried over and pushed between the two of them.

"Mrs. Miller, please allow me to escort you to the contestant transportation. It's been a long day and I'm sure you'd like to relax in your room."

"Mick, come with me for your after-the-show interview." Brenden led Mick out of the building.

"This isn't fair," Tabitha hollered over her shoulder while she walked beside Travis. "I'm not the one who did anything wrong." She leveled a look at Harrison as they passed by our quartet.

Harrison ran a shaky finger under his collar and loosened his tie. Then he strode away in the opposite direction.

"What was that all about?" Shannon turned to Skylar and me.

Skylar shrugged. "Wannabe stars? I'm out of here. Fourteen hours is enough for me."

Me too, yet I still had a cobbler to bake. "I don't know." I had suspicions, though I wouldn't share them with Shannon. Our friendship was new, and I didn't want her to think I was paranoid. However, between last night and today's interactions, I had a feeling the trio did know each other.

"Do you know Mick? He acts like you do." Shannon's tone was tentative.

I shook my head. "I plan to confront him about that tomorrow." I needed to talk to Eric first. We could approach Mick together as a unified front.

"Want to walk back together?"

"I'd like nothing more, but I have a cobbler to bake as soon as I change." I walked to the stairs. "See you tomorrow."

I made record time getting out of my wardrobe and contemplated calling Eric to come to the set. I really wanted to talk to him, yet it had been a long day. Baking my cobbler and collapsing in my room

took priority tonight. I'd tell Eric about Mick's innuendos first thing in the morning.

The cleaning crew entered when I stuck the heavy,
cast-iron skillet filled with bubbling cherries and dol-
lops of sweet batter into the oven. I sat in a chair out
of their way. It was interesting to see all the dirty dishes
and baking gear loaded into tubs and replaced with
clean counterparts. The crew efficiently wiped down
the surfaces and floors. They were in and out faster
than my cobbler baked.

"What are you doing in here?"

Travis's curt tone startled me.

"I'm baking a cobbler for my live show tomorrow."

The baking timer chirped, vouching for my statement.

Lips pursed, Travis shook his head. Everything I
did seemed to irritate Travis. I rose and started to the
oven.

"I meant, why are you here so late? I'm trying to
secure the area." His tone hadn't improved.

"Filming ran over." I bent over and peeked into
the oven, hoping my cobbler hadn't done the same.
Whew! It hadn't. I didn't have the energy to try
again.

"I'll make one more loop over the grounds and
come back. You'd better be out of here."

"Excuse me, but it's in my contract," I said to no
one. When I stood to make eye contact, Travis had
gone. I hadn't even heard him slip through the door.

I was tired of his attitude. I was tired of defending
the on-location shoots. I was, well, just tired. The
only way to rectify that was to finish this cobbler.

Turning my attention back to my dessert, I opened the oven door until it stopped. The top was golden brown. I turned the oven knob to Off, silicone-gloved my hands and pulled out the pan by the handle.

Using both hands, I sat the heavy pan on a trivet to cool. I'd pick it up tomorrow morning before filming started.

I headed to the door and pondered if I should leave the lights on. After searching around the doorframe, I didn't find a switch. Shrugging, I left the lights on. Travis could turn them off. I stepped out into the cool evening air. A shiver sent a current of fear through me.

It was dark.

Really dark. This city girl wasn't used to so much darkness. I looked up hoping to see a bright array of stars. No luck; clouds blocked the moon and stars. I hurried down the path.

Ahhwhooo . . .

I jumped. Was that an owl or a coyote? I glanced over my shoulder and saw nothing on the path behind me. I listened for the purr of Travis's vehicle over the frenzied beat of my heart. If he was close, maybe he would give me a ride to the castle. Then again, he probably wouldn't, or he'd lecture me all the way. At this point, I'd take my chances.

The only non-nature noise I heard was my own heavy breathing.

I began to walk.

A twig snapped.

I walked faster.

Another snap echoed through the still night.

I stopped and looked in the direction of the sound. A shadow loomed in the darkness, large and menacing.

My neck hair bristled. Then I ran.

# CHAPTER FOUR

I breathed a sigh of relief when I heard a knock on the door of my suite. I stopped in front of the full-length mirror on my closet door. My makeup artist had her work cut out for her today. I looked like a football player. Dark circles underscored my eyes. "Pasty" described my fair complexion and fatigue etched my features. Yesterday, I'd falsely assumed after a long day of filming topped off with an extra two hours of preparing my cobbler, I'd have fallen asleep as soon as my head hit the pillow. I hadn't accounted for the adrenaline surge brought on by the fear of a possible wild animal attack. When I did sleep, it came in fitful spurts. My dreams startled me awake. Each time I'd been running from closing sharp talons or nipping pointed teeth, all while a soundtrack of the chilling howl I'd heard played in the background.

After a couple of hours, I stopped trying for shut-eye, ordered a pay-per-view romcom and sat zombi-fied in front of the television, counting down the hours until five o'clock to send Eric a text inquiring about wild animal noises. You can take the boy out of the country, but you can't take the country out of the boy. Now, instead of doing farm chores in the wee hours of the morning, Eric worked on our show.

Closing the door that separated the bedroom from the living room and office area of my suite, I hurried to answer the door. Checking the peephole, I cranked the handle while I unlatched the security bar on the door.

Eric smiled and held out a coffee. "Good morning."

He'd made a stop at the coffee shop in the lobby. The heavenly aroma of hazelnut delighted my nose. My favorite. I grabbed the coffee and took a sip. The creamy java wrapped around my taste buds. I needed caffeine. I took another sip to stifle my urge to tell Eric to stop showing off that he'd had a good night's rest and felt like making himself presentable to the world. Where I'd pulled on a pair of yoga pants and a promotional T-shirt from my show, he'd paired navy trousers with a navy pin-striped, long-sleeved shirt. With his black loafers, blond hair styled trendy and laptop bag slung over his shoulder, no one would ever guess the man standing before me was a farm boy at heart.

"What's with the cryptic text, Courtney?" Eric strolled through the door and dumped his laptop bag on the sofa.

I closed the door, sighed and flopped down on a couch cushion, thankful Eric had the good manners not to point out my haggard appearance due to lack of sleep. I took a long, bracing sip of coffee. "On the way back to the castle last night, after making my practice cobbler, I heard a noise."

"Ah." Eric breathed the word. "You got spooked in the dark."

I caught the tremble in the corner of his lips. He was fighting a smirk. Had I not needed his help identifying the howl, I might have pointed out that this was no laughing matter.

"And didn't get any sleep?" He gave me a once-over and stopped the fight. His lips curled and the corners of his eyes crinkled.

So much for good manners. I twisted my lips into a lopsided pout. "In my defense, it was really dark. There are no lights along the path until you get closer to the resort."

"City kids. We used to turn out our car lights and drive down a gravel road by the light of the moon." Eric chuckled and shook his head. He set his own cup on the glass-topped coffee table and traded seats with his laptop bag. "Let me get this booted up and we'll see what you heard. I'm sure it was an owl."

Eric was probably right. I was out of my element and an owl's screech had scared me. I had overreacted. Another sip of my nutty brew soothed my nighttime foolishness. "Thank you for the coffee. It was just what I needed this morning. Well, and your help identifying the noise I heard."

"That's what friends, and producers, are for." Eric's gentle gaze, no longer holding mirth, met mine before he opened the laptop. The screen brightened the dim room. "Naturally." Eric looked at me and shrugged. "It's starting an update."

"I hope it's a quick one. I have to report to makeup in thirty minutes." I finished off my coffee in one long gulp. "I need to talk to you about something else anyway."

Leaning back into the deep sofa, Eric bent one leg in a triangle, so he could face me. "What's up?" Although his tone was upbeat, he tapped the foot that remained planted on the floor. His tell, for he knew he wasn't going to like this conversation.

"Well, I'm pretty sure. No, I'm very sure." Maybe this wasn't the right time to broach the topic because I was tired and cranky. The last thing I needed was a lecture, which I would get because I hadn't heeded Eric's many warnings and watched what I said. Yet he needed to know about Mick's innuendos. I sucked in a deep breath.

The swish of his pant leg against the sofa's upholstery picked up speed. "What?" he pressed.

I heaved a sigh. I had enough of being a coward last night, so I dived right in. "The man in the coffee shop reading the paper." I raised my brows.

Eric answered with a slow nod.

"He's a contestant."

Another slow nod.

"He overheard our conversation." The words rushed out of me. "He inferred our secret is safe with him."

"Right." Eric snorted the word. "I told you." He held up his index finger.

I countered with a halting palm. "I know. It's my fault. His name is Mick Henderson. I think he's trouble."

"Wasn't he the reason filming was stopped yesterday?" Eric lowered his lifted index finger and tapped the laptop's keyboard.

"Yes. The other contestant involved in that scene was Tabitha Miller. I think Mick and Tabitha know Harrison. I saw them in a tense conversation. I'm wondering if they are trying to rig the contest, or if he is trying to blackmail a win and Tabitha is on to him."

"You're not a judge, though, so what would he gain from blackmailing you?" Eric frowned. "Maybe coercion? He thinks a television celebrity brings home a big salary?"

I shrugged and rubbed my temples. "I'm really sorry. I've learned my lesson."

"Should I talk to him?" Eric patted my back, his tone soothing rather than seething.

I wrinkled my nose and found Eric's gaze. "I don't know. Maybe I should let it play out a little more. He knows I'm not a farmer's daughter and I find my show stale, yet he hasn't threatened me in any way. Or maybe he's going straight to the press or network."

Eric changed positions and logged into his system. "I doubt that." Eric glanced my way. "He has no witnesses to corroborate his story. It'd be hearsay. I'll leave it alone for now. But you," Eric's index finger wagged at me, "watch what you say and keep me informed of anything he says or does concerning this issue. Stay out of trouble."

"I will. I promise."

"Okay, now let's find out just what noise you heard last night."

* * *

Eric had walked me down the main path to the building because the sun hadn't risen. I opened the heavy wooden door. One fluorescent light at the top of the stairs illuminated the staircase, while the set remained dark. With last night's scare fresh in my mind, I opted to pick up my cobbler once the set lights brightened the room.

Wardrobed up, I plopped my tired bottom in my makeup chair. "Sorry I missed our time to walk to the set together. Eric and I got wrapped up in some . . . um . . . business details." I threw Shannon an apologetic look.

"We'll do it tomorrow. I know all about business meetings." She waved a perfectly manicured hand in the air. Wardrobe had dressed her in brown jeans and a turquoise print top. I felt certain a matching jacket hung somewhere close. Her hair was pulled back into a ponytail, I suspected to show off her turquoise-and-silver dangle earrings.

I swallowed hard. Guilt twisted through me. I'd just told Shannon a white lie. I hated it. This was not the way to start out a friendship, but if I divulged the nature of Eric's and my meeting, she would question me. A farmer's daughter would know the difference between a coyote's yelp and an owl's screech. Sadly, not one animal hoot, growl or squeal Eric played sounded like the horrible noise I'd heard. We ran out of animals indigenous to the area, leaving me to wonder what I had heard.

"Courtney?" Shannon snapped her fingers, pulling me back to the present.

Skylar chuckled. "Hey, we're all tired after yesterday's long day of filming. She zoned out. Give her a break. Her day didn't end when ours did." Skylar sported a long-sleeved, black polo shirt with black dress pants, which made sense because they'd dressed me in a bright green sheath with platform stilettos to make up for the height difference between us.

I flashed a weak smile at Skylar. "Thanks. My cobbler turned out great. I can't wait to show everyone."

I looked past Skylar at Harrison, dressed, as always, in a suit and tie, who made no attempt to join the conversation. I righted myself in the chair. The makeup artist stuffed tissue paper around the neck of my dress to avoid makeup stains. Skylar rolled his eyes at me.

"Well, I for one," Shannon enunciated the words and looked in Harrison's direction, "am anxious to see your creation."

She smiled and gave me a wink.

Harrison sighed, long and loud. "Okay, I'll play along. Courtney, I can't wait to see your cobbler. I'm sure it's unlike any cobbler I've ever seen before. Shannon, how did you spend your evening?" He didn't attempt to hide his sarcasm.

Shannon smiled like a cat ready to lap up cream. Sarcasm or not, she'd pushed the right button and won. "Well . . ." She drawled out the word. "I worked too. I'm in the throes of recipe arrangement for my new cookbook, and I Skyped with my husband. Bless your heart for asking, Harrison."

I ducked my head so Harrison wouldn't see me snicker.

Eyes wide with innocence, Shannon leaned forward a smidgeon. "What'd y'all do last night, Harrison?"

Harrison's pursed lips told us he knew Shannon was asking to aggravate him, not out of interest. "After an adequate dinner in the resort's steak house, I power walked around the grounds for over an hour. It helps me relieve my aggressions." He cocked a brow at Shannon before sticking his nose back into his magazine.

"Doesn't anyone want to know what I did?"

"Mr. Daily," Harrison said, never looking up from his reading, "of course, we want to know. Do tell." Harrison's tone as dry as week-old bread.

Skylar shot Harrison a look that, in truth, he didn't see, and turned his chair toward Shannon and me. "I ordered room service and vegged out watching a movie."

Briefly, I wondered if it was the same romcom I'd ordered.

"I found an old horror film on a classic network. The effects were so cheesy."

"I'm sure that is something you know a lot about." Harrison's tone hadn't improved.

In that instant, the air in the makeup room thickened. Again. Skylar's cheeks blazed red and Shannon rolled her eyes at me. Harrison had managed to stop all conversation except that of the makeup people, who talked in hushed whispers to each of their assignments.

The time Kinzy arrived to get us yesterday came and went. Thirty minutes later, she burst through the door. "Sorry, we're running late. Brenden's ready for you now."

Obliging, we all followed her, with me leading the group. I wanted to get my cobbler. If we were ready to film, bright lights would flood the set. Painful as it was to admit, I still had a case of the heebie-jeebies from last night. I did hope my cobbler wasn't in a contestant's way.

A worry I didn't need to have. The set remained dark and eerily silent. Still about twenty minutes before daybreak, the natural light filtering through the high windows made everything look shadowy.

I shivered, remembering last night's encounter with a looming silhouette.

"Where is everyone?" Skylar asked.

"Well." Kinzy sighed. "We can't account for all the contestants. Brenden didn't want to pay the crew to stand around, so he postponed filming for an hour. Because you're ready for filming, I'm taking all of you back to the resort to shoot some promos. Brenden is waiting in the lobby with a skeleton crew."

Kinzy started to cut a path for the door.

"Wait a minute," Harrison's tone commanded.

Stopping, Kinzy turned around.

"Who is missing?" Harrison crossed his arms and planted his feet. Making a stance, I guessed, until he got the information he demanded.

"Mick Henderson." Kinzy sighed.

Harrison's eyes widened. "You don't think he left the premises, do you?"

I shared Harrison's interest in the answer to that question. Was Mick making plans to go to the press?

Shrugging and throwing up her palms, Kinzy said, "He might have. We don't know where he is. We can't find him." Her short, quick answers reflected the frustrating morning she was having. "Now, please follow me to the castle."

"Can I take a quick minute to pick up my cobbler?" I kept my tone light and polite so as not to add more stress to her day.

"Sure. Where is it?"

"In the last kitchenette." I pointed toward the darkest corner. "Could we turn on the lights? I don't want to trip over anything." I lifted a foot to emphasize my six-inch heels.

"Um . . . I don't know where to find the switch. It's not by the door. I looked when I stepped in this morning. The crew usually turns on the lights." Kinzy shrugged.

"Use your cell phone flashlight." Skylar demonstrated with his own.

"Good idea." I tapped the app and slid my finger across the screen. The area in front of me lit up. I moved it around a little to get an idea of the circumference of the light stream. Not perfect, but adequate. "I'll only be a minute."

I kept my eyes to the floor, stepping over thick cords around the perimeter of the set. Once in the set and clear of floor debris, I shined the light at the countertop where I'd left my cobbler.

It wasn't there. I frowned and moved the beam of light along the countertop it should have been on. The light illuminated nothing but bare countertop. "My cobbler is missing."

"Maybe a mouse ate it."

My head snapped in Kinzy's direction. I spotlighted the group of people waiting for me.

"A mouse couldn't move a cast-iron fry pan." Shannon's tone held no politeness.

"There better not be rodents in this building." Harrison's command drew a frown from Kinzy.

"Who would take it?" My tone edged with panic. I didn't have time to make another one. As a matter of fact, I didn't have time for filming to be delayed. I had a show to film at six. I searched my coworkers' faces, hoping for a valid answer.

"Maybe someone moved it to the refrigerator?" Shannon called louder than she needed. Her words echoed off the high ceilings.

I shivered. For some reason, the echo of her suggestion reminded me of last night's high-pitched yowl. I shone the light on the length of the counter once again in case I'd missed seeing the cobbler the first time or it had magically reappeared. The still-bare counter propelled me down the center aisle. Heels clicking on the tile floor, I focused on my destination, the back corner of the room where the refrigerator stood.

Rounding the end of the counter I'd used the night before, the light beam caught something shiny. I stopped. I ran the light over the floor. Food. Odd; I'd watched the cleaning crew scrub. I took another step and swirled the light on the floor: more food; it was red and looked like cherries.

My cobbler! Someone or something had dumped my cobbler on the floor. Shining the light straight in front of me, I screamed and jumped back. My knees weakened, making it hard to keep my balance in my high heels. I wobbled and snatched at the air with my free hand until I found the corner of the counter to help me remain vertical.

Mick, eyes vacant and wide open, lay spread-eagled behind the counter. Cobbler splattered the tile flooring and his body. A pool of blood and globs of cherry cobbler pillowed his head. The cast-iron fry pan tilted between his misshapen skull and the floor, with the handle resting on his left shoulder.

"Noooooo." I pinched my eyes shut. My scream echoed through the large, open room.

My cobbler hadn't been dumped on the floor or eaten by a rodent. It had been used to kill Mick.

# CHAPTER FIVE

"What is it?"

My eyes popped open at Shannon's question and sought her out. Picking her way around cords, she moved toward me.

"Don't come closer!" I yelled. I wanted to spare everyone else the horror of never unseeing the scene before me.

"My goodness, Courtney, I've seen spilled food before."

"Not like this." Fright shook my words.

Day started to break, pushing enough light through the windows that the fixtures became shadowed forms. In no time, sunlight would brighten the room. My stomach lurched. I needed to move, get away from this scene before the sun spotlighted Mick. Seeing his battered body in the muted light was one thing. I didn't want to see the gruesome details full light would expose. I'd seen enough to last me a lifetime.

Taking a step, my knees threatened to buckle. Not

trusting my shaking legs, I leaned into the counter edge of the kitchenette for support.

Skylar must have heard the urgent panic in my voice. When Shannon didn't stop, he bolted from his spot and grabbed her arm to stop her forward momentum.

Fighting the urge to look down, I kept my eyes locked on Shannon and Skylar.

"That's right, Courtney. Walk toward us," Skylar urged.

I inched along the counter like a jumper on a skyscraper ledge who'd changed their mind.

"What on earth is back there?" Kinzy called.

"I'm guessing not just spilled cobbler," Skylar called over his shoulder.

"Call 9-1-1." My voice shook as badly as my wobbling legs. I finally rounded the edge of the counter, putting the gruesome scene behind me, and teetered up the aisle in my heels.

"Why am I calling emergency?" Kinzy had her cell phone out.

"I found Mick."

"Is he hurt?" Kinzy thumbed her phone.

"He's dead." The words came out on a long exhale.

A gasp cut through the room.

"Are you sure?" Kinzy looked up from her phone. Her thumb hovered over the screen.

I didn't need to close my eyes to recall the carnage just feet away. It was seared in my mind. I continued to walk toward Shannon. "Yes."

Just when I thought my knees would buckle, Shannon wrapped an arm around me. "Kick those shoes off, girl."

Everything stopped moving in slow motion and went back to real time with her touch. I did what I was told. She hurried me over to a chair. "You're shaking."

"Probably shock." Skylar stood beside the chair. "Are there blankets anywhere?"

"Check with makeup and wardrobe."

Shannon's command set Skylar in motion.

The legs of a chair scratched across the hardwood floor. Shannon placed it in front of mine. She sat down, leaned forward and secured my hands in hers. With a squeeze, she said, "It will be okay. And don't worry about your makeup. Have a good cry if you need one. Kinzy will find us tissues."

I shook my head, attempting to remove the fog in my mind and access my feelings. "I'm too numb to cry." I squeezed Shannon's hand, hoping to stop the trembling in my own.

"Here you go." Skylar draped a minky blanket over my shoulders.

I leaned forward in the chair, allowing it to cascade down my back.

Skylar squatted down and drew the corners of the blanket together. I grasped them to hold the blanket in place. "Thank you."

"No problem." Skylar patted my arm. "You okay?"

The concern in his eyes melted my heart.

I inhaled a shaky breath. "I don't know. I think so."

Bright rays of sunshine filtered through the windows. I realized Shannon and Skylar had positioned me in a chair with my back to the carnage. Kinzy stood, cell phone to ear, peering out the open door, while Harrison had taken a seat beside a camera. Although I wasn't surprised he showed no concern for me, the expression he wore did astonish me. Neither shock nor surprise registered in his face. Even in my numb stupor, I saw more than a hint of relief on his features.

"Shut and lock the door." Drake strode over the threshold, pausing by Kinzy. "Travis is the only one allowed entry until I determine if this is a crime scene. You shouldn't have called emergency until I gave you the go-ahead."

I frowned at his harsh tone. "I told her to call them. Mick has been murdered."

Drake turned my way. I could tell by his clothes— a blue polo with the Nolan Security logo above his heart and khaki pants—he'd been ready for his workday when Kinzy made the call. He started walking toward me. "Find a light switch and flip it," he commanded over his shoulder to Kinzy.

Expression grim, he stopped beside our trio. "How do you know he was murdered?"

"I sssaaaw . . ." I stopped and swallowed hard in an attempt to gain composure. "I discovered the body."

Light flooded the room. Kinzy had found the switch. I blinked against the brightness.

"Are you sure he's dead? Did you check for a pulse?"

The pointed look Drake pinned me with turned my shock into anger. "No, I didn't."

"Then how do you know he's dead?" Drake lifted his brows.

A picture flashed into my mind. An up-close of Mick's head. The stare of unseeing eyes. The puddled blood. "He's dead. Go look for yourself." I threw my arm out in emphasis. The blanket fell off my right shoulder. Skylar stood and pulled it back around me.

Drake held up his palms. "No call for anger, Miss Archer. A dead body doesn't always mean murder. He may have died from natural causes or," Drake paused and looked toward the corner, then back at me. "Taken his own life."

I opened my mouth to rebut his remarks, then stopped. What he said could be true. I hadn't investigated the scene. I'd backed away from it. Perhaps Mick had had a heart attack, knocked down the pan of cobbler and cracked open his head in the fall. The second scenario sent a shiver through me. I hadn't seen any type of weapon to self-inflict a death, but I hadn't looked long, and it was dark. I supposed Drake was right. It might not be murder.

"Looks like murder," Drake announced, making his way back to our group. "I am going to need statements from all of you on the events leading up to your discovery."

"Shouldn't that be left to the proper authorities?" A hint of challenge filled Harrison's voice.

Drake's phone chimed. He read the screen and looked toward Kinzy, who stood sentinel at the door. "Open the door, Travis is outside."

Kinzy cracked open the door and Travis entered, dressed in white shorts and a T-shirt. He carried a tennis racket. "I was heading to the courts when I got your text." He glanced around the room, then handed Kinzy the racket. "Hold this. I don't want to taint the crime scene."

Travis walked over to Drake. "What's up?"

"Looks like one of the contestants was murdered, blunt force trauma." Drake jerked his head in the direction of the body. "Miss Archer discovered it."

"Did the killer leave the murder weapon?" Travis stretched his neck and raised up on the balls of his feet, like that would help him see the back corner of the room.

"I think so, a cast-iron fry pan."

I shivered at the thought of a baking utensil of any kind being used in a murder.

Travis lowered himself and looked directly at me. "The pan you baked your cobbler in last night?"

I nodded.

The corners of his lips curled into a sneer. "And *you* found him?"

"Yes, I did." The situation overwhelmed me, but hadn't Drake just told him that?

Shannon and I both started when a loud pounding echoed through the room. "Open up. It's the sheriff."

Drake nodded at Kinzy. She opened the heavy wooden door. "Don't go anywhere. The police will want to take statements." Drake headed over to meet the county sheriff. Travis tagged along, one step behind.

"I think we're going to be here a while." Skylar sighed. "I need to find a chair."

Skylar crossed paths with the sheriff, Drake and Travis. Skylar nodded at whatever the sheriff said to him when they passed. He looked around, then leaned against the portable counter the crew had moved in for the judging segment of the show.

Turning in my chair, I watched the sheriff, Drake and Travis approach and examine the area where I'd found Mick. None of the men really got closer to the body than I had. The sheriff pulled a cell phone out of his belt and made a call, then followed Drake up the aisle toward Shannon and me.

"Courtney Archer, this is Carbon County Sheriff Milton Perry. He has some questions for you. Ms. Collins, you'll need to come with me while the sheriff talks to Courtney." Drake motioned with his fingers for her to follow him.

Shannon frowned. "I don't want to leave her alone." She looked at the sheriff. "She's had quite a shock."

"I know, ma'am. I need to get statements from all of you. I'm starting with . . . Courtney, was it?" The sheriff looked over the top of his plastic-framed glasses at me.

He wore a ball cap emblazoned with a sheriff's shield in the middle. Salt-and-pepper hair curled over the tops of his ears, where the cap pressed against his head.

"Yes."

The small shake of his head jiggled his jowls. He pressed his thick lips together, then blew out a heavy breath. "You can wait over there." He pointed toward Skylar.

Shannon pursed her lips, gave me a quick hug and did what she was told.

Sheriff Perry folded himself into the chair Shannon had vacated. Tall and stocky, he filled up the entire seat of the chair and had to push the chair back to give himself leg room. He took a notebook from his front pocket.

"What were you doing when you discovered the body?"

Sheriff Perry didn't speak in hushed tones by any means, so neither did I. "I was looking for my pan of cherry cobbler. I baked it last night for today's filming of my show."

"That's right," Travis said, suddenly beside us. "Courtney was lurking around the set last night when I came to secure it."

I drew my brows together. "I wasn't lurking around." I narrowed my eyes at Travis before I turned back to the sheriff. "In addition to cohosting this baking battle, I am filming episodes of my cooking show on location. I needed to bake the cobbler for the show we are shooting in front of a live audience later this afternoon."

"Here on this set? I don't think so; it's a crime scene." Sheriff Perry assessed me with his gray eyes.

"No." I shook my head. "We are filming that show in a large conference room at the resort."

"Why don't you go wait for the state crime investigators I phoned?" Sheriff Perry eyed Travis and jerked his head toward the door.

"Just trying to help." Travis shrugged and hurried across the room.

In a much lower voice, Sheriff Perry asked, "What time did you finish baking your cobbler?" His pen hovered over the notepad.

"Well, we put in a fourteen-hour day yesterday. We

started filming a little after eight, so we ended around ten. It took me about two hours to prepare and bake the cobbler. I'd say, approximately midnight." I rubbed my temples, trying to remember what time I'd arrived in my room. I'd been so frightened by the animal noise, I didn't remember even looking at a clock.

"And you found him when?" Sheriff Perry scratched his pen across the paper before peering over his glasses.

Time had stood still when I'd discovered the body, then swirled into a frenzy since. "I don't know. Maybe a half hour ago?"

"Okay. Describe your morning." Sheriff Perry hunkered down into a more comfortable position in his chair.

I decided to start from the point when Eric and I left the resort. Eric! I shivered. Was he okay? There was a killer on the loose. "I need to text my producer."

"No, you need to describe your morning." The sheriff's pointed look left no room for argument.

I hurried through the details of my morning, ending with the moment Drake entered the building.

"Okay . . . so your producer . . ." Sheriff Perry perused his notes. "Eric?"

I nodded when his eyes found mine.

"Did he come into the building?"

"No. He walked me to the door."

"Why? Is he your boyfriend? Fiancé? Husband?"

"No." I almost chuckled. "He is my producer. We were talking." I stopped. Did the sheriff really need to know that I was a city girl afraid of animal noises? I decided he didn't. Swallowing hard, I finished my sentence, "Business."

Sheriff Perry arched one brow and pondered his notes. "Thank you, Miss Archer. You can wait over by the others." He pointed to Drake, then called him over with the same finger.

I stood. The hardwood cold under my bare feet. I looked around and saw my shoes had landed in the same spot by the host tape on the floor. I retrieved them on my way to the counter. All the makeup artists, stylists and wardrobe staff had joined Kinzy, Skylar, Harrison and Shannon beside the counter.

In seconds, Drake returned to escort Shannon to the sheriff. When he came back, he motioned to me. "Why don't you have a seat on the stairs? I'm sure you're still shaken. Most people are when they see a dead body for the first time, even more so when it's murder."

He patted my shoulder in the same way Skylar had, yet it had a much different effect on me. Perhaps because my shock was wearing off? The simple gesture and his sympathetic gaze stirred my emotions and, surprisingly in this tense situation, took my level of attraction to him up a notch.

I frowned, perturbed at myself before I mentally resolved to fight the attraction, right now. Which was difficult, because Drake had placed his warm palm on my elbow and guided me to the staircase. I slipped onto a step and reminded myself why Drake and I were here.

Mick had been murdered.

As unpleasant as Mick had been, he hadn't deserved to be a victim of a violent death. My eyes misted.

"Here." Drake pulled a pocket package of tissues from his shirt pocket.

I accepted one and dabbed at my eyes. "Who could do such a thing?"

Drake shook his head. "You'd be surprised. It is one of the reasons I left the FBI. Investigating murder day in and day out wears on a person."

"What happens now?" I worried the tissue in my fingers.

"The sheriff will take statements from everyone in the building." Drake's eyes darted from me to the questioning area, then back. "The investigation team will arrive, take pictures, look for evidence and interrogate suspects. Can I get you anything? Water?"

The concern in his voice matched his expression.

"No, thank you. I'd like to call Eric."

Drake's brows drew together. "Did I meet him last night? Your boyfriend, right?"

If we'd been in a different setting, I'd have teased Drake about the sneaky way he was trying to find out if I was single. Instead, I said, "You sound like the sheriff. Eric is my producer. Nothing more. It's just . . ." I stopped. The fog on my brain lifted. My eyes widened.

Drake was playing it cool all right, but not because he was trying to verify my relationship status.

Eric had warned me to stay out of trouble. To watch what I said. Had I heeded his warning? No. Drake, like the sheriff, considered Eric a suspect because he was alone on the path this morning. By not heeding his warning, had I incriminated Eric in Mick's murder?

# CHAPTER SIX

"I'm so sorry, Eric."

He pinned me with a look and a small shake of his head. He closed the door of the small conference-room-turned-interview-room in Coal Castle Resort.

I'd waited in the hall outside the interview room while the sheriff took Eric's statement.

"Let's go to your room."

I strained against the hum of the background noise to hear his hushed tone. "But I want to . . ."

Eric pressed a finger to his lips and glanced around. Although his clothing still held its crisp creases, he looked rumpled. His shoulders sagged and worry—or dread—cut deep lines across his forehead.

I got the message.

People mingled everywhere. Some conversed in quiet conversations, others loud speculation. All of it concerning the murder on the set. Brenden had no choice but to cancel filming for the day, including any promos or show introductions, because the sheriff planned to question all the contestants and crew while the crime scene investigators did their thing on the set.

I winced when Mick's image flashed through my mind. The last time I saw him alive, he'd walked off the set flashing Tabitha a smug smile after he won the competition, prompting her poor-sport reaction.

Tabitha. I wrinkled my brow a little bit as I imagined how her interview would go. No doubt she'd speak ill of the dead, and Harrison. My next thought chilled me to my very core. Had she taken her loathing to another level since Mick won yesterday's competition?

Eric motioned with his hand, and I followed his lead. In silence, we cut a maze-type path through the hallways to the elevator, then to my suite. Once inside, relief washed through me. I'd closed the din of the resort and the conjecture about the murder out of my ears when I shut the door. It wasn't home, but it was a reasonable facsimile. My room, which had looked like a standard hotel suite this morning, now felt like a haven from the madness of the situation.

"Now, we can talk about the murder." Eric secured two sparkling waters from the refrigerator. Handing me one, he sighed long and loud before collapsing on the sofa.

I unscrewed the cap from my water and sat in the matching overstuffed chair. Slipping off the heels from wardrobe, I tucked my feet beneath me and relaxed into the comfort of the plush cushions. The sheriff hadn't allowed any of us to return to wardrobe for our own clothing this morning. When the crime scene crew arrived, he ended his onsite interviews, instructing Drake to ready some rooms in the resort to finish the job. Drake's security team spent the next few hours tracking down key people to interview, Eric being one of them, no thanks to me.

"Again, I am sorry I dragged you into this. All I said was that you walked me to work. Sheriff Perry and Drake jumped on the fact that you were alone."

"I accept your apology. I'm sure sooner or later, I'd have been questioned. Maybe not the same line of questioning as this morning." Eric took a long drink of water.

"What do you mean?" I knitted my brow in confusion.

"Their line of questioning bordered on me being a jealous lover, not . . ."

My snort of laughter cut off Eric's words. In an instant, a thread of hurt crossed his features. "I'm sorry. I didn't mean to interrupt you. Where on earth did they get that idea?" Then it hit me. If this was a love triangle, Mick would be one of the love interests. Ew. Mick was old enough to be my father.

Eric's lips drew into a poutlike frown, then he shrugged his shoulders. "Maybe it's common procedure. At any rate, I told them it wasn't true." He sighed and focused on the abstract art framed on the wall across from the sofa. "We don't have *that* kind of personal relationship."

In the next few moments, Eric took several sips of his sparkling water while studying the mass-produced artwork. Then his eyes found mine. He gave me a sad smile. The kind a person wears when they are ready to break bad news to someone. "Tell me exactly what happened last night after filming."

Eric's behavior seemed odd, out of character. Yet I knew being questioned about a murder wasn't fun. Neither was finding the body. Maybe he needed a distraction, something else to focus on, like identifying the animal I'd heard on the path.

I closed my eyes to call back the memory. "Everyone was tired. Skylar and Harrison left almost immediately. Shannon wanted to walk back to the resort together. I told her I couldn't. We all made haste to wardrobe to change. I went down to the kitchenette to work on my cobbler. Some of the crew were finishing up. The cleaning staff came and left while the cobbler was baking."

"So, you were alone in the kitchen?"

Eric broke into my memories. I opened my eyes. "Yes, but only for a few minutes. Travis came in. He was making his security rounds. He was perturbed I was still on set, like he and Drake were last night about my filming on location."

"Speaking of which, Sheriff Perry gave us the go-ahead for filming this evening."

"Oh! I thought the resort was locked down."

"They are ushering the busload of fans into a side door of the resort. Drake's security will ensure that no one from the bus wanders through the resort."

I drew a steadying breath. Could I bake another cherry cobbler in a cast-iron fry pan without seeing Mick's lifeless form? My stomach twisted. I didn't want to stumble or, worse yet, break down during filming. It was too late to change our show's menu. All the ingredients were brought and being readied for filming. I'd have to bake the cobbler. At least I had a few hours to prepare myself.

"Sorry, Courtney, our budget is tight. The show must go on." Eric gave me another sad smile. "Please continue with last night's events."

"Travis left to continue his security rounds. I pulled my near-perfect cobbler from the oven, put it on the counter to cool and left. I didn't turn off the lights because I didn't know where the switch was located and Travis would be back to secure the building. I was halfway to the resort when I heard the noise. I'd glanced back. Everything looked dark and shadowy. That's when I heard the rustling in the trees, saw a moving shadow and took off on a run." I looked around the room. "I thought we'd try to identify the animal noise again, but we don't have your laptop."

I put my feet on the floor and my water bottle on the table.

The weak smile on Eric's face remained. Sadness veiled his eyes. "I don't think we need to do that anymore." He slid to the opposite end of the sofa that my chair butted up against. He reached out and clasped my hand. "Courtney, depending upon the time of death, I think what you heard was Mick being attacked."

"No." I shook my head. "I was alone."

"Are you sure he wasn't hidden somewhere, spying on you?"

I wasn't sure. Emotion jelled into a lump in my throat. My eyes widened and sheened with moisture. Was the noise I'd heard Mick's last breath? I swallowed. The lump remained. My own breathing shallowed. A chill of fear shivered through me. Had the large, looming shadow I'd seen been Mick's murderer leaving the scene of the crime? And had the murderer seen me?

"I'm going in."

I heard Shannon's commanding drawl, then the cast and crew door to our conference room opened and she popped in, flashing me a wide, comforting smile. She'd ditched her *American Baking Battle* pantsuit, replacing it with skinny jeans tucked into black, high-shaft cowgirl boots with leather cutouts of yellow butterflies. Butterflies bordered the hem of her flowing yellow tunic, which hit her midthigh. She carried a large shopping bag.

"How are you doing?" She set the bag on the floor and wrapped me in a loose hug. "I'll give you a real hug after the show. I don't want to mess up your hair and makeup." She flashed me a knowing smile.

"I'm still a little jittery." Really, a lot jittery. My stomach knotted with the realization that whoever murdered Mick might think I witnessed it and I could be the next target. Something I couldn't share with Shannon right now. "I don't know about using . . ." I gave the counter where the cast-iron fry pan sat a side glance.

"Well, I know I wouldn't. So, if Eric agrees, I brought you an alternative." Shannon went to the shopping bag and lifted out a twelve-inch fry pan. "This is a prototype of the line of cookware I'm developing. Would you like to use it?"

I took the proffered pan and turned it over in my hands. "Retro" best described her cookware line. The coloring a definite throwback to the early seventies. Ears of corn, green peppers, tomatoes and mushrooms ringed the center of the burnt orange exterior. They reminded me of the Club Aluminum pans I'd spied in thrift and antique stores. The interior, however, was modern. State-of-the-art red copper plated the sides and bottom of the fry pan, while black silicone wrapped the handles. "I like the retro look and the weight."

"I thought you might." Shannon grinned from ear to ear. "A farm girl like you, cooking with organic food, would be partial to garden veggies."

Guilt winched through me as I tried to keep a poker face.

Shannon didn't seem to notice. She continued, "Thank you. Like my recipes, I want to pay homage to my heritage. Both my mom and grandma had the Ekco Club Aluminum cookware. It's what I used when I learned to cook."

"What a nice memory." I managed a smile while wishing I could set the record straight on my background. While tamping down the guilt, I admired the depth and construction of Shannon's cookware. When a different emotion surfaced, it took me by surprise. Finding a dead body does strange things to your psyche. Envy, sharp as skewers, poked at my heart. I so wanted a line of knives. I'd sketched out a rough—very rough, because I'm not an artist—design of an eight-piece set. Knives to carve fruits and veggies into works of art or a roast into dinner because I knew the knife set needed to be all-purpose to appeal to the public.

Did Shannon know how lucky she was to have a show based on her actual life, with the opportunity to expand into merchandising? Not that I couldn't merchandise; it'd just have to be authentic to the character of the show, my mythical farmer's daughter.

Authentic. I wanted to be authentic. Life was too short not to be. I'd learned that firsthand this morning. Well, maybe last night.

"Oh, Courtney," Shannon drawled and squeezed her hand around mine. "You will get through this. We all will."

Obviously, my thoughts had changed my expression. Thoughts I couldn't express until I was alone with Eric and could make another passionate plea to be honest with my audience.

"I know." I forced a smile to my lips. "I'd be honored to try out your pan."

"You don't have to plug it or anything. Just use it like you would have this." Shannon picked up the cast-iron fry pan. "Now, where should we put it?"

We both peered at my makeshift set. A couple of portable islands with butcher-block counters provided my workspace. An electric mixer anchored a corner of the island to my right. A hole had been cut in the butcher block to allow the cord to be tucked under and out of the sight of the audience. The electric wall oven and refrigerator sandwiched a deep country sink. They covered the wall to my left. Thankfully, the conference room had floor outlets for business attendees to plug in their computers, and our crew had designed the set's electrical floorplan, so I didn't have to maneuver taped cords while I baked. I'd be using an electric element for any stovetop preparations I needed in today's, and future, tapings.

"I'll take that," a deep voice said from behind us.

We turned at the same time. Drake entered the room through the adjoining suite's door, the room we used as Eric's office and for wardrobe and hair, his arm outstretched. Eric followed close behind, his lips pursed. Had Drake interrogated him again?

"Eric, Shannon offered to let me use this pan instead of the cast-iron in light of . . ."

"Good idea." Drake snatched the pan from Shannon. "The press got wind of the murder. The place is crawling with news reporters trying to get a story. The last thing we need is to flaunt a duplicate of the murder weapon."

"I don't know." Eric perused the pan in my hand.

"It's a prototype. We don't have to plug it or anything." I looked to Shannon.

She nodded at Eric. "We aren't even sure this will be the end result of my line."

"Well." Eric took the pan and looked it over.

"There's no branding of my name or the shows on the cookware." Shannon smiled at Eric.

He smiled and stopped perusing the pan. "All right." He handed off the pan to me.

"Good." Drake held tight to the cast iron.

"Wait a minute." I looked at Drake. "The baking battle is all about using cast iron. Are they changing the competition?"

"I don't think so."

"Then why are you confiscating my cast-iron fry

pan?" Hard to believe I was defending a pan that, minutes ago, I hadn't wanted to use.

"Because." Drake hesitated and looked around the room. "It was your cobbler and your fry pan that killed Mick. The press will have a heyday with this." He lifted the pan.

My heart softened. He had my back. I felt safer knowing this attractive man was looking out for my best interests.

"We told Brenden filming a show within a show would be a security nightmare. Now, add the murder into the mix, we have double the outsiders. Getting your audience inside requires more manpower now we have press to keep outside, although so far, Sheriff Perry's men managed a barricade at the entrance to the resort to keep most of them out. Newspeople are sneaky. They may offer an outrageous amount of money for a ticket to get into your show to have access to you for questions. I'll be sitting in on the filming just in case."

I placed Shannon's pan on the countertop before I stepped closer to Drake. "Thank you for looking out for me."

My eyes searched his. Our gaze locked. I wanted him to see my appreciation was sincere.

His brow furrowed. His expression blanked. "You're welcome, but it's my job."

Embarrassment flushed my skin. My attraction to this man was obviously causing me to misread our conversations.

I caught Eric's disgusted expression.

"Because we are talking about my job, you need to

know we are doing your thorough background check first."

"Why?" Eric's question boomed through the nearly empty conference room.

"Well, she did bake the cobbler and find the body. Until we can prove otherwise, she is a person of interest in the murder of Mick Henderson." Drake tucked my pan under his arm and strode away before any of us could argue.

Shannon spoke first. "Don't worry. No one thinks you're the murderer. It's just procedure. I'm sure." Her tone was confident and glazed with miff.

Behind Shannon's back, Eric and I shared a concerned look that had little to do with the murder and a lot to do with our show's secret. And our livelihood.

# CHAPTER SEVEN

I hurried toward the private party room adjoining The Fit for a King steak house in the main floor of the resort. Brenden had called a dinner meeting for the cohosts, judges and Security. Of course, my filming ran over, giving me very little time to get ready. After my shower, I braided my hair and wrapped it into a bun at the base of my neck. I doubted the dinner required formal attire. I decided on wearing basic black. I slipped on leggings, a long-sleeved tunic and flats. I accessorized with a wide jade belt. My jade necklace, earrings and bracelet, chunky and vibrant, set off the green in my eyes.

"I saved you a seat by me." Shannon waved me over to the table.

I slipped into the empty chair to her right, leaving two empty chairs to my right.

"Brenden's not here yet?" My question came out breathy. "I guess I shouldn't have hurried."

"Why are you surprised? Nothing around here runs on time." Harrison, seated directly across the round table from me, leaned back and crossed his arms over his double-breasted suit coat. His lips were drawn into a deep frown.

"How did your show go?" Skylar angled his head. Out of Harrison's line of sight, he rolled his eyes.

"Pretty good, considering."

Shannon snickered.

I laughed.

"Considering what?" Skylar smiled.

"I'm not used to the no-stick copper interior of the pan I used."

Laughter bubbled from Shannon and encouraged my own. "When I tipped it forward to give the audience a view of the golden-brown crust, and the cameraman a good angle shot, it started to slip out of the pan and onto the counter."

I hiccupped the words through bubbles of laughter.

Glee filled Skylar's face. He chuckled. "How did you recover from that?"

"Y'all, that was the best. She is such a quick thinker." Shannon waved a hand in the air.

"Of course I righted the pan and said, 'Cobbler is best served on pretty china, not a butcher-block countertop.' Then I ran my finger through what spilled, tasted it, and said, 'Oh my gravy, maybe not!' "

"The audience roared." Shannon waved her hands in delight.

"After that, I took the pan and walked through the audience, so they could see the finished product, explaining how they could save calories, eliminating the necessity of greasing the pan, by using nonstick cookware, and how nonstick saves cleanup time after all the tasty cobbler is gobbled up. Of course, once the audience left, we filmed what should have actually happened."

"That is a shame. Your fans enjoyed it so much," Shannon drawled. "It was perfect."

"No, it wasn't. It was dangerous."

Drake's voice pulled the levity from the room. His heavy footsteps thumped across the tile and stopped beside my chair. "There is a murderer on the loose. You could have put yourself and innocent audience members in danger." He slipped onto the chair beside me.

Nothing dampens spirits more than a reminder there is a murderer on the loose.

"Well, that could have happened anyway, even with her behind the counter." The miff was more prominent in Shannon's tone tonight.

"True." Drake shrugged his shoulders. "But it would have been easier for someone innocent to get hurt with Courtney mixed into the crowd."

Shannon pursed her lips and arched a brow.

"I wonder where Brenden is." Skylar broke into the conversation and exaggerated looking around. He was clearly trying to change the subject.

"He'll be along in a minute." Drake looked across the table at Skylar.

I noted both had dressed casually in jeans. Skylar wore a polo shirt with a popular, and expensive, brand logo embroidered on it. Drake's button-down Oxford, crisp white with the sleeves rolled up, was a contrast to the security uniform and a good look for him.

"Hello, everyone." Brenden clapped his hands together. A habit developed on the set, I guessed.

He took the seat next to Drake. "I thought we'd have a nice dinner and discuss our game plan for the next few days."

As if on cue, two waiters carried in trays filled with heaping plates.

"In honor of our show striving to be one big, happy family, I thought we'd eat family style." Brenden motioned to the waiters to put the platters on the table. "There is chicken, pot roast, rosemary potato fingerlings, mixed vegetables and dinner rolls. You may place your drink order with the waiters. And Courtney, my apologies, but there is no gravy." Brenden's eyes crinkled to slits at his teasing statement.

"Well, it's okay this time." I waggled a finger in his direction. "Besides, I said 'oh my gravy' during my show today when I tasted my cobbler."

"Speaking of which." Brenden sobered. "I'm forced to call off filming for tomorrow. The state crime scene investigators promise they'll be finished by the end of the day."

"Are there any intros you need Courtney and me to tape? We'd be happy to. Right, Courtney?" Skylar pulled a dinner roll apart, releasing steam and the fresh-baked aroma.

My stomach growled, reminding me that I hadn't eaten anything since breakfast. The swipe of the taste of the cobbler at today's filming wasn't enough to count.

"Absolutely." I took a piece of baked chicken off the platter Shannon passed me and handed it on to

Drake. His fingers brushed mine. He smiled, and I wondered if he felt the slight tingle too.

"The opening for the next show has to be rewritten due to Mick's murder. Once it is, I'll need both of you to record voice-overs. Because he won the first round, we will do a memorial to him. We will also eliminate humor from that show out of respect. Oh, and so you all know, but the contestants do not, no one will be eliminated during the second round. It seems someone took care of that for us." Brenden's gaze dropped down to his plate.

This situation proved difficult for everyone. Brenden had people depending on this show for their livelihood and network executives expecting results. Downtime for any reason affected the bottom line.

"Is there another location we could move to? Maybe a conference room or large building in the closest town?"

Brenden looked up and met Skylar's gaze before giving him a small shake of the head. "Relocation would cost more than losing a day of filming."

"Plus, we don't want anyone leaving the area. We will begin thorough questioning of everyone involved with the show." Drake stabbed a fingerling with his fork.

"Is that necessary?" Harrison placed his fork across his plate and dabbed his lips with his napkin. "It seems to me there are obvious suspects."

"Really, and who would that be?" Skylar hummed his appreciation of the food after he took a bite of pot roast.

Harrison waited while a waiter delivered our beverages. Once the waiter retreated through the door,

Harrison said, "The most obvious is Tabitha Miller and the eliminated contestant."

"Larry," Skylar inserted. "His name was Larry."

"Whatever." Harrison waved his hand in a dismissive manner. "Next in line would be Courtney."

My sharp, and loud, gasp pulled a speck of the broccoli I'd been chewing down the wrong pipe. I started to cough. I put my napkin over my mouth and reached for my water. Shannon patted my back while I sipped my water. After a few seconds, I'd dislodged the food, swallowed another drink of water and glared at Harrison. "Why would you say that?"

"You were in the kitchenette, with the fry pan and Mr. Henderson."

His sarcastic tone ignited my anger. "And you were there with me."

"Not last night." Harrison leaned forward, a coy smile on his face. "He seemed to know you."

Know me? That was the pot calling the kettle black. "Mick wasn't in the kitchenette last night. I know he insinuated he knew me, although I'd never met him." I directed my statement at Drake before I looked at Harrison and pointed my finger. Two could play this game. "He sought you out from the very first night. So, I think he did know *you*."

Harrison's face flushed. He must have forgotten I had overheard the tone of their conversation two nights ago.

"Enough." Shannon drawled out the word. "Courtney didn't kill Mick."

"Do you have proof of that?" Skylar looked at Shannon. "Were you with her?"

My eyes widened in horror. Even Skylar suspected me?

"No, I wasn't with her. Look at her, she's a wisp of a woman. Courtney is not a killer any more than I am." Shannon huffed in disgust, then pushed her plate toward the center of the table.

"How do we know you aren't?" Harrison swirled his wine in his glass before taking a sip. "None of us know one another."

"Skylar, I cannot believe you think I murdered Mick." My tone dripped with indignation.

He sighed. "It was your fry pan full of cobbler that killed him."

"Do you really think Courtney would slave over a cobbler, striving for perfection, then ruin it by clonking someone over the head with it? She needed that cobbler for her show. Besides, that would be like Harrison," Shannon flopped her hands in the air, "stabbing someone with his butcher knife and dulling the blade."

"Wait a minute," Harrison cut in.

"No." I broke into the conversation. "The point Shannon is making is that no chef would misuse their kitchen tools."

"Except, maybe in self-defense," Skylar added.

Skylar made a valid point.

"Stop." Brenden clapped after his command. "This is not the way to get to know one another. I have enough problems without all of you turning on one another. Besides, Drake asked me to host this dinner. He has an announcement concerning Mick's murder."

Drake! What had he deduced from our unprofessional finger-pointing?

Standing, Drake cleared his throat. I had a feeling we were all going to find out.

"First." He looked around the table. "The sheriff's initial questioning and time of death eliminated many of the cast, crew and outsiders."

His gaze rested on me. I assumed he meant Eric.

"Within the cast and crew, we have several persons of interest, which includes all of you."

Shannon gasped. "That can't be true."

"Well, it is. Every one of you had access to the set and the murder weapon. Two of you." This time his eyes found Harrison before he studied me. "Seemed to know the victim. All of you have weak alibis."

"Wait a minute," Skylar cut in and stood. "I told you I ordered and watched a movie. There is a charge for the movie, so the hotel can verify my alibi."

"Mr. Daily, we can prove you ordered a movie. There is no proof you were in your room."

Skylar narrowed his eyes. His lips pursed into a thin, hard line. He looked like he wanted to argue. Instead, he sat back down.

I thought about our conversation in the makeup chairs. All of us had talked about doing solitary activities. Well, not Shannon. "Shannon Skyped with her husband."

When they all looked at me, I realized I'd voiced my thought.

"Something we are verifying, along with Mr. Canfield's dinner."

"Didn't you find any clues on the set? A strand of

hair? A fingerprint?" A quiver of fear replaced the normal condescending tone in Harrison's voice.

"I can't disclose that information. You will each be questioned further. For now, none of you can leave the premises." Drake turned and looked down at me. "Especially you, Courtney."

# CHAPTER EIGHT

I pulled open the drapes and yawned. Peering through the rounded Plexiglas window, I felt like a Regency heroine locked in the castle's turret. Which was silly, because I hadn't planned on leaving the resort until the show finished filming anyway. Drake's orders for us not to leave the Coal Castle Resort's premises seemed to take away my freedom. Or maybe reminded me not to take the ability to come and go at will for granted. Either way, I felt confined.

My window faced east. Even through sleep-deprived eyes, I appreciated the breathtaking view of the sunrise. Hues of light pink gave shape to the Pocono mountain range. Minutes later, yellow illuminated the sky, sharpening the mountains into tall peaks and tree-lined valleys.

The promise of a bright, new day.

I sighed. Was it? After Drake singled me out at dinner last night, the heaviness of Mick's murder had weighed on my mind. I spent another night twisting, turning and counting down the hours until daybreak.

Somewhere in the wee hours of the morning, I'd determined I had to remove my name from the suspect list. The question was how.

I knew I was innocent. Eric and Shannon believed in my innocence. Skylar and Harrison, I wasn't so sure about. Or were Harrison's finger-pointing and Skylar's open-ended remarks intended to deflect suspicion away from themselves? Drake had mentioned we all had weak alibis. Besides, Harrison made a valid point. Tabitha and Larry must be considered suspects too.

Larry seemed way too laid-back to be driven to murder by a competition loss, but then again, the prize money was substantial. I was certain, once eliminated, the contestants were driven to the airport for the next flight home. He'd have had to find his way back to the resort, which was easily done.

Then there was Tabitha. She'd worn her feelings on her sleeve where Mick was concerned. Everyone had seen her loathing of, and temper tantrums about, Mick. Could her anger toward him have escalated and led to murder?

I gave my head a small shake. I'd run the same scenarios all night; right now, I needed coffee, strong coffee, like a double shot of espresso. I pulled on jeans, a fitted T-shirt and slipped into my memory-foam athletic shoes. Stringing my wallet purse over my head and one shoulder, I headed to the coffee shop via the stairs, pulling my hair into a messy ponytail on the way.

At this early hour, few people milled around the lobby area, with only a half-dozen customers in the coffee shop. Grabbing a protein bar, I placed my order. Movement out of the window caught my eye. Skylar trudged down the path in ratty jeans and an untucked flannel shirt carrying two fishing poles and a tackle box. Was there a lake or pond on the property? I searched my memory of the map in my room and came up with nothing. I changed my order from a to-stay to a to-go. When they set my plain latte, double shot, on the counter, I grabbed it and hurried out the exit door, paying no mind that Skylar and I now traveled on the forbidden path.

Skylar carrying fishing gear surprised me. It seemed so out of character. Yet what did I really know about him other than that he hosted a game show? I'm sure he could say the same thing about me. Which might explain his observations during our dinner conversation last night. It was easy to suspect strangers of wrongdoing, friends not so much. This would be a great opportunity to get to know Skylar better.

I thought about calling out to him but decided to linger behind. Maybe he planned to meet someone. He did have two poles. He'd topped a knoll on the path. Not wanting him out of my sight, I walked faster.

"Courtney!"

Shannon. I turned around. Dressed in bright blue yoga pants with a matching long-sleeved top, she pumped her arms, power walking toward me.

"Good morning," I called, glancing back at the path to catch a glimpse of Skylar's back.

It took her seconds to reach my side. "Want to walk with me?"

"Sure." I started after Skylar. Shannon fell in beside me.

In seconds, we topped the knoll.

"Is that Skylar?" Shannon called, loud enough to stop him. She shielded her eyes from the sun.

At the sound of his name, Skylar turned around, walked backward and greeted us with a wave.

"This path is off-limits," I said. Shannon and I stepped it up, while Skylar's pace slowed. In no time, we closed the gap between us.

Skylar flashed a sly smile. "We're all suspected of murder, we might as well be rule breakers too." He shrugged. "Besides, according to the concierge, who supplied my fishing gear, it's the only route to the pond."

"Fishing sounds like fun." Shannon clapped her hands, and I wondered if she was picking up Brenden's habits. "The pond's stocked with trout, right?"

Wow! First the pond, now the trout. I knew the history of Coal Castle Resort. I really needed to read the literature on its present offerings.

"Yes. I've got two rods, if you want to join me."

"Sure. Come on, Courtney."

Shannon and I fell into step with Skylar. I didn't bother telling them I had no idea there was a pond on the property. I followed along like I knew where I was going.

"What will you do with your catch of the day?" I asked.

"Well." Skylar laughed. "I might not host a cooking show, but I can cook."

"I didn't mean it like that."

"I know." Skylar bumped me with his elbow. "We could take over the resort's kitchen and prepare our lunch or dinner."

"I have a great trout almandine recipe. It's in the cookbook I'm working on. I decided on its placement the other night. . . ." Shannon's voice trailed off, and she didn't finish her sentence.

Silence became our companion for the next few minutes. I was certain we were all thinking about how our seemingly normal, innocent daily activities now made us suspects in a murder. Although I highly doubted Shannon was a murderer, it was the reason I wanted to talk to Skylar. I wanted to remove all doubt from his mind that I murdered Mick, and from my mind that he'd whacked Mick with my cobbler.

We'd just entered the small forest of trees when Skylar said, "Here's the turnoff." He motioned to my left.

I tried to hide my surprise. I hadn't seen this path the first morning when I'd reported to work. It wound down a hill and opened to a plush green valley. The sun glistened off the water in a large, oblong pond.

The asphalt path narrowed where the pond's border of white rock began. A short dock jutted out into the water. Benches and picnic tables sat sporadically around the pond with a large picnic shelter on the far end, a permanent grill beside it.

"If they don't let us use the resort's kitchen, we can grill the trout and have a picnic!" Skylar swung the tackle box in the direction of the shelter, then headed straight toward the dock. He set down the tackle box at the end of the dock and held out one rod. "Sorry, I only brought two. Three is too hard for one person to watch."

"Courtney and I can take turns." Shannon took the rod and pushed it toward me.

I caught the gasp in my throat. I hadn't considered that Shannon and I would fish. Well, I would fish. I didn't know the first thing about fishing. "Oh, no. You first." The words sputtered from my lips as I tried to think of a reason why. Then I realized my hands were full anyway. I held up my protein bar and coffee cup. "I haven't eaten my breakfast yet."

"I won't argue. I have fond memories of fishing with my grandpa." Shannon took the pole and turned to Skylar.

"Me too." Skylar answered Shannon without looking at her. Instead, he pinned me with an amused expression. "The bait's in the tackle box."

Shannon opened the tackle box and I tore off the wrapper from my protein bar. Taking a big bite, I wondered why Skylar kept his gaze locked on me.

"Wow, these are good ones." Shannon held out a wiggling worm, then started to bait her hook.

I choked and turned away, forcing down my bite.

"Are you okay?" Concern filled Shannon's voice. "You act like you've never seen a hook baited before. Didn't y'all have a lake or river close to your farm for fishing?"

Um . . . no, because I didn't grow up on a farm. There was a river in my town that probably had fish in it. The closest I came to the Chicago River, though, was on Saint Patrick's Day, to see the dyed-green water or to drive over a bridge. I didn't know what to say. I'd lied to her so many times now. In the end, I gave my head a slight shake.

"Oh." She frowned a little bit, then walked to the end of the dock.

My eyes met Skylar's. He raised his brows and gave me a lopsided grin before joining Shannon at the end of the dock. In a fluent, and graceful, move, he pulled back his arm and jerked it forward. His line flew through the air. The hook plopped down directly in the center of the pond. Ripple circles fanned out from the disruption of the still water.

"Where'd you learn to cast like that?" Shannon laughed. "I'm lucky to get it a few feet from the edge of the dock."

"Well, ladies, I used to play on a minor league baseball team, the Omaha Storm Chasers. They were a farm team of the Kansas City Royals."

"Really?" I walked closer to the edge of the dock. This was the type of information I was looking for. I needed to keep him talking. "I had no idea. What position did you play?"

"Outfield. I had a good arm for distance and batting."

"Why didn't you go pro?" Shannon cranked the lever on her reel.

"Blew out my arm."

Shannon hissed air through her teeth. "Ouch, body- and career-wise." She gave Skylar a sympathetic smile.

"How did you get into television?" I stuffed the protein bar wrapper in my front jeans pocket.

Skylar glanced my way before looking across the pond. "I fell back on my communications major, got an agent and started auditioning for hosting gigs. Sometimes they weren't much more than local beauty pageants and talent shows. I saw the seedy side of this business during those first few years. Then I got my big break announcing lottery numbers. That job gave me the exposure I needed, and here I am."

I marveled at how easily Skylar could talk about his career background. I wished I could. If I hadn't found Mick's murdered body, Eric and I would have had that conversation, again.

"Everyone knows Courtney demo'd cooking at a grocery store chain; it's in her bio." Skylar flashed me a sweet smile. "Shannon, how did you get started?"

"I was a nutritionist on a local television station in Dallas. I had a biweekly, five-minute program to create something wholesome to eat or share the newest nutrition fad, like kale. A network executive saw a show when he was in town and contacted me." Shannon put a hand to her heart and batted her eyes. "I guess the camera loved me." She chuckled. "Y'all, I was so green, I didn't know up from down. Lucky for me, my husband is a certified accountant. He takes care of the business end of my career, so I can focus on the creativity. He looks out for me just like Eric looks out for you." Shannon smiled over her shoulder at me.

I smiled back. I might not be holding a rod, but I'd been fishing too. I'd caught information. Skylar had seen the seedy side of this business. Mick didn't seem on the up-and-up. Perhaps their paths had crossed early in Skylar's career and left a bad taste in his mouth? After all, Skylar admitted to having a good throwing arm. Whacking someone with a cast-iron fry pan full of cobbler would be a piece of cake for him.

"I thought I'd find you here." Eric slipped through the door of the conference room doubling as my show's set. We'd both been given access keys to this room, along with Drake, Travis and the set manager.

"I'm doing a practice run on my finger pies."

Eric drew his brows together. "The next taping isn't for a few days and it looks to me like you are carving fruit."

Busted. I'd intended to work on my recipe. Instead, I picked up an apple and a knife, creating the face of a girl, then carving lines and ridges into the peel to make flowing hair.

I shrugged. "It gives me something to do."

"Which means take your mind off the murder?" Eric leaned against the counter.

"Yes." I put down the apple and started gathering the ingredients for the crust.

"Want to talk about it?"

"No." I sighed. "Yes. I don't understand how anyone can do that to another human being. And I don't like being a suspect."

Eric shrugged. "Investigations are a process of elimination. Sheriff Perry is doing his job."

It was my turn to pull my features into a frown. "It doesn't concern you, being considered a suspect in a murder?"

Smiling, Eric waved a hand through the air. "I'm

not. Sheriff Perry informed me the time of death ruled me out. Mick had been hours dead by the time I dropped you off at the workshop building. My alibi was easily checked for the time of death. I was in the business office printing off the script for our show's taping the next day. It's all on security cameras."

"I'm glad." Some of my guilt lifted, because I'd felt I'd thrown Eric into the mess with my innocent re-mark. "Security cameras? Wouldn't they have secu-rity cameras on the set or around the building?"

"One would think so."

"Well, they didn't have outside security lights." I shivered, remembering the all-encompassing dark-ness. I made a mental note to look for security cameras when the crime scene turned back into our show's set. "Did the sheriff tell you the time of death?"

Eric pursed his lips and shook his head. "He just said hours dead. Sorry, Courtney. I really think you heard . . ."

I halted Eric in midsentence by holding up my hand. "I know."

"Did you talk to Sheriff Perry or Drake about what you heard?"

"No. I only answered the questions they asked. I've watched enough crime shows on television to know there are times to keep quiet."

Eric's brow cocked.

"Hey, I learned my lesson talking about my back-ground when someone, like Mick, could overhear. But because you brought that subject up, we need to talk about removing the clause about my background from the contract. Shannon, like everyone else, as-sumes I am a farmer's daughter. We are becoming friends and I feel like a heel avoiding her questions or having to lie when she makes references to my farm life."

"We have one more year on the contract. If our show is picked up, we can negotiate. Take the clause out or no show."

"Do you really mean that? After all, it could blow up in our faces. *Cooking with the Farmer's Daughter* is our livelihood."

Nodding, Eric smiled. "I do. We both feel stalled in our careers. You are cohosting another show that the network hopes will garner high ratings. I'd be the only one on unemployment."

I walked over to Eric and took his hand. "Not for long. You are a great producer. Besides, we could put together another show. One where I can actually use my knife skills."

Eric gave my hand a squeeze. "We make a great team, don't we?"

I looked into his eyes. The emotion they conveyed wasn't for reassurance we were a great career team. It was something else.

Someone pounded on the locked door. Hard and loud. It startled us both. We broke eye contact before I could determine the emotion in Eric's eyes. Eric pushed me behind him. "Are you expecting anyone?"

"No. My purse is on the chair over there. I'm getting my cell phone," I whispered.

"I have mine in my pocket." Eric grabbed my arm and stopped me.

Three more bangs on the door echoed through the room. "Courtney? Are you in there?"

"That sounds like Harrison." Surprise filled my voice. Why would Harrison want to see me? He'd made it clear he didn't want to fraternize with the rest of us. Unless he thought I was here alone.

"Harrison, is that you?" I'd walked around Eric and headed for the door.

"I'll call Drake," Eric said, walking so close, I could feel his breath on my neck. "He might be the killer coming for you."

A chill shivered through me. I stopped by the door and shot Eric a you-could-be-right look. "Harrison, is that you?"

"Yes. May I come in?"

Eric started to dial.

"How did you know I was here?"

"Drake told me I'd find you here."

Ending the call, Eric said, "Open the door."

So, I did. There stood Harrison, decked out in a white, double-breasted chef's jacket over a pair of loose-fitting black-and-white, houndstooth pants and nonslip athletic shoes.

"Hello." Harrison nodded toward Eric. "I hope I'm not interrupting."

"No." I drew out the vowel.

Harrison caught my not-so-inconspicuous suspicion. "Please, may I enter?"

Eric and I stepped back. Harrison closed the door behind him. "Drake said you were preparing your next recipe. I wondered if you'd like some kitchen help."

"What?" Eric and I looked at each other.

"I know what you are thinking. I've distanced my-

self from the group. And . . . well . . ." He looked from
me to Eric and back.

I'd never heard Harrison at a loss for words.

"When I'm nervous or bored or stressed, I turn to
cooking."

Him and me both.

"What I am saying is, Courtney, help me keep my
sanity. Let me cook with you this afternoon."

His pleading tone surprised me. The renowned
chef Harrison Canfield needed my help. I twisted my
mouth into a pucker. I didn't plan to refuse. I did
want him to sweat for just a little bit. Besides, if he
felt as vulnerable as he looked right now, he may be
talkative and throw me a morsel I could use to clear
my name. Unlike Skylar, there was no question in my
mind that Harrison knew Mick.

"Okay. You can stay. I need a sous chef anyway."

A wide smile broke the tension on Harrison's face.
"Thank you, Courtney. What are we making?"

"Fruit finger pies."

Harrison grimaced. I knew he had an aversion to
not using silverware.

"Some people like to eat with their fingers, especially children. Plus, they are a great picnic food, and
summer is just around the corner."

"Okay. Show me to your kitchen and tell me what I
need to do." Harrison emphasized his agreement
with a small bow.

"It's this way." I held out my hand, which was silly,
because the room wasn't large, and the makeshift
kitchen was visible. "I need apples sliced."

I started to walk across the room when Eric raced

by, bumping into me. "Sorry," he mumbled. He kept going until he reached the countertop.

"What are you doing?" Harrison and I walked at a normal pace toward him.

Keeping his back to us, I saw him grab something from the counter and bring it to his face. When he turned to face us, he was chewing. "Sorry, I didn't want Harrison to grab my snack."

He'd bitten into the face side of the apple I'd carved. The remaining carving was tucked into his hand.

I mouthed *thank you* behind Harrison's back. I'd completely forgotten about the carving and would be hard-pressed to come up with a viable explanation for Harrison.

"The apples are in the refrigerator; peel and slice them into half-inch-thick wedges." I directed Harrison as I would any chef's helper. "I'll get started on the crust."

"What do you need me to do?" Eric nipped at the apple skin, removing more evidence.

"Nothing. We'll be okay. You can go on with your planned day."

Eric threw a look Harrison's way. Good thing his back was turned. "You sure?"

"Yes, too many cooks will spoil the finger pies." Harrison turned and placed several apples on a cutting board on the second countertop. He looked around and found the knife block under the counter.

"I will see you later." I knew Eric's pointed statement meant he would check up on me.

Once he was gone, I placed shortening, flour and salt in the food processor and pulsed until it was pea-sized; then I drizzled in cold water until a ball formed. I let the dough rest while I prepared my pastry mat.

Harrison pulled latex gloves from his pocket and slipped them on. His agile hands pared the skin off the apples. I admired his knife abilities and watched his technique. He used a larger knife than I'd have chosen, yet his result turned out the same.

"I like this knife." Halved and cored, Harrison placed the flat side of the apple on the cutting board. He sliced fast, cutting the fruit into quarters. "Good distribution of weight between the handle and blade."

I wasn't quite sure if he was talking to me or talking out loud.

"It's my favorite brand." Although in my mind, there were things I'd improve upon when designing my own set.

"Good taste." Harrison looked up from his work and smiled, a genuine smile, at me.

"Thank you." I began to roll my dough on the lightly floured mat. At my desired thickness, I took a large biscuit cutter and started cutting the dough into smaller circles. "When you're finished slicing, toss the apples with some sugar and cinnamon."

Giving me a small salute, Harrison found a stainless-steel bowl, scooped the apples into it, then added eyeballed measurements of flour, sugar and cinnamon. He swirled the bowl and tossed the apples in the bowl to coat them.

"Is this helping your anxiety?"

Harrison sighed a contented sigh. "Yes. Should I beat an egg?"

"Sure." Harrison had relaxed. I saw my chance

and took it. "The murder is nerve-racking." I pulled away the unused dough from the circles and laid it aside. "It's not Mick's death that bothers me. It's being a murder suspect."

Harrison used a fork and whipped the egg yolk into submission with more force than necessary.

My subtlety hadn't engaged Harrison into conversation. I decided to go the direct route. "Did you know Mick?"

Setting the bowl on the cutting board, Harrison sighed. "I came here to get my mind off this madness, not discuss it."

The distressed expression on his face matched my unstable emotions. He had a point. I'd come here for the same reason. "Okay, okay. I'm ready for the apples."

Harrison lifted the cutting board and brought everything over. "You should have used a scalloped-edged cutter. It would have really dressed up our pies."

*Our pies?* "I'm going for simple and rustic."

"Oh, that's right. *Picnic* food." Harrison lifted out two chunks of coated apples. "How many?"

"That should do. You can use a spoon if you'd rather." I brushed the edge of the crust with the egg wash and folded the circle in half, then pinched the dough between my thumb and index finger to seal the pie.

"I'm gloved." The latex squeaked when he moved his fingers up and down on his thumb in a puppet-talking manner before laying more apple in another dough circle. "It's the reason I always wear gloves in the kitchen."

My eyes widened. I stopped crimping my dough and looked at Harrison.

Harrison didn't seem to notice my reaction to his words. "Although I don't believe in eating with my hands," Harrison continued. "If you are a serious chef, you know your best cooking utensil is your hands. Plus, this helps keep your food germ-free."

I raised my brows. *Or your fingerprints off a murder weapon.*

# CHAPTER NINE

"From this point on, security will be tight." Drake stood at the front of the room and addressed the cast and crew like a teacher instructing his students, a handsome teacher all the girls would crush on.

"Sir?" Barb raised her hand. I stifled my giggle. By Barb's action, it seemed someone else was reminded of their school days. "How long will that last?"

"For the remainder of the filming schedule, unless the case is solved. Sheriff Perry and his staff are working on solving the murder. My security team is assisting in any way we can. Please cooperate with the sheriff's rules, especially the one about partnering up with someone before you go anywhere. It's proven, there is safety in numbers." Drake looked to Travis, who nodded his agreement. "Try to go on with business as usual. Thank you."

Setting a perfect example, Travis fell into step with Drake as they walked out the main door. We caught a glimpse of the security detail guarding the door before it closed with a thud.

"Everyone to their places." Brenden clapped his hands. The cast milled into the kitchenettes. The crew took their posts behind cameras, adjusting lights and microphones or slipping into the chair by the sound system. I hit my mark in front of the kitchenettes.

In good taste, Brenden decided to move all the contestants forward, leaving two empty workspaces in the back. The one where Mick was murdered. He'd also offered to let me peruse the set before they brought the cast on set. Apprehensive, I decided to steal a glance. The horrible scene flashed back in my mind—the pool of blood, the sticky cobbler—yet before me lay the tile floor free of food, stains and any remnants of a murdered body.

A woman's voice interrupted my thoughts. "I don't like being here."

I looked up to see a middle-aged, stocky woman with strands of white highlighting her hair plastering herself to the front of her counter. The only thing separating her from the area where Mick died was the countertop in the now-empty kitchenette.

"It's not like he's there," Tabitha snipped at the woman beside her. My guess was that she wasn't happy because she'd lost her original space, second counter from the front.

"Still." The woman—Rhonda Alvarez, I believed—rubbed her hands up and down her arms. "It's creepy."

"You'll forget all about it once the camera starts rolling. Everyone, places," Brenden said. He strode over to the side of the set and stood behind a monitor.

"Good luck." Shannon gave me a thumbs-up.

Brenden decided Skylar would do the voice-over for the memorial to Mick, so I would do a sober start to the first challenge of the day.

With my toes on my tape, I waited for my count-down cue. "Contestants, we've been presented with a challenge larger than cooking. One of your fellow bakers will never whip, stir, mix, bake or triumph in the kitchen again." I paused. My cameraman had panned out, and I noticed Rhonda swiped at her eyes. Tabitha walked over and hugged Rhonda. It was all I could do not to roll my eyes. She'd do any-thing for camera time, and she was getting it. An-other cameraman entered the area, getting up close to both women.

"Courtney."

Brenden's whisper prompted me to end my pause. "To honor Mick Henderson, we ask you to give one hundred ten percent today on your challenges. Your first challenge today is a hearty meat pie prepared from start to finish in your cast-iron fry pan."

Skylar stepped from the side onto his taped line. He placed a hand on my shoulder. We looked at the camera and, in unison, said with a gentle tone, "The baking begins, now."

The bakers created a frenzy racing to the refriger-ators and pantry area.

"Okay." Brenden approached us and motioned Har-rison and Shannon over. "Today, you are interviewing the bakers while they prepare their dish. Just walk among them, ask about what they are making or their background, whatever. Keep your tone and humor light. Shannon and Harrison, you take the left side.

Skylar and Courtney, you take the right. We'll switch for the afternoon challenge."

Great! We get Tabitha. I shouldn't balk at that; it'd be a great way to get information out of her. Although I'd need her alone to find out how she knew Mick, she might give something else away, as Skylar had during our conversation.

"Start in the front and go back. We can edit it in a different order later."

Skylar and I headed to the first kitchen station, where Daniel, a young man with skin the color of milk chocolate, poured oil into a deep, cast-iron Dutch oven.

"What are you making today, Daniel?" Skylar peered at the ingredients strewn on the countertop.

Daniel stopped working. A wide smile broke across his face when he looked into the camera.

"Um. I think you are supposed to keep working," I said.

"Oh, I'm sorry." He wiped his hands down the front of his apron. "Can we start again?"

"Well, they are still filming, so just go back to work and answer the question." Skylar smiled.

Daniel cranked the stove's knob. Blue flame shot out and around the pan. "Whoops." His dark eyes widened. He adjusted the flame. "I'm going to do a beef bourguignon with a buttery croissant top crust."

"Wow!" I didn't have to fake my awe. "That sounds like an undertaking."

"And yummy," Skylar added. "The recipe sounds like something Harrison would make. Are you a trained gourmet chef?"

"No." Daniel didn't look up and continued to cube a chuck roast. "I'm a travel food writer and amateur gourmet."

"I'm anxious to see your pie. Good luck."

Skylar and I moved out of the way for the cameraman to get another shot of Daniel working. Skylar leaned over and whispered in my ear, "I thought they were supposed to be making American dishes?"

I shrugged.

"Well, if there was an elimination today, it would be him." Skylar covered his mouth to direct his whisper to my ears only.

Barb, cheeks red from the steam rising out of her fry pan, glanced up and smiled. "What is more American than meat loaf?"

Skylar and I looked at each other. "We don't know. What?" we asked at the same time.

Confusion seared her features. I realized she wasn't setting up a joke. She was asking a question. "Well, nothing, I don't think."

Skylar's eyes widened with realization.

"I'm making my mother's recipe and, for the crust, I'm using hash browned potatoes." She peered into her pan of sautéing onion, garlic and celery. "I hope it works."

Our next interviewee was LeeAnne, a cookbook author. Long and lean, she wore her red hair short and spiky.

"What is filling your pan today?" I asked while Skylar stretched to see what she was stirring.

"Clam chowder pie. The crust is hush puppy dough." LeeAnne dropped her gaze to the counter, then glanced at us. She bit the corner of her lip and pointed. "I need to go to the fridge."

Skylar waved her off. "Most people want camera time."

I smiled at the truth in his statement. We moved on to Otto. The trained chef wore his jet-black hair, which I was certain wasn't his natural color because his brows were light brown, pulled back into a pony-tail. Tall and fit, he wore a chef's double-breasted jacket under the standard dark blue apron embla-zoned with *The American Baking Battle*'s logo.

"Is that lamb?" I inhaled deeply. "And rosemary?"

"It is. I used to make this stew in my restaurant be-fore I retired. It will be easy to turn into a pie."

"It looks like you have put rosemary in your piecrust topping." Skylar pointed, and the camera-man zoomed in on the speckled circle of dough.

"Meat pies are encased in crusts. Yes, there is rose-mary and other herbs in my top and bottom crust. Plopping some type of dough on the top isn't a pie. It's an à la king." Otto grabbed the handle of his pan and shook it to move around the bite-size chunks of lamb, seasoning and thick gravy with ease. With a flourish, he lifted the cast-iron fryer and dumped out the contents into a bowl.

That action dinged the baking timer in my mind. I needed two hands to empty a cast-iron fry pan. Was it the difference between a man's and a woman's strength? Or did I have weak wrists? I made a mental note to watch how the other contestants lifted their cast iron. As much as it pained me to remember the sight, I'd seen Mick and his injury. He'd sustained

one or more whacks to the side of the head. The way
Otto controlled his pan, swinging it through the air
would be effortless for him. For me, not so much.
Mick stood six inches taller than me. Not only would
I have to swing, I'd have to stretch my arms to do it.

*Is that enough rationale to clear my name?*

"Ingenious." Skylar held up his hand for a high
five.

Otto met his challenge, then returned to wiping
down his pan. "They said a meat pie in the same pan
from start to finish . . . no one said we couldn't do it
in stages." Otto winked into the camera.

Tabitha glanced up from her stovetop. She wore
her hair in a braid and reached around to pull the
plaited hair over her shoulder. A bright smile flashed
toward the camera.

"Tabitha Miller, tell us a little about yourself." I returned her bright smile with one of my own. The corners of her lips drooped a little.

"Like what?" she asked through her half smile.

"Why are you here?"

Her features sobered. "What do you mean by that?"
she snapped.

"She means, why are you a contestant? What would
you do with the prize money? Have you attended culinary school?" Skylar frowned a little.

I turned to the cameraman. "That's a scrap."

Laughter burst from Skylar. "You should have
saved that one for later."

I giggled.

The cameraman grinned.

By the look on Tabitha's face, she was seething. "It
is not a wrap, or a scrap. Why does this show like dumb

humor? You," she pointed to the cameraman, "keep rolling. We all get our share of camera time."

I fixed a smug look on my face before I addressed Tabitha. "Let's try that again. Skylar, maybe this time you should ask the questions."

I wanted to study Tabitha. Was she just an abrasive person? Was she on edge because she was hiding something? Or was her guilt over killing Mick making her defensive?

Skylar repeated the question I'd asked. Tabitha smiled sweetly into the camera. "It's always been my dream to work in a five-star restaurant. I thought the exposure might help me get a job or, if I win, it would help me invest in that dream."

Her answer seemed rehearsed to me. Well-thought-out and repeated until it rolled easily off the tongue.

"What are you making?"

"Individual chicken Wellingtons. I'm braising the chicken, potatoes and carrots in a white wine sauce, then scooping it into individual ramekins lined with phyllo dough. I'll seal the ramekin with a top layer of phyllo dough."

"Interesting." Skylar and I exchanged raised-eyebrow looks. "You are supposed to use the same pan."

Tabitha narrowed her eyes and glared at us. "I am." Tabitha snipped out the words. "I'm putting the ramekins back into the fry pan to bake in the oven."

"Aren't you bending the rules a little?" I didn't keep the condescension out of my tone.

"No. The judges awarded a hack like Mick first place. I tasted his cobbler. It was horrible. My dish is delicious, so don't go over and taint my chances by saying I'm cheating." Tabitha snapped a towel against the counter and turned away from the camera.

Although I did think Tabitha was stretching the rules, I'd also received the response I'd hoped for. Tabitha had a quick temper. People were murdered all the time in the heat of anger. Had she and Mick argued over the quality of his cobbler? Petite like me, I wondered if she could wield a cast-iron pan. She'd displayed her ability to snap a towel or bang pans against the counter when her temper flared.

Since we'd started taping this morning, my head had been churning with theories; I wanted to take a break and think. Or at least talk myself out of suspecting everyone. I turned to the cameraman. "Did we get enough?"

He nodded.

With the last interview of the morning captured on tape, Skylar and I retreated to chairs on the side of the set.

"I'm going to gain weight smelling all this food." Skylar laughed. "It won't stop me from sneaking a taste or two, though."

"Me, either."

"Hi, y'all."

Shannon took a load off in the chair beside Skylar, leaving Harrison to sit on the far end beside me. Harrison had reverted to his aloof self this morning. Since yesterday afternoon, I'd chided myself for not pushing the topic of Mick's murder with him. Somehow, I should have insisted he answer the question I'd posed or given me a chance to ask again. He'd become chatty while the finger pies baked, telling me about his restaurants and his favorite chefs who'd worked there. He did take the finger pie I'd offered, but insisted it was too warm to sample. He either needed a fork he didn't think I'd supply or didn't plan to eat it and was being polite.

"If you get a chance," Harrison leaned forward to address Shannon and Skylar, "try one of Courtney's finger pies. They're very good."

*What?* "You liked it?" I turned to Harrison. I knew my face showed as much disbelief as I'd inflected in my tone.

"It's apple pie. What's not to like?" Harrison chuckled. "I ate it for dessert last night."

"With your fingers?"

Harrison shook his head and smiled. "No. I used a fork. I can see the appeal in your recipe for children or picnics."

"Or farmers needing a break in the fields. Court-ney knows her audience." Shannon winked and fin-ger shot me.

My heart dipped. I didn't know my target audi-ence. I had no idea whether farmers took breaks in the field. If it were true and they did, where did they eat? Their tractors? Had Eric ever mentioned that? I needed to ask him. It'd be a nice addition to our script.

"They'd make a quick snack for anyone on the go."

Thank goodness Harrison had responded before anyone expected anything from me.

"You can use that on your show if you want. You know, a selling point for people to try your recipe. You don't even have to credit me with the idea." Har-rison waved his hands.

I was certain Harrison Canfield, renowned chef, didn't want to endorse anything as simple as finger pies even if he did enjoy it.

"Excuse me." Kinzy stood before me and Harrison. "I need to move your chairs to the other side of Mrs. Collins. We're having an electrical issue. They need to look at the outlet behind you."

"What about us?" Skylar started to stand. "Do we need to scooch over?"

Kinzy shook her head. "You're fine."

Harrison and I stood and backed away from our chairs. "We can move our own chairs," I said.

"No, really, I'll get them. You're the stars." The screen of Kinzy's phone lit up. She looked down. "I have to meet the electrician at the door." Her thumbs opposed themselves over the keyboard of her phone. She cranked her neck. "Josh is on his way to move your chair." She picked up Harrison's chair and placed it beside Shannon before she headed to the door.

Josh ran up and grabbed my chair. "Sorry for the wait."

"It's . . ."

A loud crack boomed through the room. I jerked my neck around, thinking something had blown up in the oven.

"Courtney." In the second it took me to respond to the urgency in Harrison's voice, he'd pushed my body a few feet, then wrapped his arms around me. When my peripheral vision caught movement, I mirrored Harrison's stance. Our bodies tensed at the same time. We lowered our heads to one another's shoulder and braced.

The crunch of glass shattering on impact with a hard surface. The scrape of the metal meeting the hardwood. The vibrations on the floor and Josh's cry of pain amplified through the room, drowning out all the other sounds. When silence met my ears, I lifted my head. Harrison did the same.

A large light fixture had fallen from the ceiling, pinning Josh under it.

Suddenly, the room burst with activity and noise. The security team guarding the door pushed past Kinzy and the electrician. Crew members rushed to Josh's aid.

Harrison looked at me, eyes wide with fear. "Do you think that was meant for one of us?"

# CHAPTER TEN

I was still trembling when Drake entered the room on a run. Shannon had, once again, guided me to a chair. My mind repeated Harrison's words over and over. Was someone trying to kill Harrison or me? Or had Harrison killed Mick and staged this incident to remove suspicion from him? Or did he intend to hurt me? I rubbed my temples to remove the troubling thoughts from my mind. The effort didn't work.

With the help of the crew, Drake lifted the large light's base off Josh, who used his arms to crawl free from the rubble.

"Are you okay?" Drake asked.

Josh pushed himself into a sitting position. Before he could respond, Travis blew into the room at the same pace Drake had, with EMTs on his heels.

"My leg hurts," Josh said. He looked down to see a piece of metal jutting from his jeans and started to fall backward. Drake caught him before his head clonked the floor. The EMTs took over, and in minutes had Josh stabilized and out of the building on a gurney.

Brenden stood with his arms crossed over his chest. He peered at the base of the portable light that had held the fixture now on the floor. "Kinzy, who assembled these lights?"

"I'll find the work order sheets." Kinzy hurried away.

"You think it's faulty equipment or shoddy assembly?" Drake stood beside Brenden, perusing the hardware.

My mind eased. I hadn't considered either of those explanations.

Brenden shrugged. "I hope so. I'd hate to think it was done on purpose."

Whoosh; anxiety filled me again.

"We'll look, but I'll have to call Sheriff Perry."

"Great. I'm not calling off filming unless the sheriff insists. The mess can stay here. It's off camera." Brenden turned to the bakers, who all huddled in a group except for Tabitha.

She stood to the side. When my eyes met hers, her lips turned into a smug smile that rattled me to the core. How could someone be so heartless when Josh was injured? Unless she was behind the light falling. Had she intended to hurt Harrison or me or both? Or, worse yet, kill us?

I sucked in a shaky breath and pulled my gaze back to the broken light.

"Do you have a ladder or boom?" Travis pulled on latex gloves. "I'll go up to see if anything is bent or looks tampered with on the upper end of the pole."

Brenden waved over a crew member. "Help Travis. Everyone else, back to their places. We need to at least finish and judge this round of competition before the sheriff arrives."

"I don't know if I can work under this duress," Rhonda offered over the commotion of the competitors. "Are we safe?"

"Let's not jump to conclusions." Brenden put his hands on his hips. "Equipment fails all the time. Remember the first day of shooting?"

All the bakers nodded.

"Okay." Brenden turned to the crew. "In fifteen minutes, the bakers will place their meat pies on the end of their counters. Get shots of them preparing their creations for presentation. Harrison and Shannon will drop by each station and judge the food on appearance, taste and if the directions of the competition were followed."

After his speech, Brenden walked over to me. "Are you all right? Can you continue filming?"

I nodded.

"Harrison?" Brenden's eyes lifted to just past my head.

That was when I realized Harrison's hand was on my shoulder. I'd assumed it was Skylar providing the comfort.

"I will make it through, but I insist on a long lunch. I know delaying filming costs money, but Courtney and I could have been injured or killed. You need to have your crew check all the lights. You can't keep exposing us to more danger." Harrison's pointed words left no room for Brenden to argue.

He nodded.

Harrison joined Shannon beside the first kitchenette. A makeup artist touched them up, and off
they went to taste, suggest and sometimes scold the
bakers.

After Brenden yelled "Cut," the contestants began
to file from the room while the sheriff and his crew
infiltrated the set once again. Drake and Travis met
Sheriff Perry beside the broken light. They spoke in
hushed tones, pointing to the ceiling or the floor. It
all seemed like standard procedure until Travis
pointed to me.


"Miss Archer, do you have any enemies?" Sheriff
Perry hitched the waistline of his trousers before
resting his hands on his hips.

I sat in my hair-and-makeup chair munching on raw
veggies, the side dish to my sandwich, turkey with provolone on whole wheat. In my mind, I'd reinvented
catering's standard veggie tray. I'd have scored the
baby carrots to give them a head and body. I'd have
cored the cucumber and carved the remaining flesh
into wings. Once the carrot was pushed into the center, it'd create a butterfly to entice children and non-
vegetable-eating adults to give it a try. Tulips were
easily made from red or orange bell peppers, with
celery spears for stems.

Skylar and Shannon had invited Harrison and me
to lunch in the dining room of the resort. Drake had
RSVP'd our regrets because the sheriff had some
follow-up questions. So, Harrison and I dined off
the set catering for the crew. Harrison had just finished his soup and sandwich when Travis escorted

him back to the set and away from me. There was no doubt in my mind Harrison and I would be grilled with the same questions.

"I'm not aware of any enemies." I took a drink of my soda. "Do I need a lawyer?"

The sheriff plopped down into Shannon's chair, turned to face me and sighed. "I wouldn't waste the money. You are a person of interest, not a suspect." Sheriff Perry rubbed the stubble on his chin. "Yet."

"How reassuring." I crumpled the napkin in my lap and tossed it toward the wastebasket three feet away. I missed.

Sheriff Perry had watched my antics and nodded his head in a thoughtful way. "So, no enemies? No jilted lovers, no coworker you beat out of a job, no neighbor or relative with a grudge?"

I drew my lips into a thin line and shook my head.

"What about secrets?"

My stomach twisted into a knot, making me wish I'd eaten a lighter, or no, lunch. I tried to keep the guilt of having a possible career-damaging secret off my face. I swallowed hard, flashed the sheriff a weak grin and shook my head. It was possible he knew. They'd had plenty of time to dig up dirt with the extensive background checks.

There was also the matter of my other secret, the shadow and noise on the night of Mick's murder. It might be helpful in the investigation. It might also incriminate me.

Sheriff Perry gave me a long look. "The silent treatment isn't in your best interest. The way I see it, Miss Archer, you are either the murderer or a target of the murderer."

I gripped the armrests on the chair, tight. I didn't need to look down to know I was white-knuckling it. I knew I wasn't the murderer. I hadn't considered, until Harrison voiced his fear, that it was possible I was the target of the murderer. I had no information. Why would they want to hurt or scare me? I covered my hand with my mouth. Perhaps my efforts to find out if Skylar or Harrison knew Mick had backfired. Had my questions during our conversations alarmed them? Did one of them tinker with the light to send me a message? I swallowed hard when a worst-case scenario flashed through my mind. Had the murderer seen me on the path the night Mick was murdered?

"What is it, Miss Archer? Did you remember something or someone?"

The sheriff! I'd been so lost in thought, I'd forgotten he'd be watching my every move, every expression. I dipped my head and hoped he didn't see my widened eyes. Scanning my brain, I came up with an answer. "No, I just remembered I forgot to ship an ingredient I need for one of my show tapings. I'll need to tell Eric to get that ordered right away."

Sheriff Perry pulled his lips into a tight pucker before blowing out his breath, making a low whistle. "It's always best to cooperate with the police."

Before I could respond, Kinzy popped into the room. "They are ready for you on set."

I lifted my brows at the sheriff.

"Go, we're done here."

I followed Kinzy down the stairs, the sheriff following me. It surprised me to see the glass and metal cleaned up. I turned to the sheriff. "I figured there'd be crime scene tape . . ."

"We found what we needed," the sheriff interrupted.

"Was the light tampered with?" I'd stopped beside a makeup artist.

Sheriff Perry drew his lips into a thin line and shrugged, then walked away. I guessed it was my turn to receive the silent treatment.

In no time, the makeup artist powdered off the shine on my face and smeared my lips with color.

"Places." Brenden punctuated his order with a clap of his hands.

Toes on tape, I stood beside Skylar to issue the next challenge of the day. Most of the contestants' faces pulled with concern, nerves or fatigue. Tabitha bit the corner of her lip. She hadn't fared well in the morning's challenge. Although her food tasted good, Shannon and Harrison deemed it a potpie, not a meat pie. She'd also received a stern warning not to bend the rules too much. As Otto had predicted, several of the contestants missed the mark on a true meat pie. The second challenge was their chance to redeem themselves, and the baking day.

"We started the day on a savory note and we'll end it on a sweet note. You'll be making another dessert."

I took up where Skylar left off. "You'll find a sheet of paper on your counter. It's Harrison's grandmother's Dutch baby pancake recipe."

"How sweet." Skylar pulled out the vowels, then raised his brows several times to enunciate the pun.

The contestants chuckled. I smiled at Skylar, then turned to the cast. "It's up to you to fill Grandma's basic recipe with a sweet memory of your heritage. Maybe something your own grandmother used to make."

Either tension puckered the contestants' faces or certainty washed over their features.

The next line of the script was written to heighten the anxiety of the contestants. Skylar and I read the monitor in unison, "Harrison's grandmother didn't have big teeth, but she does have big shoes to fill. The baking begins . . . NOW."

Papers flipped over. Bakers scrambled to collect ingredients, while trying to avoid the cameraman hot on their heels, trying to capture tense moments.

"Okay." Brenden approached us. "Time for interviews. Do the opposite side as this morning."

With our cameraman by our side, we started in front with a plan to work our way back.

"You had a confident smile when you heard the challenge."

Brenda, a fit fortysomething, tucked her blond blunt cut behind her ears and welcomed us with a smile. She owned a boutique doughnut shop specializing in creative flavors like dill pickle and caramel corn. Her shop had been covered on our network and in several magazines as a destination stop while vacationing in Oceanside, California. "I know exactly what I'm going to fill it with, and I might," she winked, "be making a tiny adjustment to Grandma's base recipe." She held up a container of cocoa. "I'm thinking a mocha base with a hint of cayenne pepper."

"Sounds yummy. We're coming back for a taste of this one," Skylar said.

I smiled while Brenda went to work, knowing she'd lose points for changing the base recipe.

The next contestant, Steve, an ex-Marine, still wore his brown hair in a buzz cut. He'd won several barbecue cook-offs throughout the United States and, since our baking challenge announcement, had looked worried. "I've never heard of a Dutch baby pancake." He scratched his billy-goat chin whiskers. "I'll have to keep it simple."

"Time is ticking away, you'd better figure it out." I hated to heap coals on his worry fire, but he needed to come up with some type of filling for the pancake.

Steve stood staring at the paper, so we moved on to Melissa Wong. Her mixer whirred. She drizzled oil into the cast-iron fry pan and put it into the oven to preheat before adding her batter. Apparently, this wasn't her first Dutch baby pancake. She returned to her mixing bowl and stirred the wet ingredients into the dry. "I need to get this baked and cooled. My grandma made the best lemon meringue pie. It is the first American dish she mastered after immigrating here. I'm going to mimic her pie by making a lemon curd filling and drizzling it with a raspberry sauce."

"My mouth is watering. We should have been judges." Skylar rubbed his palm over his stomach.

I nodded my agreement. "You are off to a good start."

It was a brief stop interviewing Anthony. Trained as a chef, his batter and pan were prepared. We got a great shot of the batter hitting the hot grease in the cast iron. Once he slid the pan into the oven, he started smashing strawberries. "I'm making a strawberry rhubarb sauce, then topping it with whipped cream infused with lemon grass." Native American, Anthony had made a regional name for himself by revitalizing Native American cuisine.

Next came Rhonda. "I'm keeping my filling basic. Powder sugar."

"What?"

Rhonda dumped pancake ingredients into her blender and pushed the button. She and I stepped back so the cameraman could get a good shot. She whispered, "I don't like being here since there was a murder. I'm trying to fail on purpose. I want to go home. I used too much salt in my challenge this morning for the same reason."

I cringed at her confession and wished she hadn't chosen me as her confidante. As a host, I had an obligation to the show and would have to tell Brenden before tomorrow's filming. At the end of the day, I planned to watch Rhonda's expression, because no one was being eliminated this round.

When Rhonda returned to her blender, I started to follow. The heel of my shoe slid, turning my ankle a little. I stumble-stepped. As I recovered, I hoped no one saw or got it on tape. I didn't want to be part of an outtake reel. My eyes searched the floor for a spill that needed to be cleaned up before someone experienced a slip-and-fall and injured themselves, always a danger in a kitchen. We'd had enough tragedy on the set. No food or liquid to be found. I did see something shiny sticking out under the edge of the kitchen counter. Perhaps a discarded foil or plastic wrapper had gotten lodged between the floor and the counter?

I squatted down and retrieved it. It was not quite half of a glossy business card. I couldn't tell from what. It looked personal. The only black, bold letters listed in the middle where a name should be printed were the letters "one." Underneath, in smaller print, was "orter." I shrugged. I looked around. Rhonda blocked the nearest trash can. I pocketed the torn card to throw away later.

Skylar and the cameraman decided we'd gotten enough speaking takes. We made our way to the front of the set. Our chairs resided in an open area now. I knew there was a trash receptacle near the coffee service. I headed that way, fingering the sharp edges of the business card in my pocket. I pulled it out again.

It was an odd item to find on the set. I was ready to drop it in the container when it hit me. Was this a piece of evidence the crime scene investigators had missed? Had it slid under the counter and a broom or mop from the crime scene cleanup loosened it? I turned it over in my hands. No blood or food stains. Really, no dirt of any kind. I looked at the face of the card. It was black print on ivory glossy, nothing fancy. I should find the sheriff or Drake and turn this over. They could decide if it was evidence.

Then it hit me. My fingerprints covered it now. I dropped it back into my jacket pocket.

I had enough problems.


"Most of the contestants were surprised and relieved there were no eliminations, don't you think?" Shannon folded her jacket over her arm.

We walked on the approved path toward the castle while birds serenaded us. The day had turned out warm, almost hot. The sun still blazed bright and hot, even on its downhill slide to the west.

"I do." Rhonda didn't hide her disappointment when the announcement they were all safe for another week was made. I toyed with the idea of telling Shannon about Rhonda's admission. Would it change the outcome of her elimination? She wasn't cheating to win; she was throwing away her hard-earned spot in the contest. Maybe I should leave it alone. The only person she was hurting was herself. Still . . .

I'd worn skinny jeans and a long-sleeved tunic when I reported to the set today. Even though I knew I'd put the business card in my pocket, I patted the front of my shirt laying over the pocket of my jeans. My fingers found the outline of the torn business card and reassured me. I wanted to show Eric, see if he thought it meant something to the investigation.

"Want to have dinner in the steak house? I mean, we are both still paparazzi ready with our show hair and makeup." I mocked fluffing my hair with a hand.

"I'm sorry, I can't. I'm Skyping with my hubby. We are having dinner together. The wonders of technology." Shannon sighed. "Drake and his team are doing a great job of keeping the press away from us, aren't they?"

"Yes. Sheriff Perry too. I think his staff is heading them off at the pass at the turnoff for the resort." I felt certain the resort had their own security team onsite, aiding Drake and the sheriff with their efforts. "They both did nice interviews about it with the local television stations."

"I watched. I was sad to know they hadn't contacted Mick's family yet. It's horrible when someone you love dies. Then, if you're told days later, I can only imagine the additional pain." Shannon sighed.

We walked in respectful silence for a few minutes. A low purr interrupted the sounds of nature. In seconds, it grew louder. It was coming up behind us. I stepped behind Shannon to walk in single file, the memories of jumping out of Travis's way before being hit still fresh in my mind.

"Ladies, may I give you a lift?" Drake slowed his four-seater UTV to a crawl beside us.

Shannon and I stopped. So did he.

"As much as I need the exercise, I'm dressed way too warm for the day." Shannon looked at me. "Are you game?"

"Sure."

"I picked the wrong day to wear a dark-colored polo too." Drake nodded to Shannon.

His polo today was burgundy, with the Nolan Security logo above a front pocket paired with khaki pants, a twin to the last two days'. His standard uniform was not quite as sexy as the jeans and white T-shirt from the first day we'd met.

Shannon crawled into the back of the four-seater. I walked around the front.

"I hope you are taking the passenger seat. I don't want to look like a chauffeur." Drake flashed a hundred-watt smile and winked at me.

A thrill wound through me and chased away the weariness of my day. I obliged and slid onto the seat.

My fingers itched to smooth back his windblown hair into place. To make my digits behave, I held on to the armrest and edge of the seat. Good thing too. Drake took off, plastering me to the seat. I knew why his hair was tousled. If there was a speed limit on the path, Drake was breaking it.

In what seemed like under a minute, he zipped into a spot on the patio reserved for security UTVs in all shapes and sizes. He unfolded from behind the wheel and assisted Shannon with her exit. Shannon smoothed her hair while Drake rounded the front of the cart. He grasped my hand, helping me balance while I stepped out of the cart. I followed Shannon's lead and ran a hand over my hair.

"We can use the security entrance." Drake pointed to a door marked "Employees Only" a few steps away. He swiped a key card and opened the door when the light blinked green. Shannon and I crossed the threshold and found ourselves in unfamiliar territory.

"Where are we?" Shannon peered down the long, windowless hallway.

"Behind the front-desk office." Drake walked down the dimly lit corridor.

Shannon followed him. I pulled up the rear, even though I was a little creeped out by my surroundings. "Is this a standard design in all hotels or resorts? It feels like a secret passageway."

Drake stopped in front of a door and flashed me a bemused look. "It *is* a secret passageway."

"For security purposes?" Shannon stopped beside him.

I guessed Drake was waiting for me to catch up before he opened the door. I stepped up my pace. I wanted out of this area. It felt like a trap. Drake had given me no reason not to trust him. Yet the circumstances surrounding Mick's murder put me on edge. I'm sure, like Sheriff Perry, Drake suspected me.

"At one time. It's part of a secret passageway built into the castle. I'm told Mr. Cole had several of what we'd call today safe or panic rooms. Supposedly, this corridor leads to an underground tunnel to his workshop. The resort kept it in place for employee and catering use. Keeps the staff out of the hallways."

Interesting. I hadn't read anything about the secret rooms, passageways and tunnels when I brushed up on the resort. The historical articles I read had stated the Cole family lived lavishly. What could be more lavish than a tunnel to and from your workshop? I wondered if the manager could be talked into a tour.

Again, Drake used his card and opened the door into the office area. He led us to the grand lobby, coming to a stop in the center of a mosaic-tile design on the floor and under a gigantic crystal chandelier. The impressive entryway delighted guests upon their arrival.

"I'm really sorry I can't make dinner tonight, Courtney. Rain check for tomorrow?"

"Of course."

"As of the moment I parked my vehicle, I'm off duty. I could be your dinner partner." Drake turned to me, a hopeful look on his face.

My insides swirled. I managed not to say "oh my gravy" before I said, "I'd like that."

Shannon, a mischievous grin plastered on her face,

wrapped me in a hug, then whispered, "You can tell me all about it on our walk to work tomorrow." When she released me, she wished us both a good evening.

Drake looked down at me. I raised my brows. "Is the steak house okay?"

He exhaled and smiled. "Yes. I'm starved. I thought you might want to try the sushi bar and happy hour menu."

I wrinkled my nose.

"That's right! You grew up on a farm. You're a meat-and-potatoes girl."

I hoped he didn't see me swallow hard. I tried to smile but knew the guilt associated with the lie made it a weak one.

"Oh." He waved his hands in front of him. "I didn't mean that in a bad way. I meant, you're probably a hearty eater."

I sucked my lips together. He'd misread my expression.

"No. What I mean is . . ."

I laughed. "I know what you mean. I, like you, want a tasty, filling meal after a hard day's work."

"That's it." Drake put out a hand. "Ladies first."

"Thank you." I cut a quick path to Fit for a King with Drake at my side.

The hostess led us to a booth in the back of the restaurant, promising privacy from fans, then she asked for my autograph and gushed over my show.

"Do you get that often?" Drake pushed his menu to the edge of the table.

"Not really. We are in a contained area, though. I'm sure she's asked for everyone's autograph." I opened my menu and perused the offerings. "You know what you're having?" I peered over the top of the menu.

"I've tried everything on the menu because I've eaten here every night since our security team moved in. It's all good. Tonight, I decided on steak." Drake rolled the napkin filled with silverware back and forth with the palm of his hand.

Was he nervous? I was. My insides had jittered since he'd offered to dine with me.

"What was the special?" I cranked my neck to no avail. Our secluded booth didn't have a view of the specials board.

"Sirloin tips or chicken cordon bleu."

I closed the menu and stacked it on top of the other one. "Sirloin tips sound good to me. If you have tried everything on the menu, how long have you been here?"

Our waitress greeted us when she set water on the table. She took our drink and food order, promising to be back in a minute with our wine.

Drake pulled a long drink from his water. "Travis and I came out about two weeks before filming started to get the lay of the resort's floor plan and grounds. Once Brenden provided the names of the cast and crew, we assigned rooms according to the best security or surveillance."

"You assigned our rooms?"

"Yes. You didn't get the turret suite by chance." Drake smiled wide. I noticed the slightest divot of a dimple in his right cheek.

My heart fluttered. Was he a fan giving me special treatment? I returned his smile. Before I could say thank you, he continued. "Mrs. Collins's business manager/husband insisted her lodging be in a turret suite. We couldn't give one lady a large room and not the other. We had to keep it fair."

My smile faded, and I fought a scowl, disgusted at myself for always thinking Drake may be attracted to me. His tone implied that they'd avoided a cat fight by giving Shannon and me matching rooms.

The waitress placed our wine on the table, along with a bread basket and wedge salads. In typical steak house fashion, we had limited choices for our sides. We'd both gone with wedge salads. I'd chosen Italian salad dressing, while Drake went heartier, with Thousand Island. A baked potato would accompany my sirloin tips. Drake ordered steak fries with his New York strip.

I took a longer sip of wine than I should have, then reached for the bread. I needed to fill the time it took to temper my emotions, to have the bubbles of my expectation burst. This wasn't a date. Drake wasn't interested in me in a romantic way. This was purely business. He probably planned a light interrogation over dinner. Well, two could play that game.

I buttered my wheat roll, took another sip of wine and looked into his pretty, caramel-colored irises. "So, any leads in Mick's murder? Am I still a person of interest, or has my status been upgraded to suspect?"

My timing could have been better. Drake had forked a bite of salad and choked at my questions. After a sip or two of water, he cleared his throat. "I didn't plan to talk business tonight." He put down his fork and rested his arms on the table.

I decided to counter my two long drinks of wine with some bread. Several bites into my roll, Drake continued. "Because you brought it up, though, you are still a person of interest, along with several other people. No new leads." Drake drew his lips into a Cheshire catlike smile. "Your thorough background check is finished."

He'd been baiting me with his earlier farm-girl references. I gasped. Bread crumbs caught in my throat. Guess it was my turn to choke.

# CHAPTER ELEVEN

"Why did you even go out to dinner with him?" Eric spat out the word "him" as if it was rotten food on his tongue.

"I know you view him as the enemy . . ."

"You don't know how I view him."

I didn't like the sound of Eric's voice when it was snapping out words in disgust. I usually found Eric's voice soothing. Had something happened between Eric and Drake during Eric's questioning? I hadn't planned on Eric's reaction to my news as disdain for Drake. Of course, he didn't know the news because he kept interrupting me.

I reached for the coffee he'd surprised me with this morning. He pulled back his arm a little bit, taking the cup of coffee with it.

"Go on." He quirked a brow and sneered.

"My thorough background check is complete."

"Grrreat." Eric set the coffee cups on the glass-top table in front of the sofa and flopped onto the chair.

I put a hand on my hip. "You are in a mood this

morning. If you'd let me finish, you'd find out it's not as bad as it sounds." I tried to get to the sofa, but Eric didn't move his outstretched legs. The expression on his face dared me to try to cross my barrier. I didn't accept the challenge. I walked around to the other end of the table and took a seat on the end of the sofa farthest away from Eric. I reached for the coffee, leery he might slap it out of my hand.

"To tell you the truth, I'm a little relieved someone else knows the truth." My fingers gripped the cup and slid it away from Eric.

He rolled his eyes.

"Stop." I hissed out the command. "He won't tell. He doesn't care that I don't have a farming background. He cares that there are no felonies or connections to Mick. He said it should help get my name removed as a person of interest."

"Except you left the workshop building alone at the approximate time of death. I don't see how not knowing Mick clears your name. Not every murderer knows his victim." Eric frowned a little. "I'd guess most don't know their victims."

I didn't like Eric's enunciation of the word "alone." "I didn't kill Mick."

"I know," he scolded. "I'm trying to point out that you trust Drake yet know very little about him." Eric cocked a brow and reached for his coffee cup. "Except he's the kind of guy all the women go gaga over."

"That's not true." I took a sip of coffee and wrinkled my nose. I set the cup on the table. Today, the coffee left a bitter taste on my tongue. Which, I was certain, had little to do with the coffee and a lot to do with my producer.

"Which part? You don't know him, or you're not attracted to him." With his back ramrod straight, Eric leaned forward, palms on knees. Confrontation clouded his features.

I wasn't in the habit of discussing my dating life with Eric. Although Drake's and my dinner last night wasn't a date in my mind because we went Dutch treat. A fact I wasn't feeding Eric at this point. "It is true Drake is very nice-looking." I did a good job of delivering my comment in an even tone. "As for knowing him, well . . ."

I stopped. Eric was right. Once we'd cleared the air on my background, we'd stopped talking about the murder and tried to get to know each other. Every time I turned the conversation to him last night, he'd guided it right back to me and my work on both shows. All I knew about Drake was what Brenden had divulged. He was the head of his own security company and retired from the FBI.

I palmed my forehead. Drake was a slick interrogator. He'd said he didn't want to talk business, but now I thought about it. He'd verified everything he would have found in the thorough background check. I'd let my attraction to him, and my desire for his interest in me, fog my better judgment.

"Aww . . . the light bulb moment." Eric sighed. "Courtney, I really don't think you should socialize with anyone on the security crew or the sheriff's team until you know for certain you've been ruled out as a murder suspect."

"Person of interest." I stood and paced between the sofa and the coffee table. "I'm sorry, Eric. You tell me and tell me, and I still open my mouth when I shouldn't."

"What did you tell him?" Eric took a sip of his coffee.

"I confirmed my background and told him about the clause in our contract."

Eric's expression turned sour. His eyes held disbelief.

"He did promise that it wouldn't come out." I offered the information in an upbeat tone.

"All of this went on in the steak house?"

I nodded.

"Anyone could have overheard, maybe even a reporter. I think I'll call the higher-ups and explain what is going on." He rubbed his forehead. "I don't want any surprises."

"Oh! I'll be right back." I slipped through the sliding door to my bedroom and retrieved the torn business card from its hiding place, the compact mirror in my purse. I banged the door shut and hurried over to the end cushion of the couch. "I found something yesterday on the set. It might be nothing." I held out the card to Eric.

"No, wait." I hurried back through the door and returned with a tissue. I'd incriminated Eric once, I didn't need a repeat performance.

"Where did you find it?" Eric looked straight down at the card, then angled his head before he took ahold of it by the corner with tissue protection. He held it up just above eye level, then shrugged. "I'm sure many people on the set have business cards."

He laid the card on the table in a bed of Kleenex.

"I found it at the edge of the kitchenette counter where Mick was murdered. Which seems odd, because the area had been cleaned while I baked my cobbler, then again after the murder. I guess it could have been under the counter and the cleaning crew loosened it with a broom or mop."

"Did you tell Drake?" Eric lifted his eyes from the card and found mine.

Lips in a grim line, I shook my head. "I'd touched it before I thought better of it. If they ran it for prints, I'd look even guiltier than they think I am now. Mick was murdered with my cast-iron fry pan, and then it seems only my fingers have touched this."

"Well, there isn't enough information on it to tell who it might belong to. Some people tear a business card in half if they don't want it before they pitch it into the trash. It's probably nothing."

"I'm keeping it anyway." I pulled the tissue until the card was in front of me. "None of the letters match Mick's name. Maybe it matches the murderer's?"

"But we don't know who that is."

"I've been thinking, trying to piece together who might have killed Mick."

"Don't do that. As much as I dislike Drake, let him and Sheriff Perry figure that out." Eric's gaze held a warning.

I ignored it. "You have been cleared. I haven't. To remove my name from the top of their list, I've been asking some questions. Did you know Skylar, who hasn't a verifiable alibi, played baseball on a farm team? He told Shannon and me he had a good throwing and hitting arm."

"Why isn't he still playing?" Eric picked at the cardboard sleeve on his disposable coffee cup.

"He blew out his arm. The point I'm making is, he could easily swing a cast-iron fry pan and bludgeon someone."

"True." Eric rubbed his chin. "Did Skylar and Mick interact much?"

"No. Mick spent all his time annoying Tabitha and, I think, threatening Harrison. That doesn't mean they didn't know each other." I tapped my chin with my finger. "Harrison avoided answering my probing questions when he helped me make finger pies."

"Courtney, you need to stop your speculation and questioning. It's not up to you to find the murderer." Eric stood. "I'm going to go make a phone call. Again, watch what you say and try to stay out of trouble."

I locked the door behind Eric and leaned against it. Staying out of trouble was easier said than done because trouble had found me. It was time for me to face the trouble head-on. After all, questioning and sifting through suspects in a murder couldn't be much different from figuring out ingredients in a new recipe. Could it?

"Sooooo, girlfriend, how was dinner last night?" Shannon snapped her fingers and gave me a suggestive look. She'd waited for me by the commissary table on the set. After Eric's visit, I'd texted her that I was running late and not to wait to walk with me.

Had my dinner last night really been a date, I'd have been giddy with excitement to share some girl talk with Shannon. Instead, I heaved a sigh. "All business." To save my pride from another hit, I refrained from saying it was a Dutch treat interrogation.

"I'm sorry." She swung a hand toward the table. "Have some sugar or carbs. They always make me feel better."

I eyed the chocolate doughnuts and frosted cinnamon rolls. Odd, how I never ate breakfast before I met Shannon, and now I couldn't imagine not eating a good breakfast. I felt so much better during the day. "No, thanks. A blue mood is no reason to ruin a waistline, or my health." I snagged a plate and filled it with turkey bacon, scrambled eggs and fruit.

"Who did you have dinner with?" Skylar grabbed a plate and went down the buffet table on the opposite side of Shannon and me.

"Drake." I glanced up at Skylar, who had loaded his plate with sausage and French toast sticks.

His lips drew into a deep frown. "Why isn't he out looking for the murderer? I think he and the sheriff are wasting too much time focusing on us."

"Why do you say that?" Shannon scooped oatmeal from a warming pot into a bowl, then sprinkled brown sugar, nuts and dried cranberries on top.

"He's been poking around in our past. I don't see what my baseball stats have to do with Mick's demise."

Keeping my expression stoic, I smiled inside. For never trying to solve a murder before in my life, I'd been on the right track with Skylar's baseball abilities; now, did he have a motive?

After we all secured a cup of coffee, we took the stairs up to the wardrobe and makeup room. Harrison sat in his chair, thumbs thumping on his phone.

Our breakfast group sat around a small, round table off to the side of the makeup chairs to enjoy our first meal of the day.

"Were you questioned again?" Shannon directed her question at Skylar.

He shook his head while he swallowed a forkful of sausage. "No. We met at the coffee shop by accident. He asked to join me and then revealed what came back in my thorough background check."

"Did he buy your coffee?" I blurted out the question, which drew a strange look from both Shannon and Skylar. Guess my pride stung more than I wanted to admit about paying for my own dinner.

"No. He actually waited until I'd ordered and paid before he suggested we chat." Skylar laughed. "I knew it wasn't a friendly chat, but an informal interrogation."

Shannon turned to me. "Is that what your dinner was?"

I nodded. "I'm afraid so."

"Oh, hon, I'm sorry."

"What are you talking about?" Harrison, no longer focused on his phone, twisted his chair to face us.

"The murder investigation. I hate to tell y'all this, but my alibi checked out. Thank goodness my husband and I Skyped an extra-long time that night." Shannon spooned the rest of her oatmeal from the bowl and popped it into her mouth.

The sheriff had eliminated Eric and Shannon. I wondered who the other suspects or persons of interest were besides Skylar, Harrison and me.

Pushing away his plate, Skylar stretched. "I think

they should focus on Tabitha. She seemed to hate
Mick and he seemed to . . ." His voice trailed off, and
his cheeks took on a strawberry glow.

"Dislike me?" The sarcasm in Harrison's voice
couldn't be missed. He slipped from his chair and
began to pace.

"Has Drake spoken to you about your background
check?" I asked the question even though I knew he
wouldn't like it.

"Is that any of your business?" Harrison stopped,
an incredulous expression on his face. "Just because
the three of you share private information doesn't
mean I will. Personally, I think all of you should stop
speculating on this incident because no good comes
from conjecture." At the end of his speech, he turned
and marched back to his chair. Sitting down, he
swiveled the chair until his back was to our group.

Certain my expression mirrored Shannon's and
Skylar's, we confirmed Harrison had managed to
thicken the tension in the makeup room. Again.

Our stylists entered as I was finishing my breakfast.
Once the morning greetings and hair ideas were
shared, our group went silent. The quiet, although
tense, gave me time to reflect on the situation. Eric
had warned me not to investigate, yet I'd thought
along the right track where Skylar was concerned.
Had anything in his background check led to a connection with Mick? Mine had not; Drake had said as
much.

Harrison thought we shared everything, but I hadn't.
None of them knew my country-girl image was a false
persona, that I'd found the business card and had de-

cided to do a little sleuthing to clear my name. Although I wouldn't rule Skylar out, right now my interest was in Harrison.

Was he always so standoffish? If so, how had his restaurants thrived? It was clear by his actions that both Mick and Tabitha unnerved him. Why? That was the question I wanted answered. Tight-lipped Harrison wouldn't answer it. Drake and Sheriff Perry couldn't answer it. I decided finding out the connection between the tense trio was as good a place to start as any.

As soon as today's show was a wrap, I'd head to my computer and do some internet searching on Mick Henderson, Harrison Canfield and Tabitha Miller.

"The baking begins." Skylar and I waited for a three-, two-, one-finger count to add anticipation to the cast's day. "Now." When our camera turned off, we stepped away from our marks.

The contestants flurried around their kitchenettes to take advantage of every second on the timer, except for Rhonda. I guessed her plan for the day was not to complete the challenge, sweet or savory baking powder biscuits, with a complementing spread.

Brenden approached us. "Back to wardrobe for you two." He hitched his head and eyes toward the stairs. "We're going to shoot the opening while the contestants complete their first challenge of the day."

Unlike Skylar, Shannon, Harrison and me, the contestants didn't get retakes. Cameras rolled all the time from the moment we said "now." Brenden wanted to catch the bakers' every move. During editing, he would decide what clips to use.

Once I was in costume, Kinzy led me to a far corner in the workshop where I hadn't ventured before. It was far enough from the set; the microphones wouldn't pick up the noise. A wall façade, painted orange and adorned with what would film as floor-to-ceiling white love beads, stood to one side of the room with a round, cushioned chair in front of it.

I started to giggle when I saw Skylar decked out in hippie garb: striped pants and a suede vest with tassels over a full-sleeved shirt. To top off his look, he wore a wig. The hair hung past his shoulders.

I walked toward him, fingers displaying a peace sign. He laughed out loud.

I feigned indignation, even though I looked ridiculous in my orange-sequined minidress with white, patent-leather knee boots. I didn't need a wig. My stylist had smoothed my straight hair into a middle part for the show this morning. To make the style even more era friendly for the opening, a leather headband was tied across my forehead. "I can't believe our grandparents dressed this way."

We both roared with laughter.

"Get it out of your system." Brenden smirked. "Let's try to get this in one take. I can't afford to lose more money."

We did several run-throughs of our lines, changing our voices or voice tones. Brenden listened, then gave us our direction. Once on our marks, Skylar slouched in the chair, with me standing beside it, and Brenden yelled, "Action."

"Hey, baby," my voice nagged. "All you do is loaf."

Skylar's shoulders sagged, and in a lackadaisical way, he said, "Don't be a crusty chick."

Opening a man's wallet, I delivered my next line. "This proves you're a crumb. No bread."

The camera panned in on the empty wallet.

"Give it a rest, chick. I know where to find some groovy jam." Skylar stood, took my hand and started to pull me out of the frame. I panned to the camera and said, "And biscuits too?"

"Got it. Go get out of those costumes." Brenden chuckled and waved a hand at us.

Kinzy walked us in a haphazard path through the building back to the stairway.

"You do a good job portraying a character," Skylar said.

"Thank you. It was my first time."

Skylar gave me a questioning look. "Is it? Don't you do it every week? Pretend you are a farmer's daughter?"

My heart dipped down to my stomach, then sprang up to my throat. Had Drake said something to Skylar during their coffee interrogation? "Why would you say that?" I managed to whisper.

Taking hold of my elbow, Skylar assisted me up the stairs. He kept his voice low. "Most farmers' daughters don't wear Jimmy Choos or Chanel clothing."

I made no rebuttal until Kinzy left us at the door to our respective dressing rooms. "How would you know what farmers' daughters wear?"

"I guess I don't, but I see how uncomfortable it makes you when anyone brings up your background. You know nothing about fishing. You were surprised to learn that during planting and harvest season, farmers sometimes eat in the field. That, combined with your taste in designer clothing, tells the story."

"I don't wear designer . . ."

Skylar used his palm as a stop sign. "You do. I recognize designer clothes and shoes because my mother wears them. She is a society woman who taught me to appreciate the finer things in life, and my grandparents on my father's side were farmers. I know the lifestyle differences."

I opened my mouth to deny his statement, but something different came out. "Don't tell anyone."

Moisture sprang to my eyes. I tried to blink it away.

"Oh, Courtney." Skylar wrapped me in a hug, then held me at arm's length. "I won't tell anyone. Your secret is safe with me." He smiled and winked, then disappeared into his individual dressing room.

My legs trembled, making my knees wobble. If Skylar had guessed my background, could others tell too? I grabbed the knob of the door to steady my balance. I glanced at the dressing-room door. Who was I kidding? My reaction wasn't from someone knowing and possibly spilling my secret. It was because the last man who said those same words to me and punctuated them with a wink had ended up dead.

# CHAPTER TWELVE

While changing out of costume, I talked myself down from Skylar's words and expression. His turn of phrase had to be a coincidence. An eerie coincidence. There was no way he could have heard Mick whisper those words in my ear. He'd stationed himself across the room from us during the meet and mingle. Now, I focused on his ability to see through my farm-girl façade.

Returning to the set, I pulled my set chair into a far corner, away from people and equipment. I needed to think and talk to Eric. Obviously, my lack of farming background showed. Or was it just to a trained eye? Could Skylar tell because he'd been schooled in designer clothing?

Barb's words came back to me from our meet and mingle the first night. She'd believed I was raised on a farm. A farm girl herself, I'd convinced her. Or had nostalgic memories clouded her vision, not allowing her to see the fine nuances?

Or was it a fifty-fifty split? Some people saw through

me, while others didn't? So really, anyone could tip my hand. I wanted Eric's thoughts on the subject. I pulled my phone from my jacket pocket. They'd dressed me in a pink pencil skirt with a matching jacket. Paired with a light gray tank and strappy gray sandals with kitten heels. Skylar's clothing, gray trousers and a lightweight gray sweater, coordinated with my outfit.

My thumbs tapped on my screen. I wasn't certain Eric would answer or even walk to the set, as out of sorts as he was this morning. Besides, he was trying to stay away from this show's taping because he had nothing to do with its production and didn't want his name thrown back into the hat of suspects. I couldn't blame him; I wanted my name removed from the derby too.

When my phone didn't vibrate immediately, I decided to people watch and think. My line of vision landed on Skylar first. He sat a little slouched in his chair, legs outstretched, reading a book. Clean-cut and handsome, he didn't fit my image of a murderer. Yet many murderers did have those characteristics. Between his flimsy alibi and strong throwing arm, he could very well have killed Mick. But why? Had their paths crossed early in Skylar's career, as I'd previously pondered? Somehow, I had to find out if he knew Mick.

My thoughts switched to Harrison. I'd bet money he and Mick knew each other, maybe not friends, and not acquaintances either. The thin line in between. They knew each other well enough that Mick knew what buttons to push to fluster, anger and, in my opinion, intimidate Harrison. Speed walking late at night to relieve stress had been Harrison's activity the night of Mick's murder. Was it Harrison's shadow I saw lurking in the tree line? A trained chef, I'm sure he could heft and heave a full cast-iron fry pan. Although Harrison's and Mick's physiques were in opposition—Harrison lean and trim, while Mick carried more than a few extra pounds around his middle—they were even in height.

My eyes sought out Harrison. His thumbs skimmed over his smartphone. His proper chair stance, back straight with both feet planted on the floor, matched his tailored navy suit. From this view, he looked confident, cool and in command. I'd tried to get him to open up about Mick to me in the kitchen. Instead, he'd shut me down. I learned nothing about him I hadn't already known. He had expert knife skills, his gloved hands a blur while slicing the apples.

*Gloved hands.* I did find out something! With everything that had happened, it had slipped my mind that he'd told me he always wore gloves in the kitchen. He'd carried the pair he wore as my sous chef in his pocket. Did he have a pair tucked away on his person now? Or the night he'd been jogging? If only my fingerprints were on the pan, the murderer wore gloves.

Had Mick underestimated Harrison? Had a blackmail attempt gone wrong? Or was it a love triangle involving Tabitha?

"Miss Archer."

My body started at Kinzy's words.

"I'm sorry. I thought you saw me walk up to you. They're ready for you on the set. They want you and Skylar to call the challenge time."

I hurried behind Kinzy to my mark. Skylar pulled up beside me. "Courtney, you're standing on Shannon's tape line."

"Oh!" I'd been so deep in thought, so preoccupied with the murder and the lack of Eric answering my text, I'd stood on the first piece of tape I'd seen. "Sorry." I moved around Skylar to the green tape.

"That's better. This is my best side. Maybe stand closer; gray washes me out. I need some color reflection from your pink." Skylar made a disgusted huff. "I wish wardrobe would listen to me."

I sidestepped toward him until our arms grazed.

The makeup artists brushed away our shine. Brenden drew a chair close to give us instructions. "Courtney, start the countdown with ten minutes. Action."

"Bakers, you have ten seconds left." I grimaced. "No, sorry. Keep rolling. Bakers, you have ten minutes left."

"Cut." Brenden stood and approached us. "It's important we get these lines right. It is the only warning the bakers get for the countdown. Skylar, be ready at five minutes." Brenden looked at me when he enunciated the word "minute." "Courtney, take one minute. Skylar, you say, 'Stop baking.' Got it?"

I nodded and drew in several deep breaths. I needed to clear my mind. Focus on the job at hand.

"Five minutes," Skylar warned.

Yet I kept going back to those gloved hands. Was anyone looking for gloves? I suppose it was obvious to Drake and Sheriff Perry, yet when they'd interviewed me, they'd stressed my fingerprints on the pan. Should I bring it up to either of the men?

"Courtney," Brenden's voice hissed.

Drat, I'd missed my cue. "One minute, bakers."

Nervous muttering erupted around us. Cameramen went in for close-ups of stressed faces.

I watched Barb put the finishing touches on her biscuit presentation.

"Come out," Tabitha yelled. My gaze flew to her in time to see her lift her cast-iron fry pan over her head one-handed and whack it, hard, open side down, on the countertop. She didn't seem to notice the direct stares or sneaked glances from the other contestants. She peeked under the pan. Something must have loosened. Grabbing a spatula, she poked it into the pan.

"Stop baking."

All the contestants raised their hands at Skylar's command. Except Tabitha.

Tabitha looked up at us, wild-eyed. She checked the clock before she whacked the pan against the counter again. This time, biscuit fragments splattered the countertop and floor. She swore. Fury reddened her face. She lifted the pan again, then noticed the cameraman. She dropped the pan and hid her face in her hands.

"Cut!" Brenden yelled. "Hands off the food. We will take five and get reset for the judges to visit and sample each challenge. Courtney, you are accompanying them. Feel free to sneak a bite or ad lib a comment or quip." After his announcement, he cut a straight line to Tabitha, who now tried to clean up the mess. "I said, hands off the food. Leave the mess. You are being judged on what you accomplished."

The icy glare Tabitha shot Brenden made a chill run down my spine. Shannon and I traded a worried glance.

Working from the back to the front, we started with Rhonda. She'd displayed her biscuits on a rustic, wooden cutting board in a tiered, cakelike fashion. She'd chosen a small, cut-glass bowl for her spread.

"Your plating is lovely." Harrison broke open a biscuit and spooned a dollop of her sauce on the edge.

"Tell us about your biscuits." Shannon took the other half of the biscuit and spread the topping across it.

"I went savory, with diced ham inside my dough, and a brown sugar, pineapple chutney." Rhonda's lips trembled before breaking into a strained smile while she listened to Harrison and Shannon talk about her fluffy dough and the slightly runny consistency of her spread.

Due to my insider information, I passed on trying a taste.

Shannon and Harrison took a bite and began to chew. Both of their expressions soured. They swallowed hard.

Clearing her throat, Shannon put a hand on her chest. "I believe you made an error in your recipe."

Harrison coughed and looked around. "We will need some water over here."

Kinzy came on the run with two bottles of water. After both judges took long swigs of water, the critique began.

"Like yesterday, you used too much salt. What did your recipe call for?" Harrison asked.

Rhonda shrugged. "I used a recipe I know from heart. I must have added the salt more than once." She wrung her hands. "I am nervous about the competition and," Rhonda tilted her head to the kitchenette behind her, "the murder."

Harrison pursed his lips. I wasn't sure if it was from the oversalted food or Rhonda's excuse.

"I'd say you failed this challenge. Next time, measure out your ingredients into individual bowls to avoid this error." Harrison didn't wait for Shannon or Rhonda to respond; he moved to the next station while pulling a long draw from his water bottle.

I glanced back at Rhonda, who wore a satisfied smile. I shook my head. It made me sad to know someone would sabotage their baking and a chance for the top baking prize.

Barb had baked a sweet dough biscuit with a thick strawberry jam.

"This is good. Add whipped cream and you'd think you were eating strawberry shortcake." Shannon licked her lips. "You're a country girl like us." She drew me into a side hug. "I can tell because that's how we like our strawberry shortcake, over a sweet biscuit. Isn't that right, Courtney?"

I checked my shock and guilt before I smiled wide into the camera while nodding my head in affirmation. In truth, I'd always eaten that dessert on pound or angel food cake.

"You have my stamp of approval too." Harrison dipped a spoon into her jam. "Unlike Shannon, what makes the dish for me is the jam. Kudos."

Barb beamed.

I snatched a biscuit and some jam. The light, airy biscuit melted in my mouth. The jam burst with freshness, like biting into a ripe strawberry. "This is delicious. I could eat it every morning for breakfast. Is it a family recipe?"

"No." She giggled. "I've been hungry for strawberry shortcake, so I thought, why not try it for my biscuit challenge? To be honest, it took days to perfect the recipe. I sure wasn't hungry for strawberry shortcake anymore."

"I'll bet you weren't." Harrison chuckled.

Anthony had prepared a bacon-infused biscuit with a maple butter spread. It was tasty. Harrison and Shannon thought the biscuit needed more leavening. Daniel had overcooked his biscuits. In what I thought bordered on the rude side, and a little too showy, Harrison banged one on the counter to see if it would break. It didn't. Daniel did win praise for the blueberry-whipped honey spread.

"Brace yourself," Shannon whispered.

I took a deep breath. Tabitha was next. Harrison's demeanor changed completely. Instead of a chip on each shoulder, he sported blocks of wood. He met Tabitha's glare with more bravado than I'd seen him display since we'd arrived.

"What happened here?" He threw out his hand over the counter.

Pinch-lipped Tabitha opened her mouth; then she must have remembered the cameras were rolling. "I had trouble getting the biscuits out of the pan."

What I knew was anger or resentment toward Harrison would come off as tension on camera.

"We can see that. Did you not temper your pan?" The pointed look with which Harrison pinned Tabitha told me he was really referencing her anger. I wasn't certain she understood.

"I don't know. This was my second batch. The first batch didn't turn out of the pan either."

"Well, usually, biscuits lift right out of the bottom of your pan even if it isn't greased." Shannon's raised brows asked the unspoken question.

Tabitha hung her head.

Did she feel bad? Or was that for the camera's sake?

Harrison's lips pursed. He pulled a bit from what was left in the pan. "This tastes like flour and baking soda."

"I tried to make a lighter version. A skinny-girl-friendly version." Tabitha looked up and spat out the words. "I wanted to present a calorie-friendly biscuit and spread. Obviously, what I substituted for short-ening didn't work in the biscuit. I'm sure the spread is good. I whipped spreadable olive oil with cinna-mon and nutmeg."

Shannon picked up the funky plastic bowl Tabitha had used for presentation. She dipped in a spoon and took a small taste. "The taste is passable, and the texture is good. I understand what you were trying to do here. It wasn't a bad idea; however, you had plenty of time to perfect this recipe before the com-petition."

Harrison must have considered the interview with Tabitha finished. He moved on to Otto.

The remaining contestants had few flaws in either their biscuits, spreads or sauces. The offerings were as varied as the contestants with either sweet, savory or a mix of both. It seemed to me that Shannon and Harrison would have a hard time choosing the win-

ner of this round, and an even a harder time deter-
mining whether Tabitha or Rhonda had the biggest
failure. Of course, they both had a chance to redeem
themselves in the afternoon challenge.

We broke for lunch. The contestants' commissary
was somewhere in the resort. Kinzy herded them off
the set. Shannon, Harrison, Skylar and I shared a
buffet table with the crew. I guessed the segregation
had to do with a judge becoming friendly with a contestant and playing favorites.

Shannon and I filled our plates with mixed greens
and all the trimmings. She chose an Italian dressing,
while I went with a lemon and olive oil dressing I had
requested when filling out our preference sheets for
catering. I'm sure the resort's kitchen staff were ap-
prehensive feeding chefs, especially Harrison. I was
of the opinion they were doing a fantastic job.

Once I'd grabbed a sparkling water, Shannon and
I stepped up to the wardrobe room where we'd eaten
breakfast five hours earlier. This time, we were on
our own. I had noticed Skylar ate and visited with the
crew during lunchtime. Harrison always seemed to
disappear.

I pulled out my phone. Still no response from Eric.
Always the professional, even when we disagreed, he
returned my texts and calls.

"What's with the frown?" Shannon drawled.

"Eric hasn't answered my text from midmorning."
I sighed and laid my phone on the table. I drizzled
my special-order dressing over my salad before I
forked some arugula and a chickpea.

"He's probably busy tying up loose ends for taping

tonight. I'm looking forward to coming. I need to do something besides work." Shannon nibbled at a snap pea.

"Yeah." I picked up the phone and checked it again. Nothing. I sent him another message. What I really wanted to talk to him about still felt important to me. I wanted his take on Harrison always wearing gloves in the kitchen. Would Eric think that included if he planned to murder someone there? I put the phone back down and looked at Shannon. I really wished I knew her well enough to confide my suspicions. Maybe someday.

"Wow. That is your second sigh since you sat down. Did you and Eric have a fight?" Shannon sipped from her bottle of sweet tea.

"I don't know if I'd call it a fight." I picked through my salad and absently stabbed a green pepper with my fork tines.

"Was it about Drake?"

My head snapped up. My gaze met Shannon's blue eyes filled with knowing.

"It was." She nodded her head, her lips pulled into a grim line. "He found out you and Drake had dinner together last night."

It took me a second to realize my mouth hung open in surprise. I closed it. What else did she know? Had Drake told others? Or had someone else eavesdropped on our conversation, the way I had on Harrison and Mick our first night here? "How do you know that?"

A puzzled expression crossed Shannon's face. She leaned back in her chair. "It's obvious."

"What is obvious?" I drew my brows together.

"Courtney, are you being serious?"

I nodded.

"Eric likes you. It shows all over his face when he looks at you."

It took a second for her words to sink in; then I burst into laughter. "No, he doesn't. I mean, I know he likes me, but not in the way you are indicating."

Shannon reached across the table and palmed my forearm. "I am serious. He does. Up until the moment you met and flirted with Drake, I thought you two were a couple."

I stopped laughing. "No." I shook my head.

"Yes," Shannon said, nodding. "He takes care of you the same way my husband takes care of my needs."

I opened my mouth to rebut her statement, then closed it. Eric did bring me coffee every morning. He knew my likes and dislikes. What I was comfortable cooking on our show. He stuck close to field uncomfortable questions. He texted me often when we weren't together to see what I was doing. We had shared many lunches and dinners where he paid. I'd assumed the show reimbursed him for those. He'd never said they were dates. Had he assumed I knew?

I studied my salad.

"Don't look so sad. Eric's a looker who respects you and is interested in your career. Believe me, friendship is the best start to a lasting relationship."

"I don't know." I lifted my gaze to meet hers. "He's never said anything or done anything more physical than a hug."

"Maybe he's waiting for a signal from you. Most

men won't pursue a woman unless she acts interested." Shannon gave my arm a squeeze, then returned to eating her salad.

I followed her lead. How could I read attraction into Drake's and my interactions, always coming away disappointed, and not see Eric was attracted to me? Because he wasn't. I'd known Eric a long time. Shannon didn't. She might have misread something he did as personal interest instead of professional interest. After all, we were business partners.

And she didn't know the secret Eric and I kept about my background that Drake and Sheriff Perry now knew and Skylar had figured out. Eric wasn't jealous about me having dinner with Drake. He'd been worried we might become the next network scandal. We'd witnessed the firing of a popular show host when a former employee spilled the beans that all his recipes came from the original *Betty Crocker Cookbook*.

Shannon was wrong. Eric had no romantic feelings for me. He just wanted to keep his job.


Back on the set, Harrison announced the second challenge of the day: the contestants had to prepare a casserole their morning biscuit creations would complement.

Barb threw her hands in the air.

"What's the matter, Barb?" Harrison asked with a gentle tone.

"I would have made rosemary biscuits with lemon curd had I known about this challenge."

Harrison smiled. "You're inventive. You'll come up with something."

His statement earned a smile from Barb and a glare from Tabitha.

"You set this challenge to eliminate me." Tabitha pointed at Harrison. "It's not going to work. I'll make a casserole so spectacular, you'll hardly notice the biscuit bits." *Snap.* A tea towel met the countertop.

Had she forgotten the cameras were rolling?

"I hope you do. I wish all of you luck." Harrison turned to Skylar and me.

We read the plea in his eyes. Everyone was tired of Tabitha's outbursts, and to avoid another, we wasted no time in saying, in unison, "The baking begins . . . NOW!"

Our cameraman turned and joined the others, capturing the cooks.

Brenden approached us. "Great ad-libbing, Harrison. I'll have to edit out Tabitha." He grimaced and rubbed his neck.

My cell phone vibrated in my pocket.

"I'll need you to report back to the set by four." Brenden called Kinzy to him by flicking two fingers.

I slipped my phone from my pocket and tapped the app.

**Security man's minions won't let me in.**

My thumbs sent a brief message. I hurried up the stairs to slip out of my wardrobe and into my skinny jeans, a *Cooking with the Farmer's Daughter* T-shirt and tennies. I might have a break, but my work wasn't done. We were blocking out tonight's show this afternoon.

I skipped down the stairs, opened the door a crack, got a nod from Security and stepped into the bright sunshine. Taking the main path, Eric fell in step with me when I reached a large oak tree.

"Sorry, I've been tied up on the phone or on your set all morning."

I braced. "How did the phone call go?"

He exhaled a deep breath. "They aren't happy. Your ratings are terrific. They reminded me that your demographic is the heartland."

"I'm so sorry."

"It is amazing to me how Sheriff Perry shut this down with the local and national press. No one at the network had any idea a murder had happened. They did understand that, in this case, there is not much you or I can do. They are more concerned you are considered a person of interest. They will get their public relations and attorney alerted to the situation. By the way, their attorney will call you with instructions on how to proceed if you're questioned again." Eric stopped walking and faced me. "Promise you will not socialize with Drake anymore."

I searched his all-too-familiar face. His blue eyes pleaded. Tension showed on his face in the drawn lines around his mouth. "I promise. I want this murder resolved. I've been thinking about something Harrison said. He always wears gloves in the kitchen."

"So?" Eric drew out the vowel.

"They only found my fingerprints. The murderer must have worn gloves."

"Courtney!" Eric threw his arms in the air. "Stop speculating and questioning. Leave it alone. Let law enforcement do their jobs."

I didn't like Eric's scolding tone. "I have to clear my name."

"No, you don't. You are innocent. You will get ruled out. Give them time to process everything they found at the crime scene. Even the smallest hair can detect the murderer."

I couldn't argue with his reasoning, so I changed the subject. "While you were on the phone with the higher-ups, did you tell them if they'd remove this clause, we'd have no problem? People would know I'm a trained chef who can cook wholesome and healthy, rib-sticking food in addition to fruit and vegetable art." I hissed the words through clenched teeth. I knew better than to raise my voice. Whether Eric thought so or not, I'd learned my lesson.

"Yes, we talked about it. They are reluctant. I warned them that in a year, there would be a renegotiation."

"What'd they say?"

"'We'll see.'"

We'd reached the resort.

"Let's concentrate on getting our show blocked so the people who paid to watch the live taping aren't disappointed. Okay?" Eric held the door open and I passed through.

"Agreed." I turned to Eric. "I love my fans. I don't want to hurt them, but I feel like I am by not telling the truth."

"I know." Eric guided me by the elbow. "Maybe I need to take you to the family farm for a month or two, turn you into a real farm girl."

We walked down the hall in silence, and I wondered what exactly he meant. Was it an innocent statement? Turn me into a farm girl to alleviate my guilt and have a plausible cause to explain away my past? Or could it be something else? To meet his family? My heart raced at my last thought, which was silly.

I cast a sideways glance at Eric. He was boy-next-door good-looking, successful, articulate and kind. All qualities I considered when I dated a man. A sigh built in my chest. I tamped it down before I released it. I gave my head a shake. I was reading more into everything Eric said. I knew Shannon meant well, but I wished she hadn't planted this romantic scenario in my mind. I didn't have time to spend weeding through Eric's words or actions. I had more important things to worry about: dealing with the aftermath of Mick's murder and getting my name off the person of interest list. This was one warning of Eric's I didn't plan to heed.

# CHAPTER THIRTEEN

Skylar had accompanied the judges on the second round of tasting and judging the contestants' casseroles. We'd been filmed sitting around a white bistro table, part of an outdoors set used by the judges, weighing the pros and cons of the dishes prepared in today's competition.

Now, we stood ready to make the announcement. I glanced at Skylar. "The baker leaving us today is . . ." I stopped and slowly swept my gaze over the contestants, starting with Rhonda and ending with Tabitha, who picked up on the gesture and sucked her bottom lip under her front teeth. "Rhonda," I said, casting what I hoped was an apologetic expression her way. "The judges had a tough choice between two contestants. Tabitha managed to salvage her spot with an outstanding skinny-casserole version of chicken Marsala. Rhonda, for some reason, your seasoning was off today, with too much salt in the biscuits and overpowering heat in your chili bake." It was hard to keep my expression neutral when I knew her overuse of seasoning was intentional.

While the cast hugged, cried and bid her farewell, I wondered if Rhonda really was unnerved by the murder, or if she could have committed the murder and now wanted to leave the premises. Two contestants had left the resort. Had we unsuspectingly released Mick's murderer back into the world?

"Now to deliver the happier news." Glee filled Skylar's voice, creating tension and anticipation on the faces of the remaining nine contestants. "The baker of the day is . . ." He paused. "Barb."

"Oh my!" Barb shouted and lifted her palms to her cheeks, her surprise genuine.

As the remaining contestants gathered around her, Shannon addressed the group. "Barb's use of simple ingredients to create vintage comfort food, shepherd's pie and strawberry shortcake, reminded us good food and meal preparation needn't be hard or complicated."

"Well done," Harrison added with a smile.

For a full minute, we remained on our marks while the cameras caught the congratulatory celebration of the contestants. Then Brenden hollered, "Cut."

The crowd dispersed. Barb still beamed, which was more than I could say about Otto. Stony anger settled on his features. In a loud voice, he said, "There is no way her food was better than mine."

He ripped off his apron and stalked for the door through which they ushered the contestants. Melissa followed, her demeanor mirroring Otto's. The remaining contestants removed their aprons and walked to the exit. The only expression their faces showed was fatigue from a long day of stress-filled cooking. Kinzy beelined to Barb, whisking her off into a corner. Probably to film her interview about the win.

"I have to go." I started for the stairs. I needed to do a quick change from their wardrobe to my clothes, only to get to the resort to make another wardrobe change for the taping of the *Cooking with the Farmer's Daughter* episode.

"I'm coming too."

After Shannon and I changed, we hurried from the building.

"Let's go this way." Shannon pulled at my arm.

"That path is off-limits." Sometimes I do learn my lesson.

She shrugged. "It's shorter. You need to have a little bit of downtime before you begin your taping." She started to walk, pulling me along with her.

I hoped we didn't run into Drake or, worse yet, Travis. I didn't think I could stand another one of his scoldings or insinuations. I hadn't had a run-in with him in a day or two and figured I was due. Come to think of it, I hadn't even seen him around the set or the resort. I surmised he was either covering the graveyard shift for Security or doing the background checks. I hoped it was the former.

To my relief, we didn't run into anyone. Shannon and I said our goodbyes. I made it to the conference-room-turned-television-set in enough time that I could relax with a cold drink in a comfortable chair with my feet propped on a box.

As I sipped, I thought about the murder and my frightening thought, that the show could be sending the murderer home scot-free. Yet the show had done a good job of segregating the contestants from the cast and crew. I had never run into any of the competitors at the coffee shop, steak house or even in the halls. So, could one of them have been able to slip away? Somehow, I needed to find out that information. Although Tabitha was the only one who seemed angered by Mick, most of the contestants seemed bothered by his antics in the same way serious classmates viewed the class clown, as a nuisance.

"Hi, Courtney."

I jumped at Eric's greeting, sloshing iced tea on my jeans.

"Sorry, I didn't mean to startle you. I let the door slam." Eric rummaged around the area, found a paper towel roll and presented it to me. "Glad you weren't in wardrobe."

"Me too. It wasn't your fault. I was lost in thought. Do you ever see the contestants milling around the resort?"

Eric shook his head. "Why?"

"I just wondered if they'd be able to sneak . . ."

"I told you to stop trying to solve this murder." Eric pulled a chair next to mine. "Don't put yourself in any danger."

"I'm not." I blotted the wet spot on my jeans with the nonabsorbent paper towel.

"Not what?"

Sheepishness crawled through me. I was certain it showed on my face. "Putting myself in danger."

"Well, you are if you get in the middle of this murder investigation."

"I just wondered if the contestants were free to roam

around the resort. I'd hate to think they weren't. It's such a lovely place."

"My understanding is, they are in another wing of the resort. They have certain paths on the property where they can walk, and their food is catered in to them. They are under surveillance. The show has security measures to check for cheating."

"So, say, Tabitha couldn't get out and sneak back to *The American Baking Battle* set?" I wadded up the paper towel and pitched it toward the wastebasket. It fell short by about four feet.

"You must not have played basketball."

In unison, both Eric's and my head jerked toward the door. Sheriff Perry's voice had taken us both by surprise.

"How long have you been standing there?" I stood, picked up the towel and walked it to the wastebasket. No sense in showing my lack of throwing abilities again.

"Long enough." The thoughtful expression on his face changed to pointed.

I swallowed hard. "It's just I think . . ."

"Courtney!"

Eric's voice reminded me of my promise. I stopped talking and sat down.

Sheriff Perry walked farther into the room and stood beside Eric's chair. "Everyone has a theory when it comes to murder." The sheriff looped his thumbs through his belt loops. "I'd like to hear yours, Miss Archer."

My eyes widened. "Really?"

"Yes."

Eric vigorously shook his head. I felt I was on the hot seat either way. I cleared my throat. "I think it was a blackmail scheme gone wrong."

Sheriff Perry chuckled.

"Love triangle?" I tried again.

I received the same response, which sounded a little practiced on his part.

I drew my mouth into a pout and looked to Eric for support. Instead, he met my pleading with a what-were-you-thinking look. I cold-shouldered Eric by angling my body a few inches. "Is this an official visit?" I asked.

"It is." Sheriff Perry shot Eric a glance and huffed. "Even though your network attorney called my office, I intend to continue to question you. Are you sure that you didn't know Mick?"

I glanced over my shoulder at Eric. His eyes beseeched me to keep quiet. I drew my lips into a grim line and shook my head.

"Ah, the silent treatment." Sheriff Perry clicked his tongue and paced the floor. "After reading your thorough background check, we know you have a secret. The public doesn't always take kindly to little white lies, now do they?" The sheriff air-quoted "little white lies."

I turned to look at Eric. He gave his head a small shake.

"Mr. Iverson isn't a person of interest anymore, but you still are, Miss Archer. If Mick threatened to reveal your secret to the world, would you have killed him?"

"No!" My rebuttal, involuntary, echoed through the quietness of the room. "What makes you think

Mick knew my personal background?" Eric and I knew he'd overheard and suspected, but how would anyone else know? He was murdered within twenty-four hours of his eavesdropping.

"Well." He clicked his tongue again. "When the tech guys broke through the password on his computer, they found a file marked 'Courtney Archer—bonus story.' Combine that with the fact that your pan of cobbler, riddled with your fingerprints, killed Mick all point to your theory—a blackmail scheme gone wrong."

Sheriff Perry touched two fingers to his ball cap and saluted a wave. Then he was gone.

"I can't believe . . ." I stopped. My stylist entered the room. A quick look at the clock let me know I didn't have time to debate what the sheriff had said. I had to get ready for the taping.

I hurried to the dressing room. My thoughts roved over the information Sheriff Perry had delivered. What could that mean? Bonus story? The last thing I needed to hear before my taping was the sheriff's announcement of additional evidence pointed at me. My nerves jittered. I'd fumbled with the buttons on my gingham blouse, popping off one. Now I forced myself to stand still while my stylist scrambled to sew it back on while I was in it so we could begin filming.

She'd secured my hair into a braid and added a headband in the same yellow print as my blouse. Today, I wore skinny jeans, the legs neatly tucked into a pair of low-heeled western boots, plain leather stitched with yellow thread in a daisy-chain design.

"Are you ready?" Eric called through the collapsi-ble wall separating me from the set.

"Just about." My stylist managed to secure the button and buttoned it without dismantling another. She pulled up the shirttails, tying them in a knot at my waist.

"You need to know the sheriff and Drake are in the audience, along with Shannon and Skylar." Eric cracked open the door and spoke in a hushed tone inflected with agitation. I knew Eric didn't like the evidence bomb the sheriff had dropped either.

"Friend and foe," I muttered. My stylist stood back, gave me a once-over and a thumbs-up. "I'm ready."

"I'll cue the music."

When the familiar twang of my theme song started, I opened the door, pasted on a smile and waved to the audience as I walked onto my set. It was a full house. Not one vacant chair. Via a microphone, Eric introduced me. The crowd stood and applauded.

I couldn't help but think of the opposite reaction if they knew I was a fraud. Boos, hisses and empty seats. I felt the corners of my mouth droop and forced them back up. If my secret leaked, it could ruin my chances for any other type of cooking show. I really wanted to tell my fans. Hearing it from me in a sincere and apologetic way would lessen the damage. Wouldn't it?

Off to the side, Eric waved at the crowd to take their seats, then explained a little bit about how the show was taped before he turned the show over to me. I had a rough start with some minor mess-ups in lines. I'd scanned the audience. I knew Drake and Sheriff Perry each occupied an aisle seat on opposite sides. Shannon and Skylar sat in the back. Finally, I focused on the camera and found my groove.

While the finger pies baked, the filming stopped. To pass the time, we opened the floor for questions and answers. Most questions revolved around food: my favorite, what kind of apples I used in the recipe, who was my influence in the kitchen. Then a middle-aged woman stood.

Eric took the microphone to her.

She sniffled, then said, "How do you feel about being a suspect in a murder?"

The audience gasped. Some began to whisper among themselves.

The woman looked around. "How have you not heard? It was the lead story on the national news."

*What?* Panic sliced into my heart.

Continuing, the woman said, "I am just sick my favorite cooking show host is being accused." She stopped and looked at the sheriff. "Of murder." She turned back to me. "I want you to know, you have my support." Her attention went back to Sheriff Perry, who stood. "I don't believe for a minute that a wholesome country girl like Courtney committed murder."

My stomach plummeted downward and I swallowed hard at her description of me.

"Ma'am, I have to ask you to step out of the room." The sheriff jerked his head at Drake, who was on the move. He beckoned the woman with a wave of his hand.

By the panicked expression on the woman's face, she had no idea stating her opinion and support of me might get her into trouble. Her head bobbed left, then right, as the men closed in on her.

"No, please." I walked around the counter. "She didn't mean any harm. She was only showing her support, and for that I thank her." I looked at the woman and smiled. "I appreciate it." I directed my gaze to Sheriff Perry. "Please, let her stay."

"All right." Sheriff Perry joined me in front of the crowd. "There will be no more discussion of this topic. For the record, Miss Archer is a person of interest, not a suspect. She is not the only person of interest, and no one has been accused of murder yet. The investigation is ongoing. Your questions from this point forward must pertain to cooking. If anyone mentions the murder, you will be escorted from the room and building."

Thank goodness the timer sounded and we could finish the last portion of the segment. Drake and Sheriff Perry remained standing, one on each side of the crowd. The sheriff did allow the short meet-and-greet included in the admission price of their tickets. He stuck close by me. No one uttered a word about the murder. I felt certain it'd be the only topic covered on the bus ride home.

"You wait here." Sheriff Perry pointed at me once the last audience member had exited. "Drake will be back to escort you to your room."

Despite the situation, my heart fluttered.

Eric snorted. "Is that necessary?"

"I believe it is. Someone leaked our situation to the press. Anyone could be a press person disguised as a fan. Drake knows how to handle the press." Sheriff Perry turned the pointed look he'd pinned on Eric to me. "You don't."

"Don't worry, bud, I'll take good care of her." Drake winked at Eric. He turned to me. "Do you need to change?"

"Yes."

"You have five minutes." Drake looked at his fitness tracker, then lifted his eyes to me.

I hurried toward my makeshift dressing room as he pulled his phone from his polo shirt pocket; today, it was navy tucked into blue jeans. Before I closed the door, I heard him say, "I'm going to get Travis to do a search of the internet. See if he can find the leak. I'm sure Sheriff Perry will make a search on the fan's name when he gets back to his office."

With my stylist's help, I disrobed and redressed in record time. I walked into the room, where only Drake waited.

He grimaced when he saw me. My heart plunged to my stomach. When would I admit to myself that I did not have the same effect on him as he did on me? Sadly.

"Do you mind finding a jacket or turning your shirt inside out? I don't want to attract any more attention than necessary."

Pulling on the hem of my T-shirt, I looked at my logo. It might draw attention if someone were looking for me. I considered his request. Was it for my safety, or to make his job easier? Still annoyed at myself for being attracted to someone who was clearly not into me, I took it out on Drake. "No, I don't have a jacket. I'm not wearing my shirt wrong. And before you ask, I can't wear my show's wardrobe."

One side of his mouth curled. "Feisty tonight, are we? Head toward the office. We'll use the secret hallway. It will get us close to the elevator and out of the prying eyes of the public. Until we can investigate the extent of this leak."

"Or if maybe the fan was the murderer." I said the words absently.

Drake shrugged. "Could be. Some killers like to come back to the scene of the crime. See the mayhem it created." He opened the door, checked the hall and motioned for me to exit. I did. He placed a hand on my elbow and set our pace down the short hallway to the hotel office. He nodded a greeting to the night clerk when we walked past. A swipe of a card and he opened the door, and there we were, alone in a spooky hallway.

Maybe I should have protested.

Drake pointed. "Head this way."

I turned in the direction Drake had indicated. "You don't think we've sent the murderer home already with a contest elimination?" I might as well put this time to good use.

"I can't answer that question. I can tell you that the eliminated contestants are under surveillance until we find the killer."

The hallway was wide enough that we could walk side by side without touching. It was well lit, yet all I could hear was Eric saying he didn't trust Drake. And I shouldn't either. No one knew where I was. Panic sped up my heart rate.

"While we are on this subject, do you think your boyfriend leaked the information to the public?"

"What? I don't have a boyfriend."

Drake stopped. I did too. He faced me. "Eric's not your significant other?"

My brows furrowed. I shook my head. An emotion sparked in Drake's eyes. Interest maybe? My heartbeat took a dramatic turn, going from a panicked to an excited rhythm.

"Why would you think that?" I started to walk.

"Well, you're always together. No one else's producer came with them." Drake fell into step, more leisurely than in the public hallway.

"No one else needs to film their show to keep their contract commitments. For the record, Eric wouldn't leak the information."

"He did call the network, and they called an attorney." Drake cast a sideways glance at me.

"True. No one there would leak this to the public."

"I know the top brass at companies keep secrets. Entry-level employees, maybe not. Everyone wants their fifteen minutes of fame." Drake's biceps brushed mine, making the spot swirl with heat.

"Maybe. Why would they put their job at risk? Leaking this information would look bad for the show." I sneaked a sideways glance.

"In more ways than one, right?"

I knew he was insinuating my background. I sighed. "I suppose." I thought about the bonus story file Sheriff Perry had mentioned. Could Mick have leaked anything before he was murdered? Called a family member, friend or coworker?

We approached a door. Drake slowed. "This is our stop."

A quick swipe and we were back in the main hallway. I noted the door marker said "janitor closet" as it closed behind us.

We were only a few steps from the elevator. In a few short minutes, Drake delivered me to my room. "You should stay put. If you need dinner, call room service. I'll wait here until I hear your door lock."

He leaned against the doorframe.

I studied his face, the chiseled features that gave him a rugged, outdoorsy look. So very opposite from most of the men I knew or dated. My insides went soft. It wasn't the time and I knew it, but somehow, I couldn't stop myself. "Don't you want to sweep the room to make sure it's safe for me to go in?" I asked in my best flirty voice.

"Nah; one of my guys did that already." He lifted his phone from his pocket and wiggled it. "While you were changing." His lips curled into a sly smile. "Good night, Courtney."

A thrill swirled through me at the sexy way he said my name. I pulled my phone from my pocket to take my key card from the case on the back when Drake swiped his security key. My door light winked green and I opened the door to a sliver big enough for me to slip through. I turned just in time to flash Drake a smile.

Had he been attracted to me all along but thought I was taken? After I twisted the dead bolt and flipped the security bar, I eyed the peephole. My timing perfect, I enjoyed the view. Drake's backside walking away. A wide smile stretched across my face. I leaned against the door for a moment, savoring the prospect of Drake returning my romantic interest.

It was only a moment. The word "interest" chased away any butterflies fluttering inside me. Mick had interest in me too, and not in a good way. Why would a baker and bakery owner from a small Minnesota community mark a file "bonus story"? Only a writer or a reporter would think my secret would make a good story. I searched my mind for other occupations that would refer to a situation as a story and came up with nothing.

Warned to stay in my room, I decided this was a perfect time to do a search on the internet. I perused the room service menu, made a choice and a call, then hunkered down in front of my laptop. I started with a search for "Mick Henderson, author." Nothing. I tried "Michael." More hits popped up on the browser. The face or age didn't match.

I tried several searches at online bookstores; still nothing. I ruled out "author" and moved on to "reporter." I felt more hopeful. Mick's demeanor—aggressive, especially with Harrison—fit the bill of a reporter after a story. Or a blackmailer. Or a jilted lover.

I came up as empty as a hungry hand in a dieter's cookie jar. Sure, there were a few Michael Hendersons in the business. They were local television anchors or meteorologists; again, their pictures not a match to Mick's face.

I shivered and swallowed hard, thinking of Mick on the floor of the set, splattered in blood and cobbler. Even if he rubbed me the wrong way, he didn't deserve to die in such a manner. And he deserved justice.

I typed in his name and "baker." The browser found one solitary entry, other than the network's promotion for *The American Baking Battle* show. The bakery website. I clicked on the web address. The header picture was his storefront. A small building sandwiched between an insurance agency and a gift shop. The store sign, painted in pastels, read "Baked Goodies." Doughnuts, cookies and cupcakes personified with arms, legs and faces danced around the words.

I wrinkled my nose. Mick didn't seem the pastel or cartoony type. Then I shrugged and continued to read his bio. He'd owned the business for ten years after taking it over from another party. That might explain the sign.

Odd. He listed nothing about his baking experience or schooling. Nor did it say how or why he came to own a bakery in small-town Minnesota. Was it his hometown? A second career? A woman? I clicked through the site, which was mostly pictures. There was a "contact and comments" page. Most people raved about the long johns. I went back to the original search and chose the "images" option. Two pictures appeared: the picture of his bakery and the promo photo of him for the show. Would it behoove a businessperson to have such a scant digital footprint?

I leaned back in my chair and stretched. My search had provided no useful information or insight into who may have murdered Mick.

It still seemed to me that the obvious choices were Harrison and Tabitha. I wouldn't dismiss Skylar and his powerful arm, yet he'd really had no connection or interaction with Mick. Tabitha and Harrison had interactions: terse interactions. There must be a connection there. After all, Mick's innuendos struck fear in my and Eric's hearts about the end of our careers. Not enough to make us blind with rage and kill him, though.

I was missing a vital ingredient in this recipe. Starting tomorrow, I'd corner Harrison and befriend Tabitha, if I had to, to try to find out what it was.

# CHAPTER FOURTEEN

Shannon had texted me that she was running late this morning. Which fit perfectly into my plan. Harrison was not getting off easy today. I arrived on set early. Hovering around the catering table, I breakfasted on vanilla yogurt topped with coconut and fresh peaches while I kept my eye on the door.

Harrison came waltzing through the door, newspaper tucked under his arm. He stopped for a bite to eat. "Good morning, Courtney."

"Good morning." I threw away my empty bowl, re-filled my coffee cup and snagged a small cinnamon roll. How had I ever gone without breakfast all these years? I stepped back and waited for Harrison to make his choices. He helped himself to coffee and a protein bar before heading up the staircase to wardrobe and makeup.

Well, makeup for him. He wore his own expensive suits. He also got to choose the color, and then wardrobe coordinated Shannon's outfit. I guess when you are a renowned chef, you can make demands and get your way. If a person was used to that lifestyle and someone, say Mick, didn't give in, you'd probably want them eliminated from your life. Plus, if Mick had a file that said "bonus story" on me, he must have had a file on Harrison. Harrison seemed to be Mick's focus of attention when he was alive.

I waited until Harrison vanished through the door to step up to wardrobe myself. When I entered, I saw he hadn't disappointed me. There he sat, in the chair farthest from the door, like always.

I didn't know a lot about Harrison, but I did know he was a creature of habit. I walked over and took the chair beside him.

He flashed me a frowny face. "That's Skylar's chair."

"This isn't school, Harrison. We don't have assigned seats." I sipped my coffee and tried to keep up my nerve under his scrutinizing glare. After all, I did suspect him of murder. Being brave wasn't easy.

After a long drink of bracing coffee, I cleared my throat and turned my chair to face him. "You never answered my question the other day. Did you know Mick?"

Harrison's agitated expression morphed into anger. His nostrils flared. "Why do you keep asking me that question?"

"Because I think you did, and I think he tried to blackmail you and . . ."

The creak of the door opening stopped me.

Shannon, smile wide and bright, burst into the room. "Good morning. I am running so late." She stopped in her tracks, first looking at me, then at Harrison. Her eyes widened a little and she slipped into her usual chair.

"Good morning, Shannon," Harrison said, tone curt. "Courtney, who somehow knows more than the sheriff, was just about to tell me why I killed Mick."

Shannon gasped. "Is that a confession?"

Harrison snorted. "No."

"So far, I said nothing about the murder. Do you have a guilty conscience? I asked if you knew Mick. I suggested, from overhearing a terse conversation between you, he tried to blackmail you." My tone turned snotty rather than conversational.

I noticed Skylar slip through the door. "I could hear you both when I crested the stairs."

"I do not have a guilty conscience. Nor am I afraid of anything Ber . . ." Harrison's eyes bugged. He cleared his throat. "I was not afraid of anything Mr. Henderson implied, said or did."

My brow crinkled in confusion. I'd asked if he knew Mick. I'd never accused him of being afraid of him. His body language indicated it when Mick was around. Had someone else brought up that matter? Drake? Sheriff Perry? Tabitha?

"You still haven't answered my question."

"I don't intend to. You are not a private investigator or the law. Stop nosing around in this case and let the sheriff handle things."

"As long as I'm a person of interest in this murder, I'm asking questions." I knew I should stop grilling Harrison. His face and scalp glowed like hot coals, making his white hair stand out more. I was on a roll and, quite frankly, tired of his condescending treatment of the rest of us. "Did you know Mick?"

Harrison drew a long, deep breath. I braced, waiting for the fury to roll out of him on the exhale. Instead, it propelled him from his chair. "I am not listening to this anymore. I am finding Brenden. I am tired of being treated like a common criminal instead of respected because I am the only chef on the premises. I am tired of the person whose fingerprints cover the fry pan used to kill Mick, trying to interrogate me. Tell me, Courtney, is this a ploy to deflect your own guilt?"

His question was rhetorical. He didn't wait for an answer. He huffed out of the room, banging the door behind him.

I smiled.

"How can you smile after an argument like that? He implied you murdered Mick." Shannon's face shone with disbelief.

Skylar pursed his lips and his eyes narrowed, studying me.

"Because he does anything he can not to answer my questions, including picking a fight so he can make an exit. I think Harrison is a very moral person."

"What?" Skylar eased his features.

"He can't out-and-out lie, yet he doesn't want me to know the truth."

"And that is?" Shannon leaned forward in her chair and looked around Skylar.

"He knew Mick."

Both Shannon and Skylar wore thoughtful expressions. Neither responded because our stylists entered the room, which made me glad. I might have blurted out the additional information I had gleaned before they came in. Harrison's slip of the tongue. He'd almost said the wrong name. I really believed this was a blackmail scheme. Perhaps Mick worked for someone else and the name that almost rolled off Harrison's tongue was Mick's boss.

Why would anyone blackmail a chef? Had Harrison fudged and claimed an established recipe for his own, like the network chef who was fired? Had he borrowed money from the wrong person to open his gourmet restaurants? Had he cheated in the contest win that gave him his big break in the business?

So many scenarios raced through my mind while my face and hair were done up. Of course, they were only my speculations. I did know one thing for certain: I'd hit a dead end researching Mick. I needed to scour the internet for information on Harrison.

Kinzy, looking grim, led Skylar, Shannon and me to the set. Harrison had never rejoined us in makeup. When we got on the floor of the set, he was also AWOL.

"Courtney, Skylar, get to your marks," Brenden commanded. His ruddy cheeks and deep frown told me Harrison had found him and voiced his concerns.

Skylar raised his brows at me and in a terse whisper said, "Guess he believes in peer punishment."

"I'm sorry," I whispered back.

Toes to tape, Skylar and I stood waiting for Brenden to decide what camera angles he wanted today.

Brenden always had two cameras aimed at us. A camera, mounted on a boom, filmed distance shots. Another camera, mounted on the shoulder of a crew member, recorded most of our shots and zoomed in close when Brenden directed.

Our wardrobe people used this time to adjust our collars and jewelry or smooth a wrinkle. Skylar wore a navy suit, double-breasted, and I was dressed in a nautical print sundress with a navy shrug. My jewelry and Skylar's pocket square in red added splotches of color.

Currently, Brenden, perched on the end of his chair, watched a monitor and hollered directions to the boom operator. In almost slow motion, the height and angle of the machine changed. Skylar and Barb exchanged greetings. I brushed my gaze over the contestants. I forced a smile I didn't feel to my lips. I hadn't meant to set the tone of the day. All I'd wanted to do was get Harrison to admit he knew Mick. I hadn't accused him of murder; however, I did think his rage over my asking indicated guilt.

Most of the competitors smiled or nodded back. Not Tabitha; she scowled when I made eye contact. Her expression before our eyes met hadn't been pleasant. Her narrowed eyes flicked from me to Brenden and back as she drummed her fingers against the countertop. In a split second, she was on the move. Straight up the center dividing aisle toward me, whacking the wooden spoon she held against each kitchen counter she passed.

Again, I hated to think of kitchen utensils as ways to inflict violence, but horror stories of mothers spanking their children with a wooden spoon popped into my mind. I was trapped. So was Skylar. We couldn't move from our mark or they'd have to recheck the camera angles.

Her heavy steps stopped in front of me. Anger blotched red patches across her face. In my heels, my eyes were elevated enough, she had to tilt her head to look me in the eye. She leaned in, lips pursed.

"What did you say or do to put Harrison in such a bad mood?"

"Pardon?" This was not the question I expected.

"You heard me. Don't pretend you didn't." She waved the spoon very close to my cheek.

"Tabitha!" Brenden hollered, quieting the room.

I broke eye contact long enough to see everyone watching with interest.

She turned her head for a quick look at Brenden. Maybe to check his whereabouts. Then she turned back to me and through clenched teeth said, "Stop badgering him about Mick. Stop making him angry and putting him in a bad mood before we start filming. Our," she moved her arm and waved the spoon in a circular motion into the air, "careers are riding on this show."

The arm and spoon rebounded back just inches from my cheek. "You are trouble and have been since we arrived."

Once the words were out of her mouth, she turned on her heel and ran back to her assigned area, avoiding Brenden, who came around the outside of the kitchenettes.

Skylar's hand fumbled around the fabric of our clothes, seeking my hand. When he made contact, he linked his fingers in mine and squeezed.

"You okay?"

Looking into his eyes, I nodded.

Brenden came over, and in a low, clipped tone, asked the same question.

I met his eyes and nodded again. Then I exhaled and realized I'd held my breath since the spoon came close to my cheek the second time.

"She is such a hothead. I almost hoped she'd be the one sent home last time," Brenden huffed in a low whisper. "Then one of my problems would have been gone. The shot is set, if you're up for it. If you need to regain composure, we can take fifteen."

I'd caused enough trouble this morning. I didn't need to delay filming. "I'm fine. We can start filming." Skylar's hold helped steady my rubbery legs.

"You're a trouper." He patted my shoulder, then moved to his chair in front of a monitor.

"I wouldn't have let her hit you with the wooden spoon." Skylar clenched my hand again, then released it.

"I know." I smiled his way. I also knew something else; Tabitha not only had a hot temper, she was an eavesdropper, or she and Harrison communicated on the side. How else would she know I was the one who'd angered him?

It took three tries for Skylar and me to announce the challenge, baking a cake in the cast-iron fry pan using lemon in some form, and kick off the time. The contestants scurried and so did we. The corner where we'd been hippies now looked like a table in a quaint tea shop. No costume change was needed for this taping.

We read through the short script and practiced

the expressions Brenden thought went with the words. Then we switched parts. Brenden thought Skylar's facial expression delivered with the punch line worked better than mine. We went with the original reading. After several tries, we nailed our timing, and Brenden cued us and the camera.

"Would you like lemon in your tea?" I lifted a red, midcentury teapot from its matching warmer.

"No, thank you, but I'll have it in my cake." Skylar indicated with his hand at the plate sitting in front of him, shaped like a lemon.

"You'll have to wait until our competition ends today." I poured the tea into his cup, then in mine.

"Oh?" Skylar arched a brow at the camera. "Will today's contest be a piece of cake for our bakers?"

"Maybe if they get their ingredients right." I looked into the camera and raised my brows.

"If they don't, their results will be a . . ." Skylar lifted the lemon-shaped plate and pulled his face into a pucker.

"Cut. Good job, everyone. You can head back to the set. Courtney, you did a good job. I know Tabitha's confrontation probably rattled you. You are a professional, always smiling for the camera." Brenden's tone had improved. His eyes crinkled at the corners with his wide smile.

"Thank you." I inflected my appreciation and sincerity in the two simple words.

"Skylar, I'll have you accompany the judges during the tasting. Courtney, you relax on set." Brenden checked the time and hurried toward the main set.

Skylar and I walked away. Skylar leaned close. "He

must not know it was you who made Harrison angry. You know he got an earful before we started filming for the day."

"I do. I am sorry Harrison took his anger at me out on everyone."

"It happens." Skylar shrugged.

Once back on the main set, Skylar grabbed a magazine. I took my chair and pulled out my cell phone. I could start poking around the internet to see what I could find out about Harrison. I noticed a text from Eric. He'd stopped by my room with coffee and wondered if I had to be on set early or if everything was okay. There was a second message, asking me to let him know what was going on. I did, omitting the part about me confronting Harrison and searching the internet for clues to how he and Mick knew each other.

It really bugged me that all I could find on Mick was the bakery. Most businesses had social media pages. Thumbing the information into the internet search feature on my phone, I pulled up the bakery website again. On a whim, I pressed Call on the contact page. I had no idea what I'd say. I listened to the ringing, ringing, ringing, waiting for someone or a voice mail to pick up. After fifteen or so rings, I hung up. Odd. I checked the time on the phone. Even with the time difference, a bakery in Minnesota would be open for the day. Surely he wasn't a one-man show. He had to employ staff to run the business in his absence. Unless it was a family-run business and they'd shut down due to Mick's murder.

I stared down at the phone, studying the email address. If no one was answering the phone, would they reply to an email? I had to try. I thought a minute. I wanted a response. Something that might give me an insight into Mick's past, or at least to be pointed to his obituary. Committing the email address to memory, I tapped the app on my phone and started a new message. I jotted a quick message expressing my sympathy at their loss and asked where I could make an in-memory-of donation. I hit Send.

Glancing up from my screen, I watched Skylar, Harrison and Shannon finish tasting Daniel's creation. After a brief interaction, they moved on to Tabitha. Had she failed the first competition again today? Would there be an outburst? Shannon and Skylar did most of the talking. Harrison stood a step behind them. Shannon gave her opinion and looked to Harrison. I couldn't hear them. Harrison, face stoic, delivered his opinion. Tabitha frowned a little. Shannon, Skylar and the cameramen moved on. Harrison, still hanging to the back of the group, lingered. Tabitha reached across the counter and grabbed Harrison's hand.

From this angle, he didn't appear surprised. I read his lips. He'd said, "Thank you." A genuine smile stretched across Tabitha's face and she nodded her head slightly. What was that all about? Had anyone else noticed it? It wasn't on film because the camera was pointed at Steve.

Something wasn't right between the two of them. They either acted like they hated each other or were close friends. Their interaction today confirmed my theory. There was a conspiracy between these two, a relationship of some sort.

The hinges of the heavy entry door squeaked. I saw Drake and Travis enter, their expressions grim. Was there another murder? I swallowed. Or was Sheriff Perry ready to make an arrest? Yet he hadn't followed them inside, so I guessed that wasn't it. It must have something to do with the background checks.

Drake smiled when he saw me, which gave my heart a lift, and made me feel secure that he wasn't here to see me. Travis, as always, glowered my way. At that moment, I decided he thought a person was guilty until proven innocent.

"How are you today, Courtney?" Drake pulled up beside me, closer than an uninterested party would.

I smiled. "I'm well. Hello, Travis. Long time, no see." Thank goodness, I added in my mind.

"Hello." His curt tone matched his sour expression.

Now, I wished I'd made the snarky comment out loud. I knew I wasn't everyone's favorite flavor. I wasn't asking him to be my friend. I was just extending a polite greeting. Would it hurt him to do the same?

"Is Brenden getting close to breaking for lunch?" Drake's words pulled my attention back to him, where it should have been instead of dwelling on Travis's apparent dislike of me.

"Soon. They have three more contestants to judge." I pointed in the direction of the set and realized I didn't need to do that. I dropped my arm in an awkward manner, hoping Drake hadn't noticed.

Travis wandered toward the commissary table.

My phone jangled, indicating I'd received an email. I tapped the message from my provider. An email hadn't been delivered. I perused the message. The email I'd sent to Mick's bakery had bounced.

I double-checked the address with the bakery website. It was correct. Had his family shut down the business completely? Could they do that in less than a week?

"Weird," I said absently and out loud.

"What?" Drake stretched his neck to get a non-glare look at my phone screen.

Busted. I held it up. "I emailed an expression of sympathy to Mick's family via his business email. It bounced."

"What a nice thing to do." Drake flashed me a smile.

A little guilt drizzled through me, because I hadn't been completely honest as to why I'd sent the condolences. "His family must have shut it down."

Drake's smile faded. "Doubtful."

"What do you mean?"

Drake flicked a glance around the room, bent down a tad and leaned toward my ear. "We can't find any family to report the death to."

"What?" my voice blared out.

Drake's eyes grew big and his lips pursed.

We both cranked our necks and found no one on set seemed to be paying any attention to us.

"You heard correctly. We have followed up in every way possible. It's like Mick Henderson magically appeared on earth."

Drake opened his mouth to say more, but his cell phone rang. He pulled it from his pocket and stepped away from me. I pocketed my own and massaged my forehead above my eyes, where a dull pounding had started to form.

What did this mean? No one could magically appear unless . . . I stopped the massaging. Unless they were part of the witness protection program. Yet, in the case of a death, wouldn't there be some record leading law enforcement to know the identity?

I hadn't even absorbed this bit of information when I noticed Drake and Travis waiting by the door. The door opened, letting in natural light and Sheriff Perry.

The sheriff conferred with Drake and Travis. The trio passed me and headed straight to Brenden.

Frowning, Brenden stood and motioned for the cameras to keep rolling. Together, the men walked to a secluded corner of the set.

Fear wrung the moisture from my mouth. They knew who murdered Mick. Sheriff Perry must be ready to make an arrest. Even though I knew I didn't murder Mick, did they? My pulse quickened. My breathing was shallow.

Brenden nodded and walked back to his chair. The judges finished with Barb. Brenden hollered "Cut." The contestants began to remove their aprons. After only four days of filming, they knew the drill. Get out of the so-called kitchen so it can be reset for the next round of cooking and judging.

"Everyone, I need your attention." Brenden waved his hands. "Everyone, gather around."

I walked toward Shannon and Harrison. Skylar had pulled up alongside Brenden. Drake, Travis and Sheriff Perry were on the move. We all arrived in

Brenden's vicinity at the same time. "Thank you," Brenden said. "The sheriff has an announcement to make."

"Is it concerning Mick's murder?" Barb asked. "Have you made an arrest?"

Lips in a grim line, Sheriff Perry shook his head. "We haven't. We have learned some vital information."

I heaved a relieved sigh. They'd found his family or, at the very least, a close friend to claim the body.

"It seems Mick Henderson wasn't who we thought he was." Sheriff Perry made a point to move his gaze to encompass the crowd.

Shannon and I involuntarily looked at each other. I was certain my features twinned her surprised and questioning expression. Maybe only the questioning part, because Drake had spilled the beans about not being able to locate Mick Henderson. Had my thoughts about witness protection been spot-on?

Sheriff Perry tugged up the waistline of his pants, bringing his utility belt along for the ride. What I now recognized as a nervous habit. "We were having trouble finding next of kin for Mick Henderson. After someone leaked the murder that happened on set—which, by the way, we are not happy about, and we will find the mole." The pointed look Sheriff Perry flashed our shocked group left no room for doubt. He was serious. "However, the leak also aided us in a discovery. When the story hit the national press, we received a phone call from a news editor of a network affiliate. At first, we thought he was trying to get a scoop. He wasn't. What we learned from him

was, he hadn't heard from his star investigative journalist in a few days." Sheriff Perry paused. "The man
we knew as Mick Henderson wasn't a bakery owner
from Minnesota."

A collective gasp punctuated the sheriff's words.

A small voice that was hard to recognize as my
own, squeaked out, "Who was he?"

# CHAPTER FIFTEEN

Sheriff Perry hitched his pants, pursed his lips at me, then focused on the entire group. "The man who was murdered was Bernard Stone."

Surprised gasps filled the room, followed by murmuring questions or confusion.

I belonged to the surprised-gasp group. But instead of verifying I'd heard correctly, like most of the contestants, I watched Harrison's and Tabitha's reactions. Neither made a peep, though they'd locked gazes.

Harrison smirked.

Tabitha smiled.

Some secret message passed between them that had nothing to do with disbelief. Had they both known Bernard's true identity? Had Sheriff Perry or Drake caught their reactions?

Bernard Stone was an investigative journalist with a stellar reputation. He'd discovered and uncovered many social, corporate and political scandals, all while keeping his anonymity with voice and face distortion television techniques. His body of work was reminiscent of Bernstein and Woodward with Watergate. In short, Bernard had assumed an identity to gain another notch on his reporter belt.

The sheriff's voice droned on with warnings and instructions to everyone, while my mind wandered with the possibilities.

Both Harrison and Tabitha seemed happy to learn Bernard Stone had met his demise. Add that to their being friendly during the last judging and being involved in the tense conversation with Bernard in the opening mixer solidified my opinion that they should be moved from persons of interest to suspects.

Events over the past few days filtered through my thoughts. I swallowed a small gasp, which sounded like a hiccup in my throat. Harrison did know Bernard! The first syllable of "Bernard" had almost slipped off Harrison's tongue earlier today.

I needed to call, or at the very least, text Eric this breaking news. I felt confident the sheriff would scratch my name off the person of interest list now. I had absolutely no ties to Bernard Stone, and my thorough background check should prove that. I pulled my phone from my pocket and started to peck out a message with my thumb.

"So." Sheriff Perry's raised voice jolted me back to his conversation. "The background checks take on a new meaning. People will be questioned again." Sheriff Perry rested his eyes on Harrison. Smug satisfaction rolled through me until the sheriff's gaze landed on me. "Starting with Mr. Canfield and Miss Archer."

*What?* Astonishment overpowered my satisfaction.

Shannon squeezed me into a side hug. "Breathe," she whispered in my ear. "You are innocent."

I turned. Belief in me shined from her eyes and support etched her features. In a short time, she'd turned into a good friend. I couldn't—no, wouldn't—continue to lie to her about my background. She'd keep my confidence; I was sure of it. That is, if she didn't ditch me as a friend. "Thank you."

"Let's go." Sheriff Perry motioned to Harrison and me.

We followed behind him, with Drake and Travis bringing up the rear until we were out the door. Sheriff Perry stopped at a UTV with room for four and motioned with his palm for us to take seats.

"Why are you focusing on us?" Harrison managed an indignant tone when he hissed out his question.

Sheriff Perry turned. "Because Bernard had two files on his laptop. One belonged to you, Mr. Canfield. Miss Archer's name was labeled on the other."

"We don't have to answer your questions without legal representation." Harrison drew up close to me.

Now he wanted to present a united front?

"That's right," I added for good measure.

"Fine. You can call your attorneys when we get back to the resort. For now, get in."

Harrison and I obliged. In low tones, Sheriff Perry gave Drake and Travis instructions before he slid behind the wheel. He turned the vehicle around, leaving tracks in the grass, and putted down the forbidden path.

My heart pounded with panic. I pulled out my phone, held it out of Sheriff Perry's line of vision and finished my text message to Eric.

"Was that to your attorney?"

Busted. "No."

"Your boyfriend?" Sheriff Perry glanced over his shoulder.

I heaved a frustrated sigh. Not this again. "I don't have a boyfriend. I texted my producer."

I couldn't see the sheriff's features, but he shrugged his shoulders in a yeah-right way. I pursed my lips. I needed to focus on clearing my name, not on clarifying that Eric wasn't my love interest. In a few minutes, the sheriff pulled up to the same entrance Drake had used the evening before. He cut the engine, pocketed the keys and led Harrison and me into the security entrance.

Harrison stopped short when he hit the hallway. "Where are you taking us?" He took a step backward toward the door.

"This leads to the office and lobby area. Along with other areas of the castle." I hoped the confidence in my voice soothed Harrison's wariness.

Sheriff Perry turned and fisted his meaty hands on his hips. "How do you know that?" He quirked a brow.

Whatever answer I gave would get someone in trouble. Because I believed in sharing and spreading the trouble around, I spilled the beans. "Drake brought Shannon and me through here the other evening. Then he used it again to get me safely to my room after my taping." I turned to Harrison. "This is part of a tunnel system Mr. Cole built into the castle."

"Enough."

When I turned back to face Sheriff Perry, he rubbed his chin in consideration. "Let's go."

I motioned to Harrison. "It's safe." I understood his feeling about the secret tunnel. I'd experienced the same apprehension both times I'd been led through it. "I'm told the staff uses it to deliver room service and catering."

Harrison nodded in understanding, and we walked side by side behind Sheriff Perry. Once we entered the lobby area, the sheriff led us to the rooms they were using as a base. "Wait here."

I took a chair. Harrison paced back and forth in front of me. I'd seen many of Harrison's emotions in the five long days we'd been filming the show. He paced when nervous and apprehensive.

"Are you going to call your attorney?"

He stopped pacing. "Yes." He patted his suit jacket until his hand landed on his cell phone in the upper breast pocket. He held it in his hand, staring down at it, and sighed.

For a man who seemed to know his legal rights, his hesitation seemed out of character. Unless he hadn't told his attorney the truth about the murder victim.

I was certain he did know Bernard Stone. This was the perfect time for me to ask him point-blank, and I wouldn't let him skirt around the answer.

"Did you know Bernard Stone?"

Harrison stopped staring at the phone and gaped at me instead. The storm of emotion in his eyes was unreadable. "I knew who he was. I didn't know him." He bit out the words.

Okay. I'd try a different approach. "Did Bernard know a secret about you?"

Harrison raised his brows. "I could ask you the same question."

My approach failed. He'd turned the question back to me. Sucking in a deep breath, I said, "I asked first."

A heavy sigh deflated Harrison's chest. He slipped onto the seat beside me. "I don't need a scandal. I took this judging job because three of my restaurants are floundering. I thought the salary would be a good infusion of funds." He stood back up and paced. "These background checks will not stay confidential. I don't need this leaking out to the press." He threw his hands into the air.

Money problems had led to many a murder, yet I still felt Harrison was holding something back. The first background check would have revealed his financial difficulties, wouldn't it?

The question was posed on my lips when Sheriff Perry chose that exact moment to enter the room. "Miss Archer, please follow me."

Me? He needed to question Harrison. "I haven't called my attorney."

He shrugged. "I gave you plenty of time." He set his jaw and waved me in.

A quick check of my phone showed no response from Eric either.

"Take a seat." Sheriff Perry tugged at his waistband. "Would you like coffee or water?" He flipped his hand toward a narrow table holding a catering thermal pot and fruit-infused water dispenser.

Lips pressed tight, I shook my head and slipped onto the padded chair.

"Because Mr. Stone had a 'bonus story' file on you, I can only assume he knew your secret."

Pursing my lips tighter, I stared at the sheriff.

He grasped the crease of his uniform pants and pulled up his right leg until his ankle rested on his left knee. "Had Bernard Stone confronted you about your farm-girl persona?"

I tried with all my might to keep my face free of any expression.

After a few silent minutes, Sheriff Perry went on. "Here is what I think happened. Bernard never returned with the other contestants to the resort. He managed to hide somewhere on the set. He knew you were going to use the kitchen. With no one else around, he could confront you about your secret. . . ."

A gasp escaped me before I could stop it. The murder scene flashed into my mind as Sheriff Perry started to recount his theory and he was wrong on more levels than one. Bernard didn't stay behind to confront me or anyone. He left with all the others and came back to the set.

"What is it, Miss Archer? Did a city girl like you think a simple country sheriff like me couldn't figure out a murder?"

His goading with my secret rubbed me the wrong way. Just because I grew up in the city, I didn't view people who lived in the country as bumpkins. After all, Eric was one of the smartest people I knew. I wasn't ashamed my persona was a country girl. I was ashamed of the deception. "No, that's not it at all." My words snapped out before I could stop them. So much for keeping silent.

"Then what is it?"

"Your theory called up the memory of the grisly scene and I remembered something. Something I didn't clarify in my original statement." I stared directly into Sheriff Perry's eyes.

"And what would that be?" He raised his heavy brows.

My revelation almost tumbled off my loose tongue. Biting back the information, I smirked. "You told me to stay out of your investigation. You just indicated you're capable of figuring out this murder. For the record, I've never thought you couldn't, but if you watch the show footage from the first day and compare it to the crime scene pictures, you're going to see what I just remembered. It will blow your theory about Bernard staying behind and hiding on the set."

I almost giggled at the astonished expression on Sheriff Perry's face.

Standing, I said, "I think we're done here." I started toward the door.

Bernard had gone back to the resort with the rest of the contestants and for some reason snuck back to the set. Was he meeting someone? Or looking for clues, evidence or details on whoever he planned to expose this time? Which in my mind could only be Harrison.

I reached for the doorknob and glanced over my shoulder at Sheriff Perry. "One part of your theory was right. Bernard planned to reveal to my viewers that I was not a farmer's daughter. He kept assuring me that my secret, which he learned by eavesdropping on a conversation, was safe with him. I knew it wasn't. My name atop a file is proof." I knew I should stop talking. I was on a roll now and couldn't stop. Besides, I felt like I might have the upper hand in this conversation. "On the night of his death, he didn't hide on set to confront me. Just the celebrity talent, crew and security knew I'd be on set baking."

Sheriff Perry stood and walked toward me. "Why don't you just make it easy on both of us and tell me what you're talking about."

I shook my head. "No, you specifically told me to stop interfering with your case. If you watch the footage and compare it to the crime scene photo, you'll find you have to change your theory."

I opened the door and stepped into the hallway. Once the sheriff viewed the footage and reviewed the pictures, he'd know. Bernard had changed clothes. He'd baked all day in a plaid shirt with cargo shorts. He'd died in a black T-shirt and jeans.


Blurry-eyed, I walked with Shannon toward the set. We'd gotten a late start because of me, so we chose to walk on the forbidden path. After Sheriff Perry's failed interrogation yesterday, I'd gone straight to my room, locked the door and tried to find a link between Harrison and Bernard Stone.

I found none. Bernard's stories centered on more scandalous material than a failed five-star restaurant. Usually, his work revealed some sort of white-collar scam that bilked trusting people out of their life savings. A few times he had uncovered key facts in a missing person or murder case. Those were early in his career, though. Unless Harrison was laundering money through his restaurants, it wasn't the type of story Bernard pursued.

I knew Harrison was the subject of Bernard's investigation, and it had nothing to do with restaurant failures. Bernard knew something so damaging about Harrison, it had cost him his life. As abrasive as Harrison could be, I really hated to think he'd murdered someone. Yet, if he was having financial problems and Bernard had tried extortion or public humiliation, he may have acted irrationally. I'd fallen asleep hunched over my laptop sometime after two in the morning trying to find some tidbit in the course of the last few years that would lead me to the truth.

As of five thirty this morning, I'd found none.

"You're quiet this morning." Shannon bumped me with her elbow. "The stress of being a person of interest wearing on you?"

I sighed. "A little." Now would be the perfect time to tell Shannon the truth.

"Understandable. We are only on day six of filming, yet it seems like we've been here months with the delays and interrogations. I'm not even a person of interest and stress is taking a toll on my body, something I can't afford right now."

I stopped walking and turned. "Are you okay?"

For a brief second, Shannon's eyes widened while her breath caught in her throat. Then she smiled and flipped her hand through the air. "Yes, yes. I just try to keep in shape and free of stress." A short laugh, filled with tension, followed her sentence.

"Don't worry about me." Shannon smiled. "The murder has everyone frazzled."

I quirked a brow, not quite buying her explanation, but let the conversation thread drop for now. I looked around the beautiful landscape. Distant mountaintops poked through clouds, reminding me of marshmallows on sharp sticks. The lush and varied greens of the countryside were a serene and calming backdrop to the elegant castle-turned-resort. The facts I'd learned about the area and the castle now seemed insignificant. On lockdown for the investigation, there was no way for me to discover hidden gems of Coal Castle Resort or the surrounding Pocono Mountains. What a shame.

"Maybe you need Skylar to take you fishing again?" I took a step and Shannon fell into the rhythm.

"No." Shannon drawled out the vowel in an excited squeal. "What I need is a girls' night. We can start with dinner and drinks and end with drinks and more drinks. After all, we're stuck here and don't have to worry about driving." Shannon laughed out loud. "Are you in?"

I glanced at Shannon's face, once again animated and happy. How could I say no? "I'm in."

"We'll do it tonight!"

"Well, let's see how filming goes today."

Shannon and I chattered happily the rest of the way to the set, making plans for our girls' night. By the time we slipped into our wardrobe, Harrison and Skylar had vacated the area. In no time, we were camera-ready and heading downstairs for the start of our day.

Harrison perched with proper posture, waiting in his chair. I cranked my neck. Skylar and Brenden were nowhere to be seen. The sound crew fussed with the contestants' microphones. A small microphone was clipped to their clothing. Another rested in their work area to pick up frustrated comments or wails of woe. Tabitha's probably broke their eardrums when sound bites were played back.

I hadn't ruled her out as the person who had murdered Bernard. Although he had no file on her, she seemed to have a relationship, albeit bad, of some type with him. Harrison too. Maybe she was the key in figuring out the murder.

My eyes sought her out. Would this be a good time to chat with her? Try to establish some type of rapport to get her to confide in me? After the wooden spoon incident, I was remiss in not trying. I needed to know on what level she knew Bernard. And Harrison. Based on her anger level alone, they weren't acquaintances. No one has feelings that strong with acquaintances.

There was no doubt in my mind that Harrison knew Bernard. I just needed to make a connection. So far, my searching had come up empty. Talking to Tabitha might provide a bread crumb to lead me to the right path.

The thought flipped my stomach. Glad I hadn't eaten yet, I swallowed hard and approached her workstation.

"How are you today?"

Her doe eyes stared at me in disbelief.

Had she intended that her outburst and threat would frighten me and I'd stay away? I stood my ground, which was easy because there was a kitchen counter between us. In the time it'd take her to hop over it, I could run to safety. Wardrobe had put me in camping clothes: cargo shorts with a matching jacket over a turquoise T-shirt. My footwear was stylish yet practical hiking boots.

She shrugged. "Fine, I guess."

I flipped the braid hanging over my left shoulder with my hand. "Me too. I hadn't counted on so much stress when I took this job."

"Harrumph. You have no stress. We do." She circled her arm again to encompass her fellow contestants. "No matter what we do, it's wrong or needs improvement. No one does it right, even the trained chefs. They just do it a little better than another contestant."

What? No stress? I'd found a murder victim. Then it hit me: we weren't having the same conversation. "Oh, right. Yes, the cooking competition. That would be stressful. I meant the murder. You seemed to know Bernard, so I thought maybe . . ."

I stopped talking. I was experiencing the expression "if looks could kill" firsthand. Fire flashed from Tabitha's eyes before they narrowed. Her breath came in huffs. Her jaw and lips set in a grim line. She raised her arm and swung it toward me. I took a step back, even though she couldn't really reach me. She held no spoon, but I wasn't taking a chance of getting an openhanded slap to the cheek.

Instead, she fisted all but her pointer finger. She waggled it so fast in the air, it became a blur. "Bernard Stone was lowlife scum. I don't associate with people like him or his kind. I had already petitioned the show to see how he got on as a contestant. He sure couldn't cook. Even though that one over there"— Tabitha swung her arm until her finger pointed in Harrison's direction—"awarded him top prize because he was scared of him."

Everyone stopped when Tabitha shouted in Harrison's direction.

Harrison dropped his magazine and glowered at Tabitha.

Wow! What a difference a day makes. Friends yesterday, enemies again today.

"You need to change your attitude if you want to work in the restaurant industry." Harrison stood and walked straight toward us. "I judge solely on the food prepared. Mrs. Miller, you are not being careful enough in your food preparation. You have good ideas but no follow-through. Chefs like that are a dime a dozen. The day Bernard, or Mick, took baker of the day was because he prepared the best food."

Tabitha's lips curled before drawing down into a frown, giving her a sinister appearance. She stomped around the kitchen counter until she stood in front of Harrison.

Anger steamed both of their complexions until their cheeks blazed red.

"What gives you the right to say that? Why do you act so pompous? You and I both know you are no better a man than Bernard Stone. You are both lowlife scum who make their living hurting other people."

Harrison drew a breath so deep, it moved his torso back. "And you, Mrs. Miller, would know that how?" he roared. "I know your background. You have hopped from sous chef to chef to dishwasher jobs for the past five years. You can't keep a job in this industry because of your attitude and the chip on your shoulder."

Tabitha's eyes widened. She took a step back.

"That's right. I am well aware of who you really are." A smugness washed over Harrison's face.

Realization washed over Tabitha's.

"And if I am lowlife scum, I guess you are too. Short of blackmail, you've done everything you could to gain my favor to secure a win in the contest or a job at one of my restaurants."

Tabitha tried to speak. Only sputters came out.

Harrison turned on the heel of his Italian leather shoe and stormed away.

His movement helped Tabitha recover from her shock. She turned. Hands fisted, she waved one in the air after him. "You ruined my life once. I won't let that happen again. I wish they would arrest you for murder."

# CHAPTER SIXTEEN

I wasn't certain Harrison heard Tabitha's outburst as he stormed through the building. To where, I didn't know. Everyone else had heard, though. The atmosphere on the set thickened like crème brûlée, only seasoned with tension instead of vanilla bean. The other contestants cast nervous glances at one another. When Tabitha turned to walk back to her kitchenette, most of the competitors dropped their gaze to avoid eye contact. A few did continue to stare, Barb being one of them.

"How could you say such a thing?" Barb admonished Tabitha like a grandmother. "Especially with a murder investigation going on?"

"It was easy." Tabitha's words hissed through her teeth. "Don't let his sophisticated manners fool you, old woman." She poked her finger hard in Barb's direction.

"Oh, my." Barb put a hand to her heart. Shocked at Tabitha's blatant disrespect of obviously everyone.

I was ready to interject when the familiar clapping of hands echoed through the set.

"Places everyone," Brenden hollered, paying no attention to the atmosphere around him.

Skylar followed Brenden onto the set. We met up at our appropriate tape marks.

"Good morning." Skylar smiled. His cargo shorts and hiking boots matched mine. His black-and-turquoise-plaid flannel shirt jacketed a black T-shirt. "For once, I won't be washed out on camera." He turned his best side toward the cameraman standing before us.

"Where were you two?"

When Skylar looked at me, an emotion I couldn't name tugged at the corners of his mouth. "Oh, we had some business, not show-related, to take care of. Why?"

"Tabitha and Harrison fought, again." I cast a glance in Brenden's direction. He was either distracted or tired of the drama on set. He didn't seem to notice the edginess in everyone's demeanor.

"Ready, set, action!" Brenden hollered.

The sound people cued the show's theme. By the time our cameraman panned in on us, we were both smiling. Our lines appeared on the monitor and I read, "With the elimination of Rhonda last week, there will be three challenges starting this week."

Skylar picked up, "As you can see by Courtney's and my attire, today's episode is a nod to our setting, the Pocono Mountains. Many people vacation here, which includes campers and hikers. Today's challenges will revolve around that theme."

"But with a twist." I smiled wide. "No regular camp-

ing food for us. You are tasked to create a gourmet
breakfast filled with protein, an energy-filled snack
and a hearty meal fit to be served by the finest restaurant."

Skylar opened his mouth to deliver the news that
they could use multiple cast-iron pans. Before he uttered the words, an earsplitting wail filled the room.
Followed by a shaky breath and heavy sobs. Everyone's head snapped in the direction of Barb's kitchenette. She'd flung her body over the counter, head
resting in the crook of her right arm. "I can't do it,"
she choked out through sobs. "I can't continue this
contest. The atmosphere is just too tense."

"Cut. Cut. Cut. Turn those cameras off." Brenden
pointed at Barb's assigned cameraman. "This isn't
part, nor will it be, of the show." On a run, he headed
toward Barb.

So did I, with Shannon right beside me. Brenden
stood on the opposite side of the counter. Shannon
and I ran around and flanked Barb. Each of us showing her comfort by patting her back and shoulders.

"Here we go again," Otto hollered. "Can't you
keep your temper under control?" Shoes thumping
hard against the floor, I knew he was headed toward
Tabitha. "You might have all the time in the world to
film this competition, but I for one do not. You have
continually delayed the filming since you arrived.
What is your deal? Are you trying to wear the rest of
us down until we quit and you are the winner? Or are
you in love with Harrison Canfield?"

"No." Tabitha's answer exploded from her and
through the room. "If you all knew the true Harrison
Canfield, your opinions of him would change."

"Enough." This time it was Brenden's voice booming through the room. "Kinzy, take the contestants back to their rooms, except for Mrs. Miller and Mrs. Tornquist. Skylar, find Drake or Travis. Shannon, take Mrs. Tornquist upstairs to your wardrobe area and try to calm her down. Tabitha, don't move an inch. I mean it, not one inch. Courtney, tell me what went on here."

Like good sous chefs, we followed Brenden's orders, including Tabitha. By the time Skylar returned with Drake, Brenden understood the situation. He had Drake escort Tabitha back to the resort after he gave her a firm dressing-down.

"We can't afford any more setbacks," Brenden muttered to Skylar and me before heading up the stairs to deal with Barb.

"What are we supposed to do?" Skylar called after Brenden while shrugging his shoulders at me.

"Whatever you want. We won't start filming until after lunch."

The crew started to shut down their equipment. Skylar shrugged again. "I'm going to head back to the resort. You want to walk with me?"

I considered it for a moment. After all, I'd like to talk to him. Determine once and for all if perhaps he knew Bernard Stone.

"What a mess this is. I thought it would be good for my career. Now, I'm not so certain. I paid a lot of dues to get this far. Now, I'm afraid our show is going to be known for scandal. If it even makes it on the air," Skylar huffed.

His words shot fear through me. In all this turmoil, I'd never once considered the show wouldn't

make it on the air. I flopped down in the nearest
chair. I'd hoped to use this show as a stepping-stone
to the network, allowing me to admit my background.

"Bernard Stone spent his life ruining other people's lives and it seems like he is still doing it after his
death."

I cocked my head. "I don't know if I agree with
that. Some of the things Bernard uncovered in his
career sent bad people to prison. He found justice
for their unsuspecting victims."

"Really?" The gobsmacked expression on Skylar's
face told me, great throwing arm or not, he didn't
murder Bernard. He didn't even know who he was.

"I thought he was one of those sensationalist jour-
nalists," Skylar said.

I gave my head a small shake. "It does feel that way
a little bit, because to gain information, he had to be
sneaky. Work from the inside."

"Gain the unscrupulous people's trust. Then his
murder is a bigger tragedy than I thought. To tell you
the truth, I had to do an internet search just to see
what the fuss was about when Sheriff Perry made the
positive identification. Are you sure you don't want
to walk with me?"

"I'll wait for Shannon. I'm sure she'll be down in a
few minutes."

Sunlight flashed in and out of the room with the
opening and closing of the door. I heard Skylar greet
the security guards before the door thudded closed.
Really, I wanted to be alone to consider the possibilities of Bernard's murder.

Although I was still a person of interest, I knew
that I hadn't killed Bernard. I'd studied Skylar dur-

ing our conversation. Over the past few days of filming, I'd learned two things about Skylar. He kept a low profile when not in front of the camera: unkempt hair, unshaven beard, solitary interests like fishing. In front of the camera, his shallow side showed. He worried about his best camera angle and the color palette of his wardrobe complementing his complexion. He wasn't lying when he thought Bernard was a sensational reporter. Skylar paid little attention to noteworthy news. It probably came from being a socialite's son and worrying more about what hit the society pages or who the paparazzi followed.

It was time for me to drop him from the suspect list, even if he did have a good throwing arm and a lousy alibi. I knew in my heart who I needed to focus on: Harrison or Tabitha, or maybe both.

I glanced up at the door to wardrobe. I didn't have to wait for Shannon. I could head back to my room and do more internet digging on Harrison and Tabitha.

My phone vibrated. The text notification jingle belonged to Eric. I pulled my cell phone from a pocket on my cargo shorts. He'd seen Kinzy ushering the contestants back into the resort and wondered what was up. When I answered, his next text instructed me to come to my makeshift set. Pronto.

After walking as fast as I could on an approved path back to the castle, I found Eric sitting on a stool beside the counter, perusing his tablet.

"What's up?" I glanced around the room for another stool. When I saw none, I walked over and leaned against the counter beside Eric.

"Good morning." His wide smile was the friend-liest thing I'd seen since I awoke. "Or maybe it's not."

"It's really not." I heaved a sigh. "With the murder and all of these delays, do you think the network will just shut down the show? I mean, we have to be cost-ing them a bundle."

"It's a possibility."

I shook my head. "I hadn't even considered that until Skylar said something." I looked at Eric. "I thought if this show was a success, we could use that to our advantage to come clean about my farmer's daughter background."

"Speaking of that. It's why I needed to see you. I talked to the show's attorneys. They gave me some pat answers if an impromptu question-and-answer should start during filming. The network doesn't want to alienate your fans. Your fans feel like they know you . . ."

"That is why I need to tell them the truth."

Eric held up his hand. "I know. Anyway, they don't want you to just say 'no comment.'" Eric slipped off the stool and walked over to a table where his com-puter bag lay.

I took the opportunity to sit. My eyes studied Eric's tablet. He'd been surfing the internet for re-views of our show. I tapped on the screen and opened another browser, accessed a search engine and entered Harrison's name.

"Here's the sheets. They tried to anticipate as much as they could, based on the questions that have been asked of other celebrities in trouble."

"What?" I looked up at him. "Do they think I'm in trouble?"

"No, no." Eric shook his head. "Those were my words. What are you doing?" Eric's eyes rested on his tablet.

"Just a little research."

"You mean digging for clues to try to solve this murder. I told you to stop that." Eric crossed his arms over his chest.

I laid down the tablet. "I'm trying to clear my name and save our careers."

"Here we go." Eric threw his hands in the air.

I didn't like Eric's tone or gesture, but he needed to know that I'd spoken to Sheriff Perry, again. "Sheriff Perry tried to interrogate me again because of the computer file labeled 'Courtney Archer— bonus story.'"

"What did you tell him?"

I smiled wide. "Not much until I sort of told him off."

"What?" Eric's eye's widened.

"Well, he implied that because of that file, Bernard stayed behind that day to confront me. We argued, and I killed him. While he was dragging out his theory, the grisly scene flashed before my eyes, and I remembered something."

"Will this help or hurt you?" Eric started to pace.

I turned on the stool so I could watch him wear out the carpet while I continued. "I don't know that it will help or hurt me, but it blows up his theory. Bernard went back to the resort with the others and somehow sneaked back to the set."

"How? They have security."

"Maybe he paid off a security guard? Or scoped out an area where he could sneak past without being seen?"

"He was an investigative journalist." Eric rubbed his chin, his expression thoughtful.

"All I can say is, if he didn't sneak past Security, he hid clothing somewhere, because he didn't die in the clothes in which he cooked."

Eric stopped pacing. The corner of his mouth turned up in a crooked smile. "Really? Did you tell the sheriff?"

"Not in so many words. I told him to watch the day's tape and look at the crime scene pictures. I wanted to mess with him a little bit." I shrugged my shoulders.

Eric pinned me with a look. "I don't know if that was wise."

I saw the amusement in his eyes and smiled. "You're probably right. By the way, I've ruled out Skylar. He was clueless about why Bernard was famous."

Eric rolled his eyes. "And you didn't do it, so that leaves who?"

"Harrison and Tabitha. They definitely knew Bernard and disliked him. One day they like each other. The next they are enemies. Is their love-hate relationship a ruse to throw off Sheriff Perry or Drake? Or has something broken down in their scheme and now it's each person for themselves?"

"Courtney, you are obsessing about this murder. Leave it alone. Let Drake and Sheriff Perry sort it out."

"I'm tired of being theorized into murder. In an indirect way, both Harrison and Tabitha admitted they knew Bernard. While Harrison and I were waiting to be interrogated, Harrison admitted to me that several of his restaurants were having financial difficulties. You and I both know that is not what Bernard planned to uncover. If I could only find out what it was, I might be able to figure out which one killed him." As abrasive as Harrison could be, I really hated to think he murdered someone. As a chef, I respected his work. Now, Tabitha was a different story.

"You do know it could be a crew member, an old flame, or personnel here at the resort?"

I pursed my lips and scowled at him. Mostly because it was a possibility.

Eric moved in front of me. He placed a hand on each shoulder. "Courtney, stop putting yourself in danger. If you do get close to figuring out who killed Bernard, you may be the next victim. Stop wondering. Stop searching for clues. Stop talking to the authorities."

I sighed. I knew he was right. Getting in the middle of the murder could cost me my life. So could being in the wrong place at the wrong time, like the path the night Bernard was murdered. I didn't remind Eric the murderer may have seen me.

"Now, let's get back to why I called you to your set. Can you use an old-fashioned pressure cooker without doing bodily harm?"

Between trying to learn how to use a pressure cooker and being called back to the set, I didn't get to scratch my research itch. I did have time to jot down some notes in an app in my phone so I wouldn't forget some of the angles I'd come up with while working with a time-saving yet possibly dangerous kitchen tool.

Thank goodness, Eric had helped his mom in the kitchen, as well as his dad with the crops. He patiently guided me through the steps of filling the cooker with water and attaching the lid for an airtight seal. I wasn't a fan of the chugging, hissing noises the pan emitted while heating the contents until it produced steam. Nor did I care for the jiggle-top pressure regulator on the vent pipe on the lid. The whole putting-the-safety-valve-on-the-nozzle when the steam started coming out. Eric did it like a pro. I did it like a scared kitten. He told me that I'd need to practice more and as long as I had the lid locked down, I'd be fine.

I wondered why anyone would ever use such a contraption. Eric had explained that the trapped steam helped to cook the food faster, and the food lost less of the nutrients because of the speedier cooking. Luckily, I was just demonstrating the old-fashioned pressure cooker, then preparing a meal in the new-and-improved version, the instant pot. I'd agreed Eric was right. Before filming, I had to be more confident in my demonstration. Then, he added, I needed to get it right or the pot could explode. The warning didn't give me a steadier hand.

With our hair and makeup touched up, Skylar and I stood on our marks, ready to kick off the show with the same routine Barb had interrupted with her sobs this morning. I was pleased to see her in her workstation, aproned up and ready to cook. I flashed her a smile. She returned my greeting with a weak one of

her own. I could see the puffiness around her eyes.
Her makeup person had covered up any reddishness
with expertise. Plus, they'd brightened up her cheek
and lip color, probably to draw viewers' eyes away
from Barb's swollen baby blues.

I hoped she didn't try Rhonda's trick and sabotage her own cooking.

Brenden cued us, we read our lines, then took a
breath and together said, "The baking begins . . . now."

I kept an eye on Barb. She wasn't scurrying around
quite as fast as before, but she was working. Tabitha,
on the other hand, was spending more time glancing
up to see what her competitors were doing; I doubted
whatever breakfast she was preparing would be finished in the hour and a half they were given to complete this challenge.

When Brenden cut our camera, Skylar and I
walked to our set chairs. Brenden approached us.

"Need us to do a show opener? Maybe something
about a lumberjack?" Skylar laughed and tugged at
his plaid flannel shirt.

Brenden managed a tired smile. "No, not today.
You can chill here, or upstairs or outside. Just don't go
far. It's going to be tight today to get filming done."

"I think I'll go outside and read." Skylar lifted a
hardcover book off the seat of his chair.

I had something else in mind. "I think I'll take a
walk. I am dressed for the outdoors, after all."

"Be back on set in an hour," Brenden warned our
backs.

I knocked on the door because we filmed on a
locked set now. A young security guard opened the
door and smiled.

"Thank you. I'm going to take a walk on my off time."

He nodded.

I knew I didn't need an explanation. The set was locked down and we were trapped at the resort, but we weren't prisoners and were free to roam the grounds. Shielding the sun from my eyes, I looked at my path choices and decided a walk to the pond would be nice. That meant I'd have to take the closed path. I shrugged and headed around the building. I knew it was off-limits, but how many times had Skylar, Shannon and I used this path and never been caught? Several, so I felt my odds were good.

I drew in several deep breaths and surveyed my surroundings. It was a beautiful place. At the time Mr. Cole built his castle home, it was an era of opulence. His success and class ranking demanded it. Did he know that in the future, his hard work would be preserved into a haven retreat to commune with nature, relax and enjoy life?

Everything the resort boasted about in the brochures were refurbished original amenities that Mr. Cole had built into his home—a tennis court, the inside bowling alley in the castle's basement, the pond and a nine-hole golf course. He'd laid a firm foundation for a lasting legacy with the matching stone buildings, the exotic flower beds moated around the castle and acres and acres of land. Of course, over time, improvements and modern updates had been made, like sprinkler systems, energy-efficient windows, paths paved with stone.

I couldn't help but feel the murder dampened most of the cast and crew's use of these wonderful recreational facilities, not to mention exploring the area around the Poconos. Sadly, many people were keeping close to the resort, tucked into their rooms.

A slight breeze, flavored with fragrant honeysuckle, lifted and twirled my bangs in a friendly dance while my steps became lighter. The physical activity was just what I needed to clear my mind and give me a fresh perspective on Bernard's murder.

I wondered if Sheriff Perry had viewed the tape and made the clothing connection yet. I didn't doubt his abilities to solve the murder. I just wanted to get my name off his person of interest list before I turned into a suspect. Even though I knew I didn't kill Bernard, I had to admit the evidence was stacked against me.

In no time, I wandered into the dense tree cover. The stark sunshine dimmed under the filter of the trees' canopies. The air, damp and thick, forced me to take deeper breaths. A twig snapped. I caught a gasp in my throat. I glanced around. Was someone here? Watching me?

I stepped it up and kept my ears on red alert. After a minute or two, when I'd only heard nature's casserole of noises, I chided myself for getting spooked. It was probably a squirrel, or possibly a deer moving through the neighborhood. My racing heart eased, and my shoulders relaxed when I saw the turnoff for the path that led to the pond.

With each step, I decided I'd relax on the bench by the pond, review my suspicions and create a plan of research action, then I'd take the long way back to the set. I'd follow this path to the castle, then return to the set via an approved path.

My mind teemed with ideas as I rounded the corner and bumped into someone, hard. I caught the blur of white and gray as I tried fancy footwork to regain my balance. In the end, I thudded to the ground, my behind taking the brunt of the fall. A jolt of shock shot up my spine. I shook my head to clear it.

I looked up and around before looking forward to see Harrison in the same position as me, legs sprawled, posterior planted and dazed. "Harrison?"

His eyes found mine. "Courtney, are you all right? I didn't see or hear you."

Recovered from the fall, Harrison's posture took form. He pulled his legs together, sat up straight and, giving himself a little liftoff with his hands, stood.

"I'm fine. I think." I wasn't quite ready to stand yet. From this angle, I noticed mud clung to the hem of his suit pants and slicked the sides of his Italian shoes.

When he extended his hand, I clasped it, grateful for his assistance to stand. I pulled my hand away and brushed off my rear. I tried to angle around to see if I'd ruined my wardrobe with smudges of grass stain. It was an exercise in futility, so I continued to swipe my hands over my shorts. "What are you doing here?"

"I could ask you the same." Harrison too brushed at his clothes before tugging his suit coat back into place.

I disliked this little avoidance game of his. "Yes, you could. And if you did, I would actually answer you."

Harrison raised his brows. "Courtney, you ask too many questions." He sighed. "If you must know, I had to walk off my anger. I stumbled upon this path. It leads to a pond. Did you know that?"

"Yes." My gaze fell to his pant legs and shoes. "Did you wade into it?"

Harrison's head dropped, and when he looked back up, panic pulled at his features. "No, I, um, found a turtle and put it back into the water. I didn't realize I'd soiled my clothing and shoes. I'd better get back to the set and change."

He quickstepped around me and was gone before I could respond. I watched him retreat into the wooded area of the path. Not believing the turtle story for a moment. My mind spun with reasons he'd be in this area. Harrison was fastidious. He'd never dirty his designer clothes and shoes without good reason.

A soft purr growing louder whisked me away from my thoughts. I turned to see a UTV made for two approaching. My heart sank.

I took a step back when Travis pulled the vehicle to a stop, a little too close in my opinion, beside me. Did he have depth-perception issues, or was this a form of passive-aggressive intimidation?

"What are you doing here?" Disgust dripped from every word. "This path is off-limits."

I pursed my lips and stared directly into his eyes. His expression was hard, cold almost, to intimidate me.

"I needed to take a walk." I didn't bother pointing out that he'd just missed Harrison, and Skylar, Shannon and I used it quite often.

"You've been told not to use this path. I guess rich doctors' daughters don't have to follow the rules."

I didn't appreciate his sarcastic tone, nor the way

he let me know I was a liar. Was the fact I came from a successful family the reason he disliked me? "That is not it at all." I allowed my anger to flavor my words.

Travis heaved a sigh when he saw I wasn't backing down this time. Although his expression and demeanor remained hard and defensive, his tone changed when he said, "Look, there is a murderer on the loose. We are using this path as an emergency access path. We need you to use the paths we are surveilling for your protection."

I blinked. "I haven't seen any surveillance people on the path."

"Really, Miss Archer, do you think we're going to be obvious and wave at people to let them know we are watching?"

I crossed my arms over my chest. "No, I don't expect that, but speaking of surveillance, there are security cameras on set. Didn't they capture Bernard's murder?"

"Geez, you just don't get it, do you? You are a television star, not a cop. None of this is your business. Then again, you have no problem lying to the public. You're pretty good at it, in fact. That tells me a lot about your character." The corners of his mouth turned up and changed his expression from cold to cocky.

Anger surged through me. I knew I couldn't take his bait or let my anger show. Besides, it wasn't all directed at him. His words sizzled my shame at the clause in my contract that forced me to pretend to be something I'm not. There was truth in his words about lying and character. Somehow, Eric and I had to convince the network to let me tell my viewers the truth, even if we faced media backlash, poor ratings and cancellation.

"Yeah, I didn't think you'd have an answer to that." Travis moved a tennis racket lying across the passenger seat. "Get in. I'm taking you back to the set."

This time I didn't argue. I did what I was told. After all, I was used to it, but after this conversation, that was going to change.

# CHAPTER SEVENTEEN

Although my ride back to the set with Travis took only a few minutes, the tension-filled silence made it feel like miles. Poised for a dismount, I jumped out of the passenger seat before the UTV came to a complete stop. I marched toward the heavy wooden door, not thanking Travis for the lift or the verbal smackdown he'd given me about my true background.

Once inside, I headed to wardrobe, so they could peruse the damage, if any, to my cargo shorts. There were some streaks of mud they wanted to wash out. I started to disrobe so they could take care of the stain removal when Kinzy blew into the room.

"There you are. They are ready for you on set."

I explained the situation, which prompted a phone call to Brenden. "He said to wear them. They will shoot you from the front or waist up from behind."

The wardrobe person held out the shorts and I slipped back into them and stepped down to the set with Kinzy in the lead.

Brenden looked at me and shook his head. "Sorry, Courtney, I can't lose any more time. Wardrobe can fix it during your next break."

Skylar had called the time as scripted. I would call it alone on the second challenge. We'd count down for the third. I was needed to walk with the judges while they sampled, and decided whether the contestant created a gourmet breakfast.

LeeAnne tried making eggs Benedict. The separated hollandaise sauce served over rubbery eggs earned some harsh words from both Harrison and Shannon. Although, they agreed, it did qualify as a gourmet breakfast.

"Scrumptious!" Harrison declared after a bite of Otto's scrambled eggs and caviar. Otto served it with toast points of brioche with a smear and a thin slice of smoked salmon.

Shannon and I took a sample at the same time. I agreed with Harrison's description. The salty caviar and creamy eggs tasted like perfection. However, Shannon gulped twice before she managed to swallow her bite, then chased it with a large bite of toasted brioche.

"The eggs texture was perfect, and the butter brioche complemented it well." She smiled, and so did Otto, from ear to ear.

We followed Harrison to Barb's kitchenette. Shannon leaned close and whispered, "I don't know how y'all ate the caviar without gagging."

"I'm afraid my breakfast casserole isn't gourmet. It's just an old, everyday dish I've made for my family during the holidays for years." Barb looked down at her cast-iron like it was a naughty child.

"We'll be the judge of that, right, Harrison?" Shannon smiled at Barb.

"Yes. What is it?" Harrison looked at the dish with genuine interest.

"It's a cremini and brie strata." Barb's tone held disgust. "It's all I could think of to make for this challenge."

Harrison's laughter boomed through the set. The mirth on his face a welcome change to his usual serious demeanor. He reached over and clasped Barb's hand. "Dear woman, I'm not sure you know the meaning of gourmet."

The surprise on Barb's face was priceless, and it was all caught on tape. When this episode was edited and, hopefully, aired, it'd make a great television moment.

She earned high praise from Harrison, Shannon and me, although mine didn't really count.

Again, Harrison led the way to the next contestant. As Shannon, two cameramen and I snaked along behind, it was obvious he was avoiding Tabitha. We sampled three more stratas with varying ingredients; though tasty, they couldn't compare to Barb's.

The only contestant left to judge was Tabitha. Harrison's demeanor changed. His shoulders and back stiffened. His lips pursed.

"Why don't I take the lead on this one?" Shannon stepped ahead of Harrison.

"I saw that," Tabitha said. "I also saw how you purposely left me for last. You've been trying to oust me since I arrived." Tabitha stared at Harrison to leave no doubt to whom she was speaking.

Harrison met her glare with one of his own.

Brenden strode over to the group. "Are you two trying to sabotage the show? We already have bad karma with a murder on our set; we don't need any more delays in filming. I am giving you two minutes to taste, judge and react to this dish." He looked at the cameraman. "I am serious. When I say cut, this segment of judging is finished so we can reset."

Tabitha's glare turned to wide-eyed surprise. She opened her mouth.

"No." He pointed at her. "The time starts now."

"What's your gourmet breakfast?" Shannon smiled through her question.

Tabitha, mouth still agape, turned her attention from Brenden to Shannon. She furrowed her brows, then Brenden's warning must have clicked a switch in her brain. She blinked and smiled. In a voice sweet as sugar, she said, "I made shirred eggs with spinach and paprika over Virginia ham slices."

Harrison used a knife and fork to cut two bites from a ramekin fit between two others in the cast-iron fry pan. He and Shannon forked the egg into their mouths.

"Hmmm . . . this is creamy. The texture is perfect, and the meat has enough seasoning in it that it flavors the eggs." Shannon laid her fork on the counter.

Tabitha smiled wider.

"Well done. Also, it was an excellent choice. No duplicates." Harrison emphasized his praise with a curt nod of his head.

"Thank you." Tabitha managed a grateful tone while blinking back the moisture that had sheened her eyes.

After Brenden yelled "Cut," the contestants filed

to the door to be whisked away for their lunch. The cleaning crew descended on the kitchen, while the rest of us hit the catering table.

"You need to grab your lunch and head to wardrobe," Kinzy prompted me.

At her reminder, my gaze dropped to Harrison's pant legs and shoes. Not a speck of mud in sight. Had he made it to wardrobe to have them clean up the mess? Or did he have several of the same style and color suits with him?

What had he been doing in the wooded area anyway? Harrison was not the outdoorsy type. I filled my plate with an herbed chicken breast and sautéed vegetables and headed upstairs. Once I'd slipped out of my shorts and robed up, I accessed a search app on my phone so I could do some research on Harrison, Bernard and Tabitha while I ate.

I started with Tabitha. She had a page on every social media site available. All were set for public viewing. I scrolled through her friends and pictures. Not one of Bernard Stone or Harrison. No surnames matched theirs either. I did learn she was married with a five-year-old daughter, which made me reconsider the love triangle theory. Every picture showed a happy, contented family.

I kept scrolling. A three-month-old post caught my eye. She'd started the post, "It happened again . . ." With interest, I read on. She'd lost her job in a four-star restaurant. By the comments of commiseration and encouragement, this was about the sixth time.

Pushing my phone aside, I finished my lunch. The post didn't say where she'd worked or why she was fired. Had it been one of Harrison's restaurants?

Had she come here to seek revenge by blackmailing or maybe framing Harrison for murder? Had she known some dirt on Harrison and tipped off Bernard?

I tapped my chin, wondering what the best course of research would be concerning Tabitha. We weren't on friendly terms by any stretch of the recipe, so bringing it up in casual conversation would be out of the question. I guess I could point-blank ask. Either way, it would turn into some kind of confrontation, like the first time I'd tried.

Wardrobe hadn't brought back my cargo shorts, so I searched for Bernard Stone stories again. Several hits popped up; all were stories on his recent investigations. I found many duplicates due to different media websites reporting the news.

The creak of the door pulled my eyes from my phone. Shannon peeked in through a narrow crack. "We still on for tonight?"

Tonight? I drew my brows together while searching my memory. "Girls' night! Absolutely!" I'd been so focused on trying to get my name off the person-of-interest list, I'd spaced on Shannon's and my plans. "Sushi bar?" I smiled. If Shannon didn't care for the caviar, I doubted she'd be a fan of sushi.

She grimaced. "I'm thinking the steak house. I could really go for some surf and turf. Besides, they have a martini bar."

I couldn't hold in my laughter.

Shannon laughed. "Stop messing with me. You knew if I couldn't eat caviar, sushi would never be a dinner choice. I have to make a quick phone call to the hubs to remind him we won't be Skyping dinner tonight. I don't know about you, but I'm really looking forward to some girlfriend time. See you downstairs."

I stared at the closed door. I was really looking forward to girlfriend time with Shannon. In just a few days, she'd become a good friend to me. I couldn't say the same thing about me. I was deceiving her, and that wasn't what friends did. I hoped I didn't ruin our night out, but I'd decided to tell Shannon the truth about my background tonight. She'd already made too many references to me being a farmer's daughter.

Before I could talk myself out of it, I tapped out my plan in a message to Eric and hit Send.

Once released for the day, I'd walked via an approved path straight to the resort. My fingers, and mind, itched to do some more internet searching. Now that the world knew about Bernard's death, many of the news media sites were running reports on some of his old exposés. I calculated I had at least an hour, maybe two, to do some online sleuthing before meeting Shannon for our girls' night out.

The day got off to such a slow start, Shannon and Harrison had to stay and film a segment discussing the cooking challenges and the contestants' end results. The special set, with the white, wicker bistro table and chairs, sat on the edge of a lovely wildflower garden. A baker's rack stood behind the table. The shelves held the bakers' finished products of the day, good or bad. It might seem backward, because we'd ended the day's filming and LeeAnne had already been sent home, but that was how shows were filmed. The chronological order of scenes came during the editing stage. Although the judges had determined LeeAnne's dinner was passable, she'd failed the breakfast and snack challenge. Otto had won the day. Of course, on camera he was a gracious winner. Once Brenden hollered "cut," he'd strutted around in front of the other contestants while uttering, "It's about time."

So much for civil reality television.

My musing made the walk seem brief. Once I reached the resort, I stopped to snag a latte from the lobby's coffee shop, then I made tracks to my room. I hunkered down in front of my laptop in hopes of finding a connection to Bernard, Harrison and Tabitha.

What I found was that Bernard had ruined some lives, and justly so. In the midnineties, he had focused on exposing crooked hedge funds and penny stock brokers. One of his more high-profile cases involved a penny stock scheme aimed at the elderly. He'd infiltrated the company to gain information that sent several people to prison. The victims recouped a large share of their money. Although I had to admit he'd annoyed me, his heart was in the right place in most of his investigations, exposing crimes and obtaining justice for the victims. Which must have been his tactic for getting on our show. His focus was pointed at Harrison and, possibly, Tabitha. What crime could they have committed that hurt someone, made them a victim? Harrison seemed too business savvy to get caught up in a Ponzi scheme, yet he'd admitted to some financial problems. In this scenario, Tabitha had to be the victim. Had she tipped off Bernard to recoup something from Harrison? Perhaps back wages, if she'd been fired from one of his restaurants? Had she and Bernard staged a volatile relationship to throw everyone off?

My continued perusal of his investigative reporting revealed he handled small, regional topics, like corrupt town governments and school scandals, yet I couldn't fathom Harrison's financial difficulties or Tabitha's job failures worth his time and trouble. It had to be something else. Bernard worked on a bigger scale, bringing justice to a larger group of people.

The buzz of my phone drew my attention away from the research. Shannon would meet me at the steak house in fifteen minutes. My heart raced a little when I wondered if she'd stay after I confessed my white lie.

Eric had texted me back. He hadn't tried to talk me out of my confession. His reply was "Whatever"; then he'd proceeded to be all business by asking me if I'd practiced putting the steam cap on the pressure cooker today. Of course I hadn't, and I promised I would tomorrow. If we had a normal day of filming.

I slipped into my pink designer dress and a pair of strappy sandals embellished with jewels. I glanced in the mirror; my hair and makeup from today's filming looked great. A quick spritz of perfume and I headed out of my suite and down to the restaurant.

Shannon was chatting with some people by the door of the steak house. I didn't recognize any as being affiliated with the show. She'd cinched a flowing western-cut minidress with a silver conch belt.

The red dress matched the stitching in her red, high-heeled cowgirl boots.

"Hi, Courtney!" She waved me over when she saw me approaching.

"I'm sorry, y'all. I have to run now. I have a business meeting. I'm glad you like my show, y'all have to work with the network on your sponsorship idea." She grabbed my arm. "It was nice to meet y'all." She smiled wide as she walked away, pulling me with her through the restaurant door.

"We need a private table for two." Shannon made her request before the hostess could even greet us. Turning to me, Shannon jerked her head toward the hallway. "I hate when that happens."

"What happened?"

"That was the barbecue-sauce guy on the show's marketing people. They want me to do a segment on my program using his sauce because I'm Southern. They feel it would give his company a boost. I have no control over those things. What am I telling you that for, you know how it works." Shannon glanced back over her shoulder.

"I thought we were here to have fun, not have a business meeting," I said as we followed the hostess to the secluded table Drake and I had shared.

Shannon laughed. "We are. If they had known this was a social dinner, they would have tried to join us. It's happened to me before." Shannon shrugged. "I told a white lie to get them to leave us alone."

As I slid into the booth, my stomach clenched. This was the perfect lead in to what I had to tell Shannon. My heart raced. I cranked my neck to make sure no one was listening. Believe me, I had learned my lesson about eavesdroppers.

"On that subject, I have something to tell you." The sudden sheen of moisture that blurred my vision surprised me. I tried to blink it away. After only a few days, Shannon's friendship meant a lot to me. I didn't want my confession to change this relationship from friend to acquaintance. I needed to spill my secret before we ordered. My honesty might make or break our dinner.

Shannon looked up from the drink menu. "Courtney, what is it? Has one of your sponsors dropped you because of the murder? Do they think you're a suspect and not a person of interest?" She reached across the table and clasped my trembling hand.

I gave my head a small shake and swallowed.

The concern in her eyes brought out more moisture in mine. I swallowed hard, then cleared my throat. "No, nothing like that. It's something else." I paused, not for dramatic effect, to gain my composure. I wanted to do this right, not blurt or blubber it out. I cleared my throat again.

"I need to tell you something about me. Something I'm not proud of and is a secret I'm being forced to keep." Fear shook my voice. I really didn't want Shannon to be angry with me. Yet, if I wanted to come clean to my fans and the world, I had to be brave and thick-skinned.

"Courtney, I've found ripping off the Band-Aid fast applies to delivering bad news." She quirked a brow. "Or a confession."

My eyes widened. I did have a confession to make,

but maybe not what she was expecting. Taking a
deep breath, I blurted out my thoughts. "It's not that
I killed Bernard. I'm not a farmer's daughter. My father is a doctor. I've lived in Chicago my entire life.
Half of the country things you make reference to, I
know nothing about. Eric has the farming background and pitched my show. The network put in a
clause that I had to 'be' a farmer's daughter and lead
the public to believe I was."

When I stopped to take a breath, I realized the
words had tumbled out of me and might not be making any sense, because Shannon's brow was knitted,
and her mouth puckered to the side. I hoped it was a
look of confusion and not building anger. She
slipped her hand from mine.

Not a good sign. Tears sprang to my eyes again.

"I'm sorry I lied to you. I'm sorry I lied to the public."

"Stop." Shannon held up a hand, then crossed her
arms over the tabletop, turned her head and smiled
like everything was okay.

"Can I get you something to drink?"

My head snapped to the side. A waitress stood beside our table. I'd been so preoccupied with confess-
ing, I hadn't been aware of the surroundings. Again,
I swept my gaze over the area around us.

"I'll have a lemon drop martini." Shannon looked
at me. "No, make that two fingers of bourbon. One
for each of us. House is fine."

The waitress hustled away to fill our order.

"Before you start talking again, I want you to know
one thing. I have never thought you killed Bernard.
When I said confession, which, given our situation, is

a poor choice of words, I meant for you to spill what was troubling you. Although . . ."

"It wasn't what you were expecting." I picked up the conversation.

Lips pursed tight, she shook her head.

"Shannon, I value your friendship. I know it's only been a few days, but I feel, and hope you do too, that we kind of clicked."

She nodded. "I feel the same way. I thought it was because we had . . ."

I waited, then I noticed the waitress heading to our table with our drinks on her tray. She placed one in front of each of us and said she'd check back later.

Shannon lifted her glass and took a bracing drink. "Aren't you going to join me?"

"I don't think I like straight bourbon."

"Ah, consider it payback?" The corners of Shannon's lips curled. "Just try it."

I lifted the glass and took a sip. Involuntarily, my face scrunched and my stomach tightened as the strong alcohol burned down my throat. "That tastes good, but burns . . ."

"Like the devil?" Shannon laughed.

"Yes." I watched Shannon polish off hers.

"Throw it back. It never stops hurting, but the after-effects are worth it."

I went for it and swallowed the rest of the amber liquid in one large gulp. The bottom of the glass banged the table when I sat it down. I stared directly into Shannon's eyes. "I'm sorry I lied to you and led you to believe I'm someone I'm not. I totally understand if you don't want to be friends."

Smiling, Shannon sighed. "I have to admit I feel foolish. I made so many country girl references."

"I know. I've wanted to tell you since the first comment. I never meant to deceive anyone, but people assumed from the show's name, I was a farmer's daughter. My demographic is Middle America and the network just ran with it. I want to tell my fans and the public in general. The network says we'll lose ratings. Thank goodness, I have Eric to help me navigate the questions. It's the only way I'm believable as a country girl." It was my turn to sigh, and I took it.

Shannon cocked her head to the right while she studied me. "Thank you for telling me, and your secret is safe with me. I understand how this business works. I am sorry to tell you this . . ."

When her voice trailed off, I braced for the worst. I was going to get the let's-just-be-coworkers speech.

"Whoa, sorry about that. The warmth of the bourbon hit me. What I was going to say is, I'm sorry to tell you that geography has little to do with who, or what in this case, a person is. A person's heart determines those things. And you, Courtney, whether you are aware of it or not, have the heart of a country girl. That is why your viewers love you. That is why you are so convincing on your program. That is why Barb and I both thought so."

I leaned back into the deep booth and allowed the warmth flooding my veins, the aftereffects of the bourbon, to relax every muscle in my body, and Shannon's words to sink into my mind. Could it be true? I'd loved the demonstration job at the small grocery stores. The local customers became my friends, and I looked forward to seeing them, and they me.

Many shared how they made a dish or asked me if I'd revamp an old family recipe. I welcomed their suggestions and input. I'd also learned some tips and techniques from these everyday cooks that I incorporated into my demonstrations and *Cooking with the Farmer's Daughter.*

And Eric and I clicked immediately when we met. We had the same career ideas and goals. And values. He thought the charity work my dad was doing was commendable, unlike their many friends in the city. Yet Skylar saw my true background, the real me.

"I don't know if that is true."

Shannon smacked her palm on the table. "It is. Believe me."

When I furrowed my brow, my eyes narrowed. "You're not angry with me? And you still want to be friends?"

"I told you. I feel a little foolish, but I understand." She lifted her coiffed bangs to expose light brown roots. "The network told me they needed a blonde in their lineup. I could have the show if I bleached my hair." She dropped her bangs. "I wanted the show."

"Do you think lying about your hair color is the same as leading people to believe you were raised on a farm? The network is worried if I reveal the truth, the show's ratings will tank. I'm worried the fans will hate me. You know how fast the public can turn on some celebrities. Not to mention the gossip programs and magazines."

"It's a risk." Shannon sucked the corner of her mouth under her top teeth. "I can tell this is eating you up inside. I think, as soon as you can, you should explain to your audience. If you handle it in a sincere manner, I think you'll be okay. What does Eric think?"

"He says next year, when our contract is up for renewal, he's going to have the gag clause negotiated out of the contract if he can. Even though he knows it might mean unemployment for both of us." I raised my palms in defeat.

For a few minutes, silence surrounded us.

"So, did you go to culinary school?" Shannon asked.

I nodded. "I'm a trained chef with an emphasis on food art."

"You carve fruits and veggies? That is so neat. I love it when I see that kind of stuff on banquet tables." Shannon flipped her hands through the air.

The waitress took that as her cue to approach our table. We placed our food choice and both decided on soft drinks to accompany our meal. "So much for a wild girls' night out for us," I said.

"Well, the night is still young. After some food, we can have a nightcap. Besides, we can share girl talk over sodas as easily as alcohol." Shannon raised her water glass as if to toast before sipping from the straw. She set down the glass. "Why don't you use your carving skills on your show?"

"It doesn't match the theme. I was hoping *The American Baking Battle* would be a hit. Eric and I thought it might give me leverage not only with the clause, but maybe another show, where I can use that skill." I took a sip of my water. Shannon's expression grew thoughtful; then she smiled.

"What?"

She flopped her hand through the air. "Oh, nothing. Just a silly thought. Tell me, have you seen Drake anymore? On a personal level, I mean."

"No, on either account. Although I do think he's interested. Just sidetracked with the murder investigation." I inhaled deeply. "Or maybe he doesn't want to get involved with a suspect."

"Person of interest. I wish the sheriff would eliminate you."

"Me too." If Shannon wasn't angry about my confession, I knew I could trust her with my speculations. "I really think they should be focusing on Harrison and Tabitha."

She nodded as the waitress delivered our beverages.

Once the waitress left, with the promise our food wouldn't be long, I continued. "I've been doing some internet research. Bernard Stone was here to investigate someone. I think it was Harrison." I lowered my voice. "Harrison confided in me that a few of his restaurants are having financial difficulties. I don't think that is the kind of thing Bernard would have been investigating."

I sipped my soda.

"Unless maybe the financial problems involve misappropriating investment funds." Shannon also took a sip of her cola.

"I hadn't thought of that. It would be right up Bernard's alley. He exposed many investment frauds. One was quite a big Ponzi scheme, according to the news articles on the internet."

Shannon looked at me wide-eyed. "You have done some heavy-duty research."

I leaned forward. "I'm afraid not enough. I can't really find anything on Harrison or Tabitha that Bernard Stone wouldn't have found a waste of time and effort. Yet the first night at our meet and mingle, they had an argument with quite a personal, and threatening, feel."

"Really." Shannon leaned forward too. "Anything in their background?"

I blinked. "Background?"

"Right, their past. Did they have past connections?"

Shannon was much more fun than Eric to bounce ideas off of. She actually seemed to enjoy it and refrained from being a voice of reason. "Tabitha is married. I'd need her maiden name to find a past link to the men. Harrison could be her grandfather, don't you think?"

Shannon shook her head vigorously. "No, father maybe. You are judging his age by his hair color. I think he's only in his midfifties. As a matter of fact, I'm thinking he and Bernard might have been in the same age group."

"Really?" During all my research, I'd never checked their ages. I'd pursued the information trying to find their names mentioned. "Maybe they are from the same hometown." I rubbed my chin, considering. This might explain why Harrison was so indignant about thorough background checks.

"Or went to college together. Could Tabitha be related to one of them?"

I let Shannon's question marinate while the waitress set surf and turf in front of her and sirloin tips in front of me. We'd both chosen the vegetable of the day for our side. Both of us tucked into our entrées. As much as I enjoyed Shannon's company, I wanted nothing more than to eat my dinner and head to my room.

After all, I had some new angles to research.

# CHAPTER EIGHTEEN

The next morning, although I'd researched into the wee hours, I walked on air. I'd readied myself to report to the set in record time after only a few hours of sleep. I didn't even mind walking on the longer path to get there.

I had discovered the link between Harrison and Bernard, and what I believed Bernard planned to investigate. What I didn't know was what I should do now. I supposed I should call Drake or Sheriff Perry to see if they were aware of this situation. I didn't think Harrison had revealed this little secret to either of them. If he had, I felt certain he'd have been moved from a person of interest to suspect. I was still perplexed at how Tabitha had played into the scenario. I had a strong feeling she was connected to all this in some way, especially after her arrest comment the other day. Everyone thought she'd meant in the present day; now, I wasn't so sure.

Yet I really wanted to confront Harrison. If this news got out, it wouldn't just damage his career, it would ruin it. No wonder he'd acted so nervous around Bernard and paced while waiting for our interrogation after the discovery of Bernard's true identity. I knew publicizing his financial difficulties wasn't that troubling. Financiers often pulled their money from restaurants.

He'd fought Brenden on the background checks from day one, with good reason.

The air smelled fresher this morning than it had in days. White, puffy clouds dotted a clear blue sky. I felt certain what I'd found would remove me from Sheriff Perry's person of interest list. I couldn't wait to tell Shannon and Eric about the scenario that linked Harrison and Bernard. Although it was a sad turn of events. Heartbreaking, really.

The whine of a UTV engine caused me to draw closer to the edge of the path. I waved as Travis buzzed past me, decked out in his tennis whites. His response was a shake of his head; not a nod of acknowledgment, more of a not-you-again reaction, and a heavier foot. The engine roared, echoing through the valley. Travis zipped out of sight.

I laughed at his antics. Even his blatant snub didn't bother me today. Plus, I knew if Travis was playing tennis, Drake would be on security duty in case I decided to reveal my findings to him instead of the sheriff. First, I planned to confront Harrison.

Quickening my pace, I made record time getting to the workshop-turned-set. The security guard at the door smiled and nodded as I passed through the door. I whizzed through the catering table, snatching a banana, a bran muffin and a large coffee before I stepped up to our makeup area.

A creature of habit, I found Harrison in the same chair with his nose stuck in a magazine. I set my breakfast on the table. "Good morning, Harrison. Why don't you bring your coffee over here and join me? There's something I'd like to talk to you about." I knew the smile I flashed was smug. I couldn't help it. I was proud of myself for digging up this information and thankful Shannon had suggested a past connection instead of a present one.

"I don't believe I will. This feels like another one of your let's-pin-Bernard's-murder-on-Harrison conversations." Harrison lifted the magazine high enough to cover his face and, with his foot, swiveled his chair until his back was to me.

"Okay, I'll come to you." I left my breakfast on the table and strode over to the wall. In my standing position, I could peer down the magazine tunnel and see his face.

Lifting only his eyes, Harrison met my stare. "I'll humor you. What have you dreamed up this time?"

His condescending tone rolled off my back. I crossed my arms and smiled. "Nothing. I found a fact. Something I wonder if you've disclosed to Sheriff Perry. I've asked you several times, and you've skirted my question with a question of your own or an indirect response. You are an honest man and didn't want to lie, which is commendable. So, this time I won't ask you the question because I know the answer. You and Bernard knew each other."

With his foot, Harrison twisted his chair away from me. He threw his magazine on the small workspace attached to the makeup mirror and stood. His glare turned icy. He drew in a breath and squared his shoulders, giving him a larger, more intimidating stance. "I have had enough of your speculations." He brushed at the sleeves of his suit jacket before letting his arms drop to his sides. Not so subtly, he fisted, then relaxed, then fisted his hands.

I'd imagined a different reaction. Two could play the intimidation game. I mirrored his body language, with the exception of making fists, until there were only several inches of air between us. "This is not speculation. This is fact. And I don't care if you are tired of me confronting you or not. I am tired of being a person of interest in this case because the murder weapon, riddled with my fingerprints, belonged to me. I didn't kill Bernard. I didn't know Bernard, but you did. You went to college with him. As a matter of fact, you were fraternity brothers."

Harrison exhaled long and loud. We were close enough that my skin caught the warmth of his breath with each huffing exhale. Fury flashed in his eyes. His features morphed between rage and fear. "How do you know that?"

"I found an old article in a newspaper archive about the court case. I paid the subscription price so I could read the article. It's printed out in my room." Maybe I shouldn't have added that last part, but I was on a roll and I had a bad habit of not keeping my mouth shut when I really should. Eric's finger-wagging warnings flashed in my mind. I pursed my lips to keep in further comments for the time being.

In a flash, Harrison's right arm jerked out. He clasped my forearm in a death grip. He stepped toward me, closing the space between us. His body pushed mine while he tugged at my arm until my back thumped against the wall. Through gritted teeth, he asked, "Have you told anyone about this?"

The frantic edge in his tone sent fear into every cell in my body. Why couldn't I heed Eric's warnings? I'd put myself in danger. If he'd murdered Bernard, he'd murder me too. Especially now that I knew his secret. Something he wanted kept buried. Was the only way to do that to kill anyone who found out?

Bernard had lost his life through bludgeoning. My eyes roved the area for heavy objects. I didn't want to meet the same gruesome demise Bernard had. I didn't want to meet my demise at all.

"Have. You. Told. Anyone. About. This?" His fingers dug deep into my upper arm.

Pain bit through my arm. My eyes jumped back to Harrison's face, red with rage. My racing heart leaped into my throat. I tried to speak. Only noises squeaked from me.

I tried again. "Not yet." My voice sounded hollow, weak. If I lived through this, I had every intention of telling. Where were Skylar and Shannon? Or our wardrobe and makeup crew? I hadn't shown up that early. Someone needed to come into the room to witness his outrage and save me.

My answer triggered Harrison's retreat. He let go of my arm and stepped away. His angry, red complexion faded. "Good." He stepped back farther. "Good. Courtney, keep this information to yourself and stop nosing around my life, both past and present. Do you understand me?"

I reached over and rubbed the pain from my arm. The attack had ended, but Harrison still blocked the only exit for me. I continued to lean against the wall. It was probably the only thing holding me upright.

"Do you?" His pleading tone held urgency.

I nodded.

"Okay. Okay." Harrison tugged his suit jacket into place. "I trust you, Courtney. Don't let me down." He raised his brows and pinned me with a stern look before turning on the heel of his Italian loafers and storming out the door.

I slid down the wall, still rubbing my upper arm. I was the last person he should put his trust in. I was telling Sheriff Perry or Drake, whoever I found first.

"Geez, what was that all about?" Shannon blew into the room, talking to herself. She carried a cup of coffee dripping from the bottom in one hand and her breakfast in the other. She set down her food next to mine, flicked her hand in the air and looked around the room. Her gaze finally seeing and settling on me.

"Courtney," Shannon shrieked. "Are you all right?" She rushed to my side.

"I am." I continued to rub my arm.

She pulled away my hand. "Are you sure? Did you fall? Your skin is red like it's been bumped."

"I didn't fall. Harrison sort of assaulted me." I reached out a hand to her for assistance standing.

She fisted her own hand to her hip. "What? Why? What kind of a man harms a woman?" She glared at the door. "This explains why he tramped down the stairs and pushed me out of his way."

"Ahem." I cleared my throat. Shannon's attention turned back to me. I waved my fingers. She took the hint and grabbed my hand, helping me to stand.

"Wait a minute. What does 'sort of assaulted' mean?" Shannon stood back and looked me over.

Other than wrinkles, my linen capris and button-down tunic appeared in good shape. "He grasped my arm hard and threatened me."

"Why?" Shannon helped me over to the table.

I slipped onto a chair and took a sip of my coffee, surprised it was still warm. Time had stood still during Harrison's and my exchange, but perhaps only a few minutes had passed. I rubbed my right temple. "I made him angry."

"That explains why he stormed past me on the staircase and spilled my coffee." Shannon swiped at the front of her light pink T-shirt, splotched with dark brown coffee stains. "What did you say this time?" She pulled on the skirt of her pink skorts, inspecting them for spots of coffee.

"The truth. I told him I knew that he and Bernard knew each other. And that I'm pretty sure I found out the reason Bernard was here. It was to investigate Harrison."

"What? Why didn't you go straight to Sheriff Perry?" Shannon slid onto her chair and began to eat a hard-boiled egg.

"I don't know. I wanted to confront him. I was a little miffed with his I'm-a-gourmet-chef-and-you're-not attitude when I am a gourmet chef." I sipped my coffee. The warm liquid calmed and comforted me. "And I thought maybe he'd have a conversation about it with me. You know, be relieved someone else knew the secret, like I am since I told you about my background and training."

"Confession is good for the soul." Shannon sighed.

My shoulders sagged. "I guess Harrison doesn't think so."

Shannon pushed my banana and muffin toward me. "Eat your breakfast. You need nourishment and fortification, because when you're finished eating, we're going to find Drake or Sheriff Perry."

While we gobbled our breakfast, Shannon insisted that I call or text Eric. I chose to text. I'd calmed down, but my emotions were still running high. I wasn't certain I'd be able to find my voice or endure an I-told-you-so lecture without crying. I had nothing against crying; I just wanted to be able to convey the story in a concise and believable way to Eric, Drake and Sheriff Perry. There'd be time to cry later.

My phone jingled Eric's assigned music. "We need to go downstairs to tell Security to let Eric in." I lifted my phone. "He said he's on his way and will break down the door if that is the only way for him to gain entry."

"How sweet. What a white knight you have there."

Shannon's eyes and expression turned dreamy. This wasn't the time to make a romance out of friendly concern. Not to mention financial. We were partners in *Cooking with the Farmer's Daughter*. She looked at me and smiled, waiting for my own romantic response. I changed the subject, fast. "We need to go find Drake or the sheriff. And Brenden. This is probably going to create another delay in filming." I cringed. If the network pulled the plug on this show, I wouldn't blame them.

"Speaking of which, where is everyone? Shouldn't Skylar and the makeup and wardrobe crew be here by now?" Shannon looked around the empty room.

She was right. "I would think so. Let's go downstairs and wait for Eric."

At my suggestion, we gathered our breakfast trash, tossing it into the waste receptacle and descending down to the first floor.

"How is your arm?"

"It doesn't hurt anymore." I stopped on a stair and looked at the skin on my upper arm. No longer red or with a hint of a bruise, I wondered if I'd imagined more pain in my fear of the situation. Skipping down several stairs, I caught up with Shannon.

We found the crew huddled around the catering table. "What's going on?" Shannon drawled over the din of the chatting.

Kinzy stepped out of the crowd. "Something with Skylar is delaying the day." She rolled her eyes. "I don't know why call time isn't noon. It's the time we seem to get started anyway."

"Why didn't anyone tell us?" I asked.

"We sent out a group text." Kinzy shrugged one shoulder.

Shannon and I checked our phones. We'd both received the text that had been delivered during the time she found me upstairs slunk against the wall. In my haste to text Eric, I hadn't even noticed it.

"Is Skylar all right?" Shannon moved closer to Kinzy.

This time both of her shoulders moved up and

down a couple of times. "I don't know." Before the words were off her tongue, she turned away from us and rejoined her conversation.

Guilt stabbed at my conscience. I'd been so concerned about myself, I hadn't considered Harrison may harm someone else. Had he found Skylar and taken out his anger on him? I thought for a minute. My theory was impossible. The text probably was sent before Harrison left the building.

What could it be? Something to do with the murder? Or totally unrelated? He and Brenden had come from some secret meeting the other day. Curiosity and concern piqued, I grabbed Shannon's arm. "Let's go see what's happening." I motioned to the door with my head. "Eric should be out there waiting by now."

Shannon's expression indicated her worry for Skylar too. Was she thinking along the same lines I was?

"You don't think—" She stopped talking when her voice shook. Her eyes misted. "You don't think Skylar was murdered?"

I wanted to say, no, absolutely not. How could I? For all I knew, he had been. I hadn't considered it because Harrison was with me. We double-timed our pace.

Once we walked through the door, I saw Eric pacing in front of our designated meeting place, the oak tree.

"Courtney!" He ran over to me and wrapped me in an embrace. "Are you all right?"

I was taken aback by his gesture. After all, in my text I'd told him nothing about Harrison and my confrontation. "Yes, I think so."

He held me at arm's length. "'I think so'? What does that mean?"

With his face directly in front of mine, I saw the panic and fear etching each of his features. Had Shannon texted the story to him? No, she couldn't have. I hadn't seen her use her phone until she checked for Kinzy's text. She'd been attentive to me since she found me in a crumpled mess on the makeup room floor. "I have a feeling we are talking about two different things."

Eric dropped his arms and looked from me to Shannon and back.

"Hello, Eric." Shannon's bright greeting, hitched with a little giggle, was a contrast to my day and his mood.

"Shannon." Eric nodded. Eyeing both of us, he said, "I thought something happened on the set when you texted."

"Why?"

"Because just I as started down here, every security person wearing a Nolan polo jumped into their utility vehicles and headed this way. Not to mention the sheriff vehicles with flashing lights taking the maintenance roads. Was someone else killed?"

"Skylar!" Shannon and I dueted the name loud enough, we drew the attention of the security personnel guarding the set door.

"Eric, filming was postponed for today. Kinzy said it had something to do with Skylar."

"I hope he's all right." Shannon's voice hiccupped.

"Did you hear any of them say anything while they were fleeing the premises?" I searched Eric's face.

"No." He shook his head.

"Are you sure?" I stretched my neck and cranked it around. The beautiful landscape of plush grass and thick leaf foliage was all I could see.

"I'm sure. They moved too fast for conversation."

"So, it was an emergency." I stated my musing. Where had Harrison gone when he stormed out of the dressing room? Had Skylar witnessed what happened in the dressing room, then followed and confronted Harrison? After all, Skylar wasn't going to allow Tabitha to hit me with a wooden spoon. Perhaps Skylar had called or texted for help?

"Yes, I guess it was." Eric answered me, thinking I was making conversation instead of trying to fit the pieces of the situation together in my mind.

"Did you by chance see Harrison in the lobby or on the path?" I turned my attention to Eric.

"Courtney, you don't think Harrison hurt Skylar like he hurt you this morning?" Shannon placed her hand on my shoulder.

Wide-eyed, I looked at Shannon. "I hope not."

"*What?*" Eric's bellow echoed through the countryside. He grabbed my shoulders again. "Harrison hurt you? How?" His head jerked from me to Shannon.

"Well, he squeezed my arm really tight and backed me against the wall in a show of intimidation."

Eric's eyes bugged out. His jaw clenched. "Why would he do that?"

Squinting, I wrinkled my nose in a bracing manner. "I confronted him about a past relationship with Bernard."

"Courtney, I told you to stop meddling in this investigation." Eric dropped his arms and some of the concern from his expression.

"But I found something. Something significant."

"Then why didn't you take it directly to Sheriff Perry or your rent-a-cop friend?"

Shannon didn't even attempt to suppress her giggle at what she thought was a show of Eric's jealousy by not using Drake's name. I shot her a look and she stifled it.

"Is this really the time to discuss this? Skylar may be hurt or . . ." My voice trailed off. I didn't bother finishing the sentence. Everyone sobered. Eric and Shannon knew what I meant.

"Okay." Eric wagged his index finger in my direction. "We will see what is going on with Skylar. The previous subject is not closed." His eyes held a warning.

I nodded. "What path did you use? Did you see anything?"

"I came on the south path. Sheriff Perry's men used the maintenance road that runs on the back of the property."

"The pond!" Shannon and I again voiced our thoughts at the same time.

Our trio hurried around the building and speed walked along the path. Visions of Skylar floating on the pond bludgeoned to death in the same manner as Bernard filled my head. The air around our group thickened with tension when we entered the wooded area. Nerves on edge, we each took turns being startled by nature's noises, mumbling our speculations of a squirrel, the wind or a bird.

Finally, we rounded the bend. Our guess had been accurate. UTVs and Security blocked the path to the pond. Flashing lights from the police cars, somewhere from the other side of the pond, cut through the leaves' denseness like an eerie beacon.

"You can't go back there." A security guard stepped into our path when we approached and tried to take the path leading to the pond.

"What has happened?" I asked.

"I am not at liberty . . ."

"Wrong. This affects all of us," I cut him off. Protocol didn't apply if I thought my friend and cohost had come to harm. "Is Skylar all right?" I stood on my tiptoes and craned my neck.

"My orders are . . ."

"I don't care about your orders. Was Skylar harmed?" I'd raised my voice almost to a shout.

"Courtney?" Brenden slipped from a four-passenger UTV behind the blockade stopping us from entering.

"Brenden, is Skylar okay? We heard filming was delayed because of him, and Eric saw the commotion in the resort." My words came out in a rush of breath. I inhaled and waited for the worst.

Brenden approached us. "You can't come any farther. It's a crime scene."

"No!" Shannon cried out.

My knees weakened. I needed support. Reaching out, I grasped Eric's arm. In an instant, he covered my hand with his. Had my need for satisfaction in telling Harrison I knew the truth caused Skylar's death?

Shock registered on Brenden's face. "Oh, no. I didn't mean— It's not what you're thinking." He swallowed hard. "What I'm trying to say is, Skylar is fine. He was fishing and found something. Well, I guess, *caught* something suspicious. He called Drake, and here we are." Brenden held out his hands.

I cringed. What could he have caught? A body? A body part? My stomach jolted when a flashback of my discovery of Bernard, bludgeoned and covered in cobbler, popped into the forefront of my mind. Poor Skylar.

"So, Skylar is okay." Shannon breathed behind me.

"Yes, yes, I think so." Brenden looked over his shoulder. "I haven't seen him either."

Movement behind Brenden caught my eye. A rainbow of Nolan polo shirts headed in our direction. "You can break it up and return to your posts. I've made assignments for those staying. Your posts may change throughout the day. Be prepared." Drake's men scattered into their respective vehicles at his direction. He walked toward our group, his usually immaculate hair tousled by the wind and humidity of the day. "What are you doing here?"

He gazed over Brenden at our trio.

"We thought something happened to Skylar," Shannon drawled.

"Something bad," I added, to indicate our concern, and our right to be concerned.

"He's fine. A little shaken up but fine." Drake turned his attention to Brenden. "He will be tied up with the sheriff for a while, though. And so will Courtney."

"Why?" Eric beat me to the question.

"Sheriff Perry wants to talk to Courtney." The corner of Drake's mouth quirked into a smile. "Alone."

Hands on my shoulders, Eric spun me around.

"Remember, you don't have to answer any questions without legal representation present."

I nodded my head.

With the palm of his hand, Drake indicated for Brenden, Eric and Shannon to get into the UTV Brenden had sat in. Side by side, we watched the retreating vehicle disappear into the dense trees on their way back to the set.

"Let's go." Drake walked beside me in silence until the path broke and opened up to the pond. Yellow police tape surrounded the dock area. Sheriff Perry's deputies walked the perimeter, heads down, obviously searching for other items.

I scanned the area, trying to catch a glimpse of Skylar. My gaze rested on Sheriff Perry staring down into the trunk of one of his cruisers. My heart sank. What had Skylar found? With more urgency, I tried to spot him. He was nowhere to be seen.

The thud of the trunk reverberated through the silent countryside and my body. I needed to see Skylar, living and breathing. Then I'd confess my findings to Sheriff Perry and Drake and not leave out any details of Harrison's actions this morning.

Sheriff Perry looked up. Although he wore sunglasses, it seemed as if our eyes met. He headed my way, the lines of his face grim and serious.

"Miss Archer, I'd like you to join Mr. Daily in the back of the squad car." My eyes pursued several cars before I saw Skylar's head leaning back against the seat. Relief washed through me.

Sheriff Perry extended his hand in an after-you fashion. With no hesitation, I took the lead. Skylar had been so supportive of me when I'd found Bernard. It was my turn to help him. Besides, I knew he'd tell me what he'd found.

It didn't take us long to cross the span of grass between the pond and the maintenance road. The hum of the sheriff's car welcomed us, as did a blast of cold air when Sheriff Perry opened the back door.

He leaned down and peered in at Skylar. "Feeling better?"

Opening his eyes and lifting his head, Skylar answered, "Yes, thank you. I'm no longer light-headed or nauseous." Sheepishness crossed his features.

"Don't worry about it, son. Even the best detectives and deputies get sick sometimes."

My own stomach flipped. What had Skylar found?

Sheriff Perry straightened, and at his hand gesture, I slid in beside Skylar.

"Courtney." Skylar reached for my hand.

"You okay?" I gave his hand a squeeze.

"Yes. A little shocked, and humiliated for throwing up."

The front car door opened and clicked closed. The seat belt whooshed as Sheriff Perry secured himself into the driver's seat. Through the rearview mirror, his eyes watched us.

"It just . . ."

I returned my attention to Skylar.

"It just smelled so bad." Skylar gagged at the thought.

"What did?"

"The plastic garbage bag full of clothes I snagged when I cast my line to the middle of the pond."

What? I scrunched my face in confusion. "Who'd throw a plastic bag full of clothes into the pond? And why would they stink so bad it made you sick?"

Sheriff Perry cleared his throat. "My guess is Bernard's murderer, Miss Archer, because they were covered in blood and your cherry cobbler."

# CHAPTER NINETEEN

Skylar and I sat across from each other at a table in one of the resort's suites blocked off for Sheriff Perry's use. I drank coffee. Skylar sipped ginger ale.

"How do you do it? You found the dead body. I can't seem to get the stale blood and rotten food smell out of my nose. If I could, I wouldn't need this." He held up his soda can. "What you saw had to be ten times worse."

Once more, my mind recalled the scene.

"Sorry, Courtney. I didn't mean to bring up bad memories."

My expression must have shifted with my thoughts. "It's okay. Some days are better than others. In time, I'm sure it will fade for both of us."

The collapsible wall wiggled with the movement of Sheriff Perry opening the door and entering. "Mr. Daily, if you feel up to it, you can head to your room and lie down. I've called Brenden. He will start filming after lunch because you've had a trying and shocking morning."

Skylar gagged. I knew the freshness of the situation, and the staleness of the murder on the clothing, flooded back to his memory at the sight of Sheriff Perry. Skylar rose and double-timed it out of the room, covering his mouth with his hand.

"Poor guy." Sheriff Perry clicked his tongue. "Just doesn't have the stomach for murder like you do."

I raised my brows in question. "You don't think finding a murdered body bothered me?"

"On the contrary. You have a stronger stomach for the gruesome aspect of the murder. The actual murder, the taking of another's life, really bothers you. It's why you keep sticking your nose where it doesn't belong in my investigation."

I puckered my lips to the side while I contemplated my response to his spot-on statement. Deep down, I knew even if I wasn't a person of interest, I'd be trying to solve the mystery.

"I should thank you, though. The change of clothing clue helped us move forward in the case. Although you were trying to be less than helpful that day, it alerted us to the fact that Brenden has quite a bit of evidence on tape. Not the murder, though." Sheriff Perry eased his ample frame onto the chair Skylar had vacated and pushed the soda can to the side of the table.

"Speaking of evidence on tape, weren't the security cameras on the night of Bernard's murder?" I heard Eric's warning and pushed it to the back of my mind, along with my visual of Bernard.

"They were off-line." Sheriff Perry removed his ball cap and ran a hand through his thick, white hair, which did nothing to eliminate the cap-band ridge around his hair.

"What does that mean?" I finished off my coffee.

"They are hooked up to the resort's network. Somehow, they'd dropped off."

"How convenient." I rubbed my chin.

"Or a coincidence. Networks go down." Sheriff Perry laid his palms flat on the table.

I wasn't buying that explanation. I doubted he did either.

"Good thing Mr. Daily casts a long line. We might never have found that bag of clothes."

"Was it weighted down?" I leaned toward the sheriff.

Sheriff Perry leveled me with his eyes. "You know I can't disclose that information, just like the security cameras. I can tell you that after this morning, Mr. Daily is no longer a person of interest in the murder." Sheriff Perry leaned back and shook his head. "Doesn't have the stomach for it."

My heart lifted with the news that someone had been removed from the list. Then it dropped. Did that mean that because he'd brought me back into the temporary interrogation room, he thought the splattered clothing belonged to me? My eyes widened.

"Relax, Miss Archer. The clothing inside the bag belonged to a man."

"Does this mean I'm no longer a person of interest too?"

Sheriff Perry laughed. "You really haven't been a person of interest for a while."

"What?" I'd been spending all my time and energy finding a way to remove myself from a list I wasn't on anymore? He could have told me sooner. I wouldn't have stopped snooping around, but I wouldn't have been so worried either. A heaping dollop of aggravation raised my temperature. I'm sure it showed on my face.

Sheriff Perry grinned and nodded. "Miss Archer, I've observed you over the past few days. You can't hit a trash can from two feet away with garbage, so how could you swing a loaded cast-iron fry pan and hit your target? You are at least a foot shorter than Mr. Stone. Couple that with little upper-body strength and bad aim, there is no way you could deliver the devastating and murderous blows that killed Mr. Stone while he was standing. Once we found out his identity I was certain his 'bonus story' on you had to do with your nonfarmer girl background. Mr. Stone seemed to like those types of stories . . ."

Sheriff Perry's voice, perhaps thoughts, trailed off, and he rubbed his chin. "Anyway . . . you haven't been a person of interest for some time. We have a theory that whoever murdered Bernard might be trying to pin it on you."

*What?* Now, instead of being relieved, I was full-fledged miffed. "So, I've been bait to lure the murderer to reveal his or her hand?"

"I suppose you could look at it that way." Sheriff Perry shrugged. "What puzzles us is why anyone would try to pin the murder on you. You don't seem to have enemies here on set or in your personal life. Several security persons were assigned to watch you, to make certain you were safe or to see if anyone tampered with anything else belonging to you. So far, nothing." He shrugged.

"How about the light on the set? Did someone rig it to fall on me?"

"Nope. Faulty product. Stripped bolts. With that said, we are still working our theory, and there are three things we'd like you to do." Sheriff Perry sobered and looked me directly in the eye.

"What if I don't want to?" My voice reflected my irritation.

Holding up his index finger, it seemed Sheriff Perry didn't notice the emotion I infused in my words, or he chose to ignore it. He continued. "Don't look around and try to spot or identify the security personnel assigned to watch you." His middle finger lifted. "Keep this between us. And the most important of all . . ."

I leaned toward him because his dramatic pause seemed to make his last point the most important of the three.

With his thumb holding his pinkie, the third digit appeared, then, with the flick of his wrist, his index finger pointed at me. "Stop your amateur investigation."

I pursed my lips. "Very funny."

"I'm serious. We know you are trying to solve this murder. We have security detail on you, and one was your waitress in the steak house. She heard your and Mrs. Collins's conversation."

When I realized my mouth hung open, I closed it, then reopened it. "Was any of my information helpful?" At this point, Eric's warning about keeping my mouth shut was a distant memory.

Sheriff Perry smiled, putting a happy twinkle in his blue eyes. "You know I can't tell you that. Now is the time to share any pertinent information you've discovered about Bernard or Harrison and their past connection."

Touché. I needed to alert Sheriff Perry on Harrison's actions this morning anyway. I might as well start from the top. Drawing a deep breath, I filled him in on their past connection. Drake entered the room and I cast a glance his way but continued. I wanted to get the story out like I was reporting facts and not a victim of Harrison's abuse. Once the entire story spilled out, including my thoughts about Tabitha, I owned up to possibly egging Harrison on to the point of rage.

Both Drake and Sheriff Perry listened without interruption or a change of expression. A few minutes of silence ensued after I finished.

"Do you want to press charges against Harrison?" Sheriff Perry asked.

Drake inspected my upper arm. "Not a trace of a bruise." When Drake touched my skin, the area warmed. I smiled at him, then turned to Sheriff Perry.

"I don't think so, but where was my security detail when that happened?"

Sheriff Perry leveled me with a look. "At the pond."

"Oh, right! What happens to the clothes now?"

"They've been sent to Forensics." Sheriff Perry eased his cap over his hair.

"I saw Harrison at the pond yesterday. His shoes and pant legs were covered in mud. He said he returned a turtle to the water."

"Really?" Sheriff Perry's brows shot up. He and Drake exchanged a look I couldn't read. Was this information helpful in making a case against Harrison?

"Again, don't tell anyone you are not a person of interest. Not your coworkers or your boyfriend." Sheriff Perry's tone negated argument.

"He's her producer, not boyfriend," Drake said and flashed me an interested smile that warmed me to my toes.

"Whoever he is, don't tell him. If you find out anything else, *anything*, contact me right away. Here is my cell phone number." Sheriff Perry slipped a business card from his pocket and handed it to me. He stood and said, "Now, I get to go deal with the press. Drake will take you back to the set."

My day had come full circle emotion-wise. I'd awakened happy; after a detour to scared and shocked, my happiness had returned. Once again, I rode in the passenger seat beside Drake in his utility vehicle. Only this time we were alone. If he drove any slower, we'd stop. Which meant Drake wanted to spend some time with me too, right?

Insides giddy, I glanced at him and smiled. He'd sneaked a peek my way at the same time. Our eyes met. He smiled wide. His eyes sparkled with interest. A full flush crept onto my face.

He flicked his gaze back to the path. His smile remained and pink tinged his cheeks. Awkward silence surrounded us. I searched for something to say. Drake beat me to it.

"Wow, this job is turning out to be as bad as working for the FBI." He whistled. "I thought I'd left murder behind me."

"Did you work many murder cases?" Not really the topic I wanted to discuss, but for right now, it was a start and our only common ground.

"Quite a few." Drake sneaked a look my way before turning his eyes back to the path before us. "The last case I worked, I realized I wasn't even fazed that someone could be so vicious in taking another's life. I realized murder had become routine to me, expected really, because it was in my job description, which disturbed me. I examined who I'd become, another callous cop, so I quit and started Nolan Security."

"How did Bernard's murder make you feel?" I twisted my body to the side as far as the seat belt allowed to put Drake in my line of vision. I needed to relish this moment. It might never happen again.

"Sad when I thought it was Mick Henderson, average Joe. Not at all surprised when we learned the true identification of the body. Bernard Stone, though for good reason many times, ruined lives and reputations." Drake sighed. "Let's change the subject. How does it feel to be a free woman?"

I laughed, a little louder than I'd intended, because I was nervous and trying to make a good impression. "I always felt free and knew I was innocent, so about the same. I am relieved to unofficially be off the person of interest list."

"You think Harrison Canfield is the murderer, don't you?"

My eyes roved the pristine landscape. This conversation had a familiar vibe and reminded me of the interrogation in the restaurant. Perhaps I'd misread his expression and motives toward me. Yet his line of conversation allowed me to glean information from him too. "He seems the most likely. He had motive. Bernard planned to ruin his life in some kind of exposé concerning their past. It's just . . ." I paused and zoned in on as much of Drake's face as I could. "I think Tabitha Miller is tied to this in some way. I wish I knew her maiden name."

"She is a firecracker, that's for sure. My staff is tired of escorting her off the set. Some have asked for hazard pay." Drake laughed. "Somehow, we turned the conversation back to my business. I intended this ride to be social. I have an important question to ask you."

"What's that?" My heart leaped around in my chest, while a mantra ran through my mind. *Ask me out. Ask me out.*

"When the murder is solved, would you like to go out to dinner with me?"

My heart picked up pace and my limbs trembled. Oh my gravy. The mantra worked.

"In a restaurant not located in the resort." Drake's fingers tapped a nervous beat against the steering wheel.

The pulsing of my heart dimmed out the white noise around us. Drake wanted to take me to dinner away from prying eyes. "I'd like that." I smiled wide, and so did he. For seconds, we gazed at each other, smiling, before the off-road vehicle bumped off the edge of the path, bouncing us up, then back down.

"Oops." Drake hit the brake, looked straight ahead

and guided the UTV back onto the path. Embarrassment turned his complexion a deep shade of red.

"Maybe I should drive when we go out?" I inflected humor in my question. It worked. Drake laughed and some of the color faded. Too soon, he pulled up to the workshop door.

"Thank you for the lift." Unbuckling, I climbed out of the passenger seat.

"See you later." Drake saluted a wave and sped off on the forbidden path. I watched him until he was out of sight, then entered the workshop.

Habit guided me up the stairs and through the door to wardrobe, never stopping to see what was happening on the set. I didn't try to fight my ear-to-ear grin. When Sheriff Perry solved the murder, Drake and I were going out on a date. Something I'd desired from the day we met. Now, more than ever, I wanted Bernard's killer found.

"That is not the expression I'd thought you'd come away with after being questioned by Sheriff Perry." Shannon arched a brow while flashing me a skeptical look.

"Drake asked me out." I shimmied my shoulders to the rhythm of my singsong tone.

"What?" Shannon grabbed me by the arm and guided me over to the chairs around the table. "Did you say yes?"

"No, I refused." When I saw some relief in her eyes, I quickly added, "Of course I said yes."

"Courtney."

I cringed at the disappointment in Shannon's tone. "What? You know I'm interested in him. He is very attractive. You think so too."

Her lips drew into a deep frown. "There is no denying Drake is handsome, but remember, someone else cares about you too. As a matter of fact, he is frantic to know what happened to you. He has texted me about every fifteen minutes since we left you."

Eric! With all the sheriff had disclosed, and then the lift and dinner invitation from Drake, I'd completely forgotten to text Eric that I was okay. I slipped my phone from the side pocket of my capris. I tapped a message and hit Send. In seconds, my phone jingled with a response.

I read the message and laid my phone facedown. Shannon's chiding and Eric's relieved concern, then his reminder that I needed to practice using the pressure cooker again, dampened my spirits about Drake and my future date.

Was Shannon right? Did Eric have romantic feelings for me? Any business partner would be frantic if the other was in danger or risked being arrested. Right? I would be if the tables were turned. Then there was Drake and Sheriff Perry's misunderstanding about Eric's and my relationship too. Did I need to take a step back and examine Eric's and my interactions? Sure, we talked about personal stuff, our backgrounds, hopes and dreams, but we'd known each other for over ten years. We'd worked and traveled together. How could we not be concerned for each other?

I rested my head in my hand. How did I feel about Eric? I'd grown to depend upon him. He was a constant in my life. A day never went by that we didn't talk either in person or on the phone, with many side conversations sprinkled throughout the day via texts.

He was my biggest career supporter and advocate. My heart gave a little twist. Had I taken him for granted? Considered him a given?

My thoughts tugged my features into a frown.

"You okay?" Shannon patted my arm.

Her voice snapped me out of my reverie. "Yes, I guess so." I lifted my phone. I should talk to Eric about this. Not on the phone, though it might make it easier. "I need to talk to Eric."

Shannon nodded. "I should say so."

I stood at the same time our makeup and wardrobe staff entered. A quick glance at the time told me I'd have to put it off until later.

In record time, makeup and wardrobe whipped us into shape. Kinzy appeared in the door to take us to the set as the last mist of hair spray floated through the air.

"We need to get you both downstairs. Skylar has the day off, so you are on your own, Courtney." She whipped her arm in a circular motion toward the doorway in an attempt to herd us out of the room. Shannon led the way. Wardrobe had dressed her in an outfit similar to the one she'd worn the night we met, only the short denim skirt had gussets that flared. Her bright yellow T-shirt under a denim vest that matched the skirt screamed summer sunshine. Her low-heeled, yellow cowgirl boots had high, leather shafts.

I guessed the recipe challenges for today revolved around a western theme. Shannon's braided hair haloed the crown of her head. They'd ponytailed my hair high, curled and brushed it into one long ringlet down my back. I wore a chambray dress complete with a lace, western-cut yoke and a wide ruffle across the bottom, along with black cowgirl boots that were the opposite of Shannon's, a dressier heel and a lower shaft.

We followed Kinzy down the staircase, and I wondered how Harrison's tailored suits fit into this theme. My gaze searched the set floor and found him sitting in his chair, his nose in a magazine. His wardrobe for today was a smart suit reminiscent of the gamblers in the Old West.

Apprehension seized my body. I hadn't seen him since this morning's kerfuffle. Would his anger flare again? Phantom pain squeezed my arm where his fingers once had. I rubbed the area and felt no soreness. Taking a deep breath, I entered the spot on set where the talents' chairs sat.

"There you are." Brenden walked away from a camera. "Skylar's under the weather." Brenden raised his brows. "So, you're on your own."

I nodded.

Brenden smiled. "We'll do a comedy set up when he's feeling better. Right now, we will do a basic explanation of the challenge and get started. Perhaps we'll finish filming by midnight. Hit your mark and review the monitor while we escort in the contestants and adjust camera angles."

Stepping over to my tape mark, I passed Harrison. He kept his head down, interested in his magazine. Had Drake or Sheriff Perry made any contact with him? Talked to him about our altercation this morning? I read through the monitor four times before everyone was in their places, including the cameramen. I about had the monologue memorized by the time Brenden hollered "Action."

"Most of you can tell by my outfit"—I pulled out the skirt with one hand, turned and bent my knees at the same time, creating a curtsy—"today's challenges have a western theme. We're going to do-si-do with food made with wild game. Unwrap the butcher paper in front of you and you will find bison. Think about feeding hungry cowboys coming in from a long day driving cattle. These aren't your ordinary, run-of-the-mill cowboys. Our cowboys yearn for gourmet food, like a rib-sticking bison Wellington." I smiled and panned my gaze over the contestants, hoping their cameraman caught some of their expressions. Viewers would love the happy, shocked and, for Tabitha, repulsed looks at the bison sirloins. "Baking begins now."

Brenden cut, and so did the light on my camera. I turned from my mark to see Harrison slouched down in his chair, while Drake hovered behind him, chatting with Shannon. Had Drake questioned him about our altercation? Drake caught my eye and waved me over to him.

"Could I talk to you for a minute?"

"Sure."

With his hand on my upper arm, he guided me toward the back corner, where Skylar and I usually filmed the opening sequence. He angled his body so he could see anyone approaching and pulled a folded piece of paper from his pocket.

"This is for you. Like Sheriff Perry, I'm trusting you to keep this quiet."

I took the proffered paper.

"Don't open it now. Wait until no one is paying attention to you or you are alone. Okay?"

"Sure." I pulled my cell phone from my pocket and slipped the paper between my driver's license and credit card in the plastic holder on the back.

"I need to get back to work. Let me know if that is helpful." Drake gave me a wink and walked away without looking back.

I remained in the area. After minutes passed, I slipped out the paper and flipped it open. In small, neat printing was one word. My breath caught. I looked up from the paper in the direction Drake had made his exit. I smiled, refolded the paper and stuck it back into its hiding place. It would have to wait until I was alone in my room tonight. I wasn't taking any chances on the set.

Harrison and Shannon judged the first challenge alone. The contestants placed their cast-iron fry pans on the end of their counters, near the center aisle. The judges zigzagged back and forth, tasting and critiquing.

I softly clapped my hands when Barb received high marks for her pepper-crusted meat, cooked to a rare perfection, slathered with a shitake mushroom pâté and tucked inside puff pastry. Otto chose to herb-crust his meat, slather it with a duck liver pâté and roll it in Parma ham before encasing the entire sirloin in puff pastry. He'd decorated the outside of the dough. Although the end product had eye appeal, Shannon and Harrison disliked the medium-cooked beef and felt the herbs and pâté were mismatched.

When they came to Tabitha, I held my breath and waited for the combustible personalities to ignite a campfire. I giggled at my thought, then realized Harrison and I shared the same type of relationship. I frowned. Why? Was it his standoffish attitude? Despite this morning's altercation, I'd seen an honest and genuine side of him too.

"Very good."

Harrison's voice pulled me back into the moment. Shannon nodded her agreement.

"I added dried chilies to my cremini duxelles to keep with the western theme." Tabitha sucked her lips together, then pulled them into a tentative smile.

"Well done," Shannon said. "And I don't mean the bison. You brought it to a perfect medium rare."

"And the puff pastry is tender and crispy." Harrison flaked off a layer of the toasted dough. "You made a brave choice not adding a pâté, yet it is not missed at all. Kudos."

The judges moved on, and Tabitha turned with a smile, hoping, like all the other contestants, to be cheered on for this victory. She was met with scowls or frowns. Her smile drooped and she blinked several times. Had she just learned a hard lesson? Her actions had made her an outcast.

Harrison stabbed at Brenda's charred piece of meat with his fork several times. Shannon rested her hand over his, so he would stop. She flashed a sympathetic look at Brenda, then said, "There is no reason for us to try the meat. It's burned to a crisp, including whatever seasoning you put on it."

"I doused it with olive oil and stuck it under the

broiler to get a better sear." Brenda sniffled. "It caught on fire."

"Well, olive oil has a low burning point." Harrison raised his brows. "Unfortunately, the puff pastry is undercooked because there is no pâté or layer of ham or prosciutto to protect it from the meat juices, making it soggy. I don't think you understand how to cook a Wellington."

Anthony and Daniel had cooked their pastry and bison to perfection in Harrison's and Shannon's eyes, but underseasoned the meat. Melissa had tenderized her bison fillet with a marinade of soy sauce. Both Harrison and Shannon loved it. The sugar in the soy gave the meat a nice crust after the sear. The mushroom duxelles complemented it. She'd covered the meat entirely, so the puff pastry cooked perfectly inside and out. Steve had opted for a mixed mushroom pâté over meat. He'd sliced the mushrooms by hand. Their inconsistent shape made some very well done, others chewy and the puff pastry soggy. Harrison gave him a stern lecture about slicing, dicing and purée-ing.

It took only minutes for Harrison and Shannon to decide who'd won the first round of the day. Brenden decided Shannon and Harrison would announce the best and worst of the first challenge.

I watched Tabitha to gauge her reaction.

Shannon led with the failing recipe, Brenda's. Harrison wasted no time naming Melissa the winner of the round.

Tabitha's lips drew into a disappointed pout. I waited for an outburst. It never came. She calmly removed her apron and stepped over to their exit door. Was praise all she sought in the competition? Or had her peers' reaction caused her to think about, and maybe regret, her outbursts? Brenden broke for a short lunch, giving the cleaning crew time to clean and reset the kitchenettes for the second challenge of the day.

Famished, I walked straight to the catering table. I grabbed a croissant, stuffed it with smoked turkey, provolone and lettuce, and snagged a bottle of water. I hurried from the building, intending to sit under the shade of a tree to eat my lunch and do research. I ate my sandwich as I walked. When I came to the tree where Eric usually waited for me, I carefully leaned against it to avoid another wardrobe snafu and polished off my lunch.

I hoped I looked casual, and normal, pulling out my cell phone and the slip of paper Drake had sneaked to me. Double-checking the spelling, I typed "Tabitha Callahan Miller" into the search engine. Instantly, her social media sites popped up, then an obituary. A quick tap sent me to the funeral home website. A lovely woman, appearing to be in her fifties, smiled beside the story of her life. Tabitha's mother had lost her life to pancreatic cancer. She'd left behind her only daughter, Tabitha, and her parents. She was preceded in death by the love of her life, Dallas Rodgers.

I stared down at the name. Why was it so familiar? I scowled and tapped back to the main screen. I scrolled through the prominent links. Most led to Tabitha's culinary training, which was impressive. I looked out across the horizon, wondering what my next search should be, when I saw Kinzy on the path, waving her arms in the air to garner my attention.

Slipping my phone into my pocket, I met her halfway. "Are they ready for me?"

"Yes." We fell into step. "It's a good thing Shannon saw you leave, and the security at the door paid attention to what direction you took. We are losing money on this show. I am afraid the network is going to close us down." Kinzy sighed loudly. "I need this job. It's my stepping-stone to something better. You know, I went to school to be a director, not a gofer."

*School!*

I almost pulled Kinzy into a tight hug. That was where I knew the name *Dallas Rodgers.* He'd gone to college with Harrison and Bernard. He'd pledged their fraternity. Unlike Bernard and Harrison, he hadn't become a frat boy because he died during initiation. I was certain Dallas Rodgers was the reason Bernard had entered the baking competition. Had he planned to solve a decades-old death and expose Harrison Canfield for what he was, a murderer?

# CHAPTER TWENTY

For the remainder of the filming day, time stood still. I'd texted Sheriff Perry and Drake that I'd need to meet with them after filming. We agreed on the interrogation room in Coal Castle Resort. Then Eric texted to remind me I needed to practice using the pressure cooker tonight. Both Drake and Sheriff Perry agreed my makeshift *Cooking with the Farmer's Daughter* set would make it easier to lure Harrison into joining us.

Really, Sheriff Perry wasn't leaving him a choice. As a favor for finding out this information, Sheriff Perry had granted me permission to be included in the conversation with Harrison. I frowned at the last text I received from the sheriff, reminding me this didn't mean Harrison murdered Bernard.

Innocent until proven guilty. The irony wasn't lost on me that I'd developed what I'd thought was Travis's mind-set, guilty until proven innocent. I justified my feelings by considering all the evidence I felt pointed to Harrison. The use of gloves in the kitchen. A midnight run on the night of the murder. Muddy pants and shoes. Sharing a life-changing secret with Bernard. A secret, if found out, that would ruin Harrison. Couple that with mood swings, although not as severe as Tabitha's. Should she be included in this meeting? If anyone might want to seek revenge, it'd be her, right?

I shook off my thoughts and refocused on the show. The sooner Brenden captured all his shots for this episode, the sooner I could turn over my evidence. With my toes on my tape, I was ready to do double duty, name the baker of the day and send the next contestant home.

The other two challenges also contained game meat: pheasant, and what I felt was a stretch, catfish. Smiling, I swept my gaze over the contestants while I gave the recap of the challenges. "Today's baker excelled at all three challenges. The superb, peppered, crusted bison."

Barb gasped.

My smile widened. I continued, "The rustic pheasant and potato chip casserole."

Barb waved her hands up and down in front of her eyes, like it would dry the moisture pooling in them.

"The scored and deep-fried catfish fillet all tasted delicious. Barb, once again, you are the baker of the day."

"Oh, my!" She clapped her cheeks with her palms.

"Now." My smile faded.

The remaining contestants sobered at the sound of my voice. "The baker leaving today missed the mark on two of the three challenges."

I saw relief on Anthony, Daniel and Melissa's faces.

"I'm sorry, Brenda, it's time for you to leave the kitchen."

Blinking rapidly, she nodded. All the bakers began to mingle, giving congratulations or condolences depending on which woman they were hugging.

As always, when Brenden hollered "Cut," not only the cameras stopped, so did the contestants' mingling, some in midsentence. Otto didn't hide his emotions. His face and body language showed he disagreed with the judges' top choice. Although to others he looked like a bad sport, I sympathized with his feelings. Barb, a home cook, kept beating him, a trained chef. Because I was also a trained chef, I knew it would sting your ego.

The other contestants filed in behind Otto at their exit door.

"Are we good?" I called to Brenden. "I have a practice run for my next on-location filming."

He waved me off. I escaped without being stopped by anyone and quickly changed from the western dress and boots into my capri set and flats. I took the time to text Eric that I was on my way to the resort. I'd tell him he might be asked to leave when everyone got there. Skipping down the steps, I managed to skirt Shannon. I'd fill her in later. I busted through the door, intending on hoofing it to the resort.

Sheriff Perry sat in a four-seat utility vehicle. "Hop in."

I rounded the back of the cart and started to slip into the passenger seat.

"Take a back seat. Harrison is going to sit there." The sheriff hitched his head.

I obliged, swallowing a comment on the tip of my tongue about walking rather than riding with Harrison. After what seemed like forever, Harrison exited the building in his tailored suit. He stopped and hesitated.

"Get in." Sheriff Perry's tone held an official edge. Harrison rounded the front of the UTV. He avoided eye contact with either of us while he slipped onto the seat.

Tension-filled, the short ride felt like a long-distance haul. Once again, the sheriff parked beside all the other utility vehicles, and we entered the building through the door marked "Security." Sheriff Perry led the way through the hallway to the office, then to the rooms designated for my set.

Eric! "Could I go in first and prepare Eric for his abrupt exit?"

Sheriff Perry turned around. "Is your boy . . . er . . . producer in there?"

I nodded and dismissed his slip of the tongue. I didn't have time to linger on everyone's perception of Eric's and my relationship.

"Make it quick." Sheriff Perry heaved a sigh. Harrison's annoyed expression deepened.

I keyed my way into the room.

"Hey, Courtney." Eric's face lit up when he smiled my way.

"Hi, Eric." He looked so happy, I hated to tell him that he was an unwelcome party on his own set. I decided the best way to do it was fast and direct. "You need to leave."

"What?" Confusion etched every inch of Eric's face.

"Sheriff Perry is having a little meeting in here with Harrison, Drake and me."

His eyes rounded. "Do I need to call the attorney?"

"No."

"What is it, then? Security breach? Or did they make an arrest?"

I glanced toward the door. Sheriff Perry had told me not to tell Eric, yet I really felt he should know. I stepped over to him until we stood face-to-face. "Eric," I whispered. "If I tell you something, do you promise not to act like you know?"

He nodded.

"I'm not a person of interest. I haven't been for a while."

He opened his mouth. I put a finger to his lips. "I just found out today. The good news is, I don't need the lawyer."

Eric sighed and smiled, then his brows drew together. "What's the bad news?"

I knew the sheepishness I felt inside showed on my face. "I ran across some vital information while doing my research."

"Courtney!" Eric's voice seemed magnified in the quiet room.

"Keep your voice down." Again, I glanced at the door.

Eric minded me. "I told you not to do that. You could be in danger," he whispered.

I didn't bother to tell him the sheriff was using me as bait. That was best saved for another day. Maybe when Sheriff Perry apprehended the murderer. Or maybe ten or twenty years from now.

"Time's up." Sheriff Perry burst through the door. "You," he pointed at Eric, "need to leave."

Eric pinned me with a look and walked past the group without a greeting. As he reached the door, Drake entered with Tabitha, who still wore her challenge-smeared clothes. Eric turned. Our eyes met. Even with distance between us, I read the emotion shining in his eyes.

"I'll be fine." I managed a smile.

"I hope so." Then he was gone. I stared at the closed door. A strange feeling kneaded my insides, like I'd lost my strength and support. Somehow, his presence always made me feel secure.

"Have a seat." Sheriff Perry's instruction and chair legs thumping on the floor drew my attention back to the other people in the room. Sheriff Perry had dragged chairs until three sat in a semicircle around one. He plopped down on the solitary chair. The rest of us sat down. Harrison and I chose an end chair, sandwiching Tabitha between us. In true Harrison fashion, he scooted his chair a little farther away from the two of us. Drake hovered near the counter, close enough to assist the sheriff if an altercation broke out. Far enough away to leave no doubt in anyone's mind who was in charge. "We have new information on both of you." He swung his hand between Harrison and Tabitha. "Miss Archer is here because she is the person who discovered the information."

"I object to this." Harrison leaned over and shot me a hateful look. "I want my attorney."

"Mr. Canfield, this conversation is to clear up some misinformation given by both of you during previous questioning. Information that may appear incriminating, so you both left it out." He stared at Harrison. "And you will cooperate, or Miss Archer may file assault charges."

Harrison's jaw dropped. He peered at me with disbelief. Did he really think I wouldn't tell?

Tabitha started to sniffle. "I'm sorry. I'm sorry. I didn't come on the show to cause trouble. I came to meet Harrison. Then Bernard Stone showed up too. I knew he'd cause trouble and ruin any chance I had to get to know or impress Harrison. I was so angry he made it on the show as a contestant when he was only here to research a story. I didn't out him because I wanted justice, after all these years, for my father. I thought if I kept insisting on background checks someone would discover Mick's," Tabitha air-quoted the name, "true identity. He didn't care about the baking challenge or what it might mean to other contestants who needed a win."

"Like you?"

She nodded and looked from Sheriff Perry to Harrison. "I want to work in one of your restaurants." A single tear ran down her face. "You owe me that for taking my father away from me." Her eyes went back to Sheriff Perry. "He should be arrested for murder. Not Bernard's, though, for my father's, from thirty years ago."

"What?" Harrison's question came out in a gasp.

"My mother is Connie Callahan."

Recognition, then realization washed over Harrison's face.

Clearing his throat, Sheriff Perry pulled his left leg over his right knee by his pant leg. He pinned Tabitha with a sympathetic expression. "I can see how you might feel that way because you don't know the truth. Mr. Canfield, I need you to tell us what Bernard planned to investigate, and don't say your finances, because a sheriff can see sealed testimony."

Harrison's posture changed from ramrod straight to spread-legged, with sagged shoulders. He rested his elbows on his thighs and leaned forward with his face in his hands. He stayed in that position for a minute or two, then he scrubbed his hands over his face and looked up at Sheriff Perry. "Bernard thought I was the cause of Dallas's death in our fraternity days and still to this day." Harrison sat up straight and looked at Tabitha. "I can assure you, I was not. Dallas wasn't my pledge. He roomed with my pledge. The night of the initiation antics, when I took my pledge to his room, I saw Dallas. He'd vomited on the floor, and well, remained there. I knew something was wrong. I ran for help, but the other frat boys laughed me off, including Bernard. When I tried to make an emergency phone call on the main floor phone, they stopped me. I ran back upstairs to see if I could get Dallas up and walking. His breath had become shallow."

Stopping, Harrison dropped his head. His shoulders and back heaved with his rapid breaths. I knew from experience, he was reliving the scene, and probably in slow motion. He started to speak again, and lifted his face. This time his eyes focused on the wall. "I used the upstairs phone and called the police. I went back to the bedroom and knelt beside Dallas. I held his hand and pleaded to God to keep him alive until help came. I was so relieved to hear the approaching sirens. I stood and ran to the window. When they came to a screeching halt, I went back to Dallas only to find . . ." Harrison swallowed hard and looked at Tabitha. "He'd stopped breathing."

Drake stepped into the group and handed Tabitha some of the soft paper towels from my set. Tears streamed down her cheeks.

I don't think Harrison even noticed. He continued to purge his past. "I ran downstairs. Bernard had answered the door. They weren't going to allow the police in, but I insisted. I thought it might not be too late to revive Dallas. But it was. After the body was removed, our fraternity brothers called a meeting and made us all swear to support our fellow brothers. No one was to tell the police anything incriminating. I went along at first."

Harrison turned to Tabitha. "I am ashamed of that. It is my biggest regret in life." He looked at the sheriff. "When the cause of death was reported as alcohol poisoning, and some of the other frat brothers laughed about Dallas not being able to hold his liquor, I knew it was time to tell the truth. So, I called my parents, got an attorney and bargained with the district attorney. My testimony was sealed. Two of the fraternity brothers were arrested, one being Bernard's cousin, and the frat house was closed. Bernard was here to expose this secret. It always troubled him how the police solved Dallas's murder without much evidence."

The room became silent except for Tabitha's sniffles. I swiped a tear from the corner of my own eye.

After a few minutes, Tabitha turned to Harrison. "I don't understand why you wanted to keep that hidden. You tried to save my father. You were the hero."

"No," Harrison said, the force of his conviction evident even though his voice cracked. "I wasn't. If I were the hero, Dallas wouldn't have died."

Tabitha reached a hand toward Harrison. "Thank you. Thank you for trying to help him."

Harrison's shaking hand grasped Tabitha's, and he nodded.

"Well," Sheriff Perry cut through the tense emotion. "That brings us to the matter at hand, because all of you were persons of interest in this case."

"What?" Tabitha's shocked tone showed she'd never considered the sheriff might suspect her angry reactions to Bernard as motive.

Sheriff Perry scowled. "You, Mrs. Miller, are no longer a person of interest, and neither is Miss Archer. You see—and this has been released to the public—Mr. Daily caught a plastic bag in the pond this morning when he went fishing. It was filled with rocks and the murderer's clothing. Men's clothing that would fall off a petite woman like both of you."

"But I didn't kill Bernard. I wanted him to go away, but not death. I've seen someone die . . ."

"Enough, Mr. Canfield. The clothing isn't your size either. All three of you can breathe a sigh of relief. You are no longer persons of interest in the murder of Bernard Stone."

"I don't understand." Harrison stood. "Why'd you make me tell them about the past?"

Sheriff Perry stood, tugged his waistband into place and said, "Secrets can lead a person to do strange things, out-of-character things. Telling the truth is always the best course of action. You probably won't admit it to me, but I'm guessing you feel better." He turned to Tabitha. "And your outlook on life probably seems brighter."

Tabitha smiled. "It does. I can't thank you enough. You either, Mr. Canfield."

"Call me Harrison." A wide smile lit up his face. "When the competition is over, you and I need to have a long conversation."

"I'd like that."

"You are all free to go."

Harrison and Tabitha beelined toward the door. Sheriff Perry followed.

"Aren't you leaving?" Drake smiled.

Would he stay and talk to me while I practiced using the pressure cooker? I flashed my most welcoming smile. "I have to stay and do a run-through of the show we're filming tomorrow night. Would you like to stay and join me?"

Drake flicked his wrist and checked his smartwatch. "Can't. Time for a shift change. I'll come to the actual taping, though."

Once Drake bid me goodbye, I pulled out the instructions for the pressure cooker. Should I call Eric back to the set? I lifted my phone and started a text. **I'm on the set and I need help . . .**

I stopped and laid down the phone. Between Harrison's emotional confession about the past and the sheriff disclosing the murderer's clothing evidence going public, I needed to relish the silence and put my thoughts in order, if only to formulate an apology to Harrison.

Sheriff Perry's words rested heavy on my heart. I hated to ruin my, and Eric's career, but I needed to tell my fans the truth. I couldn't go on pretending to be a farmer's daughter, and if I was sincere with my fans, I thought they'd stick by me. Shannon's assessment had been right too; in my heart, I loved the life and cooking style of the rural people I'd come to know. As of tomorrow, I was issuing an ultimatum to the network: Let me be honest, or I'll break our contract. I'd seen firsthand how secrets ruined lives.

Then there was the matter of Bernard's murderer. Was Sheriff Perry still using me as bait? Or had he figured out who the clothes belonged to? Perhaps through DNA tests? Who killed Bernard? I had no more names on my list to research, and I'd been so wrong about Harrison and Tabitha. I decided to leave it up to Sheriff Perry to figure out. Right now, I had something else to figure out. How to work a pressure cooker.

I gave my full attention to the kitchen appliance. I read the manual that came with the modern instant pot. Although the hour was late, I placed a pork chop into it, like I'd do tomorrow on the show, following the instructions for use and cook time. Once it was started, I took a deep breath to tackle the usage of the antiquated appliance sitting on the stove.

It didn't come with instructions, so I used my phone to search for instructions on how to use the pressure cooker. As I read through them, I recalled Eric covering everything the last time we met. Nowhere in the instructions had it said to be brave when releasing the steam when your food was cooked.

Adding water and a pork chop, I locked the lid into place and cranked up the burner heat. It didn't take long for it to hiss, sizzle and pop. An auditory reminder to me of the dangers of cooking. I appreciated the convenience the original cookware had provided housewives in its time, but I was glad to use the modern, quieter version. While the pressure cooker did its thing, I decided to sit down and go over my script.

I heard the click of a lock releasing and looked up expecting to see Eric walk through the door. It didn't open. Odd; I laid the script on the chair and started to walk toward the door when I heard one close on the other side of the collapsible wall. There was no outlet door to the hallway in that room.

Closing my eyes, I thought of the layout of the resort. My set was on the side of the security hallway. Perhaps Drake had come back for a conversation. Ready to greet him, my lips stretched into a wide smile. When the door opened, my heart and lips sagged.

Travis strolled into the room. Was he my assigned security detail today?

"Hi, Courtney."

My neck hairs bristled at his condescending and taunting tone. What was it with this guy? I doubt he'd even protect me. "Travis."

He stopped, placed his hands on his hips, and looked around the set. He snorted. "Farmer's daughter. Now that's a joke, isn't it?"

When he turned his eyes on me, I noticed they were dark with loathing.

"This whole filming-on-location has been a pain in our keister. Cost Drake a lot more money in man power." He shrugged. "Worked out for me, though."

I scowled. What exactly did that mean? He had someone else to harass?

"Anyway, I need you to come with me."

Travis stepped toward me. I realized he wasn't wearing a Nolan Security polo shirt. Something Drake's staff were never without when they were on duty. Dressed all in black, Travis wore a T-shirt, jeans and athletic shoes.

My heart rate quickened. Panic built in my chest like the steam in the hissing, popping pressure cooker on the stove. I couldn't let my feelings show. "Where?" I asked, managing to keep my tone light. I moved toward the kitchenette, where I'd left my phone.

"What are you doing?" Travis stepped toward me.

"I can't leave the stove on. We wouldn't want a fire." I didn't want to mention my phone, which was hidden under a pot holder beside the stovetop surface. I tried to keep my tone normal, conversational, until I could reach my phone. All I needed to do was send the text I'd started to Eric.

"Okay, then we're going," Travis's voice warned.

"Where, again?" Fear wobbled my knees. I grasped the countertop and deliberately took slow steps.

"Sheriff Perry wants to question you." Travis's lips pulled into a sinister smile.

I had to buy more time. I knew Sheriff Perry didn't want to talk to me. Travis didn't. It had been his day off, and judging by his appearance, it still was. He didn't know about the bag of clothing Skylar had found or that I wasn't a person of interest anymore.

"You don't have to wait for me." I used Shannon's gesture and waved a hand through the air. "I'll take care of things here and walk over to the interrogation room. You can tell Sheriff Perry that I'll be there in five minutes or so." I forced a smile.

"Sheriff Perry is at his office in town. We're going for a little ride." Travis's features turned to stone. "Get those pots turned off. That one is annoying." He reached into his pants pocket and pulled out latex gloves.

I willed my legs to move, putting me at the opposite end of the kitchen countertop. I wished we'd installed three instead of two on the set. The more space I had between us, the better I'd feel.

He snapped the gloves over his hands and started around the counter at a leisurely pace.

"What do you need the gloves for?" I failed at a conversational tone. Fear shook my voice.

"You ask too many questions."

I moved around the countertop. My phone was within reach. I grabbed it and tapped the screen. When it lit up, I hit my texting shortcut. There it was. My innocent text, which was now a call for help.

Travis made a primal noise, I hit Send and pocketed the phone, then, instead of turning off the burner, I cranked the nob to High.

"That was a stupid move." Travis hurried around the countertop and so did I. It was wide enough; he couldn't grab me.

The popping and hissing intensified the tension in the room.

"We'll be long gone by the time anyone comes. Vanished through the secret passage that comes out at the workshop." A cocky grin stretched across his lips.

My breath heaved. My legs weakened. "I thought we were going to see Sheriff Perry in town."

Travis's sinister laugh chilled me to the bone. "Yeah, okay, the car is waiting by the workshop." He shrugged and tried to fake me out by moving left, then running right around the counter. Hoping my weak legs wouldn't fail me, I ran too. Once again, I was on the side of the counter by the stovetop. The heat from the wide-open burner warmed my skin.

I felt the vibration of my phone against my leg. The noise from the pressure cooker drowned out the jingle. It had to be Eric. Was he coming? Had he called for help? I needed to buy time.

I recalled the night of Bernard's death. Travis had come to the set and been annoyed I was there. Then it hit me. I'd never heard the purr of the UTV motor. Not leaving or returning, yet the lights on the set had been turned off and I hadn't done it.

"You murdered Bernard." I stared hard into Travis's eyes.

Instead of remorse, a satisfied smile appeared on his face. "I did. He had it coming." Travis laughed like an evil villain in a movie. He kept moving his body in a fake-out fashion, yet never left the spot across the countertop from me.

"You made it easy with your pan of cobbler." Travis lifted his right hand in the air and stepped back from the counter. He assumed a tennis pose. "First, I served him some dessert to the top of his head." He whacked his empty hand through the air. "When that didn't take him down, I did a split step and a forward swing."

I knew Travis's mind was replaying the murder by his physical motions. I swallowed hard. "But why? Why did you murder Bernard?" Surely he had a reason, although I didn't recall seeing any interaction between the two men. Or was he just a natural-born killer?

"Because he ruined my life with his investigative reporting." Travis's lip trembled into a snarl. "I went from living the good life in a mansion complete with a swimming pool and tennis courts to barely surviving in run-down government housing."

Surprised, I sucked in an audible breath. Information from one of the web articles I'd read about Bernard jumped to the front of my thoughts. The Ponzi scheme. The mastermind's name was Taylor. Donald Taylor. The man Bernard took down in the Ponzi scheme was Travis's father.

"Aw, by your reaction, you ran across that bit of news in your nosy search, trying to pin the murder on Harrison."

My eyes widened. The pressure cooker bubbled and hissed, mirroring my growing panic. Drake must have confided in Travis. Why wouldn't he? Travis was his second in command.

"Here is what you didn't read about. After they put my dad in jail, my mother drank herself to death, leaving me and my two sisters to move in with our grandmother. A cruel woman who took out her public embarrassment about her son, and her loss in wealth, on her grandchildren."

"But . . ." I stopped myself. I wanted to explain in a rational way that his father took other people's life savings, leaving them with nothing too. Some of Donald Taylor's victims had succumbed to the same type of life his family had. I knew Travis wouldn't understand. He was bitter and filled with hatred. He was beyond reason. Eric had been right. By putting myself in the middle of this situation, I'd put myself in danger.

"You know too much. We are going. And so you know, not to town. Your final resting place will be at the bottom of the pond with all the evidence from both murders."

Should I tell him the clothes had been found? Would he flee in fear of being found out?

Travis's eyes darted around the kitchen until, finally, his gaze rested on something behind me.

I didn't have to turn around. I knew it was the rack holding my kitchen utensils, one of which was the cast-iron fry pan Drake had returned.

I stole a glance toward the door. Someone should be coming, yet I couldn't wait. I had to get away from Travis before I became his second victim. My peripheral vision caught movement. When I turned my attention back to Travis, he faked left, then moved right. I remained planted. I knew what I had to do. My recipe for survival had three ingredients: the spot where I stood, bravery and exact timing.

I watched him round the end of the counter. His fierce expression intent on my demise. As I expected, he reached for my cast-iron fry pan. "Kind of ironic, isn't it? Getting killed with your own pan."

Every cell in my body screamed "run," yet I knew his long legs would overtake me if I ran. I willed my feet to remain planted. My only chance was to stand my ground.

Eyes riveted now on Travis, I waited. He swung the fry pan like he was volleying a tennis ball across the net.

"Should I use the same tennis swings I did on Bernard? Or mix it up?" He sliced underhanded and let out a menacing laugh. "I'm pretty sure it will be all over when your head meets my back swing."

Travis lifted his hand, holding the pan across his chest, then lunged forward. I had only one chance. Sucking in a deep breath, I jerked out my shaky hand, hoping it didn't fail me. My fingers found the release valve and pulled hard, following the manufacturer's instructions I'd found online for a quick release of steam.

I screamed when the steam hit my hand. Not as loudly as Travis when his face took the full force of the overboiling-point heat emitting from the pressure cooker. I clasped my hand, skin burning, close to my chest. Through the cloud of steam, I saw Travis drop to his knees, and I ran toward the exit.

Halfway there, the door flew open. Sheriff Perry crossed the threshold on a run, gun drawn. He caught me in his gaze for a brief second. I saw a shadow of relief in his eyes before they broke contact and surveyed the area where Travis lay writhing on the floor, hands over his face.

"You okay?" he asked in passing.

I bit my lip, fighting back the tears from the intense stinging of the skin on my hand. "I will be. Travis killed Bernard. He confessed it all to me." I turned to watch him apprehend Travis. Between the pain from my burned skin and my fear-weakened knees, my body started to slump to the floor. I didn't have the energy to stop it. From behind, strong arms wrapped around me just as my legs gave out. I collapsed into their strength.

# CHAPTER TWENTY-ONE

I couldn't believe we'd made it to the final day of filming without further incidents. Once Sheriff Perry apprehended Travis, tension on the set had eased, and so did the delays in filming. Now, Skylar and I stood toes on tape, decked out in business casual attire. Wardrobe had dressed me in royal blue capris with a lovely white silk, short-sleeved blouse. My chunky necklace and earrings matched the capris, as did the kitten-heeled sandals.

For once, Skylar loved his on-screen clothing. His royal-blue polo brought out the deep blue of his eyes and brightened his skin, his words. Khaki trousers and leather loafers completed his ensemble. No campy costumes or jokes for this segment. It was all business for the talent, and all nerves for the remaining contestants.

Harrison, clad in a tan designer suit because business casual wasn't in his vocabulary, and Shannon, who wore a royal blue sheath with tan pumps, came from their judging chamber and joined us on their marks.

Skylar and I wouldn't know the winner until we read it from the monitor. Without much movement on our part, we could scan the remaining three contestants. All of the kitchenettes but three had been removed from the set. The remaining bakers had more counter space and room to move while meeting their challenges. Between the brutal, late-spring heat and humidity and the constant run of the ovens for the challenges, Barb, Otto and Anthony looked wilted and frazzled.

Sweaty-browed, they stood beside their counters with their last three dishes displayed on the end, a baked cheesecake, an egg custard and a soufflé. All prepared in some type of cast-iron cookware. I'd sampled all the food and knew who I hoped took home the top prize.

To build momentum and keep the surprise, Skylar and I didn't even know which one of us would send the third-place contestant out of the room and announce the winner. We would read whatever popped up beside our name.

Brenden clapped his hands. "The cameras are set. Ready?" He looked our way and received head nods. "Action."

Skylar's name appeared. I read silently while he read the words aloud. I kept a smile plastered on my face and fought back moisture from my eyes, even though I knew the cameraman had zoomed in on Skylar.

"Today, every one of you should be proud. You are a cut above the rest. You've met and exceeded the food challenges set forth. It is what brought you to this point. Although there can only be one top prize, you are all winners in our eyes." Skylar smiled. "And tummies."

The last part he'd ad-libbed. The contestants laughed. I found his hand and squeezed. He'd nailed what the moment called for to ease the tension.

He continued. "The judges had a tough choice to make. The baker leaving our kitchen is..." He flashed the camera and the contestant a bittersweet smile. "Barb."

"Oh," she cried and put her hands to her cheeks. Smiling, she said, "I can't believe I made it this far."

In an unprecedented move, Otto turned to Barb. "Dear woman, you truly have a natural talent in the kitchen. I am honored to have made it this far beside you."

I had to wonder if it was genuine after some of his earlier snide comments. He wrapped Barb in a tight hug, while Anthony patted her back. Once Otto released his embrace, Barb walked out of the kitchen with her beaming smile in place.

Harrison picked up where Skylar had stopped. "Then there were two. Otto, you are a trained chef, yet we found, over the course of a few weeks, maybe not in the use of cast iron. You got off to a rocky start, then found your groove with the cookware, creating a scrumptious pheasant à l'orange and perfect soufflé."

The cameraman caught Otto's satisfied smile.

"Anthony," Shannon took over. "You strutted your stuff through the course of the show. Although you never made baker of the day, all of your recipes turned

out well, with only a few technical errors. However, in
the last two rounds of the competition, you soared
above and beyond—especially with your desserts. While
others had trouble, you managed to turn out a dense,
luscious chocolate raspberry cheesecake, a pumpkin–
spiced egg custard—which I will be serving on my
Thanksgiving buffet—and a savory soufflé."

When Shannon paused, the camera caught Anthony's nervous smile. Anticipation kissed his features.

My name flashed up on the monitor. I smiled. "The
winner of the American Baking Battle is . . ." I
paused. Otto's chest puffed with pride, waiting for
his name to be announced. "Anthony."

Relief, then elation covered Anthony's face. Otto
reached out a hand of congratulations and Anthony
wrapped him in a hug. Otto managed to pat Anthony's back. Anthony released Otto, who stepped
back from the counter to give Anthony his well-
deserved time in the spotlight.

All the contestants, who had been brought back
for the finale, descended on Anthony from the side-
lines of the set. Brenden gave the order for our cameraman to cut.

Harrison was the first to move off his marker. "I
have a vehicle waiting to take us to the wrap party."
He moved his hand in an after-you fashion. Some of
the party would be filmed, so none of us had to return to wardrobe. As a group, we hurried through
the heavy wooden door and tumbled into the four-
seat UTV. Harrison drove. Skylar rode shotgun, while
Shannon and I relaxed in the back bench seat.

"I asked you all to ride with me for a reason." Harrison spoke over the purr of the engine. "I have hired Tabitha as a sous chef at my restaurant in Chicago. She really does have the talent to be a good chef someday. It's the least I can do for her and her mother. Had I only known about this . . ."

His voice trailed off. I'd been right all along about Harrison being an honest and moral man. Once Sheriff Perry arrested Travis, Harrison had relaxed. He enjoyed our teasing and we appreciated his keen sense of humor. The mornings spent in makeup and wardrobe turned into a good, and happy, start to our days. It turned out Harrison also loved animals and was very active in many animal organizations. He hadn't lied the day I bumped into him on the path to the pond. He had returned a turtle to its natural habitat, muddying his suit pants and shoes in the process.

Our discussion of Harrison hiring Tabitha made the trip, via an approved path, seem short. Harrison parked in a spot by Security, but we entered the castle resort through the coffee shop door. Once inside, we made our way to the same banquet room where our first meet and mingle had been held. It seemed like a lifetime ago and, sadly, for Bernard Stone, it had been.

In Travis's confession to Sheriff Perry, he'd said that he thought he'd put all the anger and resentment toward Bernard behind him until he saw him, posing as Mick, as a contestant on *The American Baking Battle*, and it all came rushing back. He'd asked Bernard to meet him on the set of the show that night to confront him and demand an apology. When Bernard denied being, well, himself, Travis had presented an old business card of Bernard's with his picture. Although younger, there was no mistaking the man on the card was Bernard. Bernard became angry, grabbed the card, tore it half and tossed it in the air, then told Travis he was going to call Drake and have Travis removed from his job. Travis snapped, thinking Bernard was going to ruin his second chance at a good life. He'd picked up the pan of cobbler and started swinging. Once Bernard was dead, Travis had picked up the business card with Bernard's picture. He stated he never found the other half, and no one ever would. Travis had confessed, and I'd disposed of the half of the card I'd found.

I hadn't seen Sheriff Perry since the day he'd called us together and told us Travis had made a formal confession, which included Travis being the leak to the press in hopes the show would be shut down due to bad press and Bernard's death would become an unsolved murder. For a brief second, I wondered if Sheriff Perry would join the party. My eyes roved the room, which showed no sign of the law.

"Let's grab a table." Shannon pulled on my arm and brought my thoughts back to the present.

"Okay. I don't want to stand at the cocktail tables, though. My shoes are pinching."

"Mine too."

Shannon and I made our way across the room, where the staff had staged several tables that would seat a party of four. I faced the door and watched as crew and contestants filed through. We'd barely taken a load off when a waiter came around with a tray of champagne.

We both snagged a flute.

"To us!" Shannon lifted her glass.

I followed suit. "To our new friendship and business venture."

Our glasses tinkled and we took a sip of bubbly amber liquid.

Oh my gravy! I knew my eyes widened. There, framed in the doorway, peering into the room, was Eric. I waved him over.

Dressed in a plaid, button-up shirt, distressed jeans and boots, I saw the farm boy in him. And I liked it. Maybe Shannon was right, I was a country girl wrapped in city packaging. My pattering heart sent a flush to my cheeks as I watched him cross the room. This had been my reaction since the day Travis tried to attack me and I fell into Eric's arms. His strong arms. Although on the surface, it seemed nothing had changed in our relationship, inside, I had shifted. I saw Eric as more than my friend and producer. He was the man I counted on. The man who had my back in any situation that befell me, whether accidental, like an eavesdropped conversation, or intentional, like getting involved in a murder investigation.

Of course, after my hand had been bandaged from the steam burn and I'd been declared okay, Eric had chided me once again for not listening to him and sticking my nose where it shouldn't be. I knew it was out of concern, and I was glad to take my scolding.

Just before Eric arrived at our table, a waiter offered him a glass of bubbly. "Ladies." Eric held his flute high.

Before he could make his toast, Brenden entered the room, clapping. "Your attention, I'd like your attention." He found a vacant chair and climbed up to stand over the crowd. "I have an announcement to make. Our show dailies, despite the rough start, or maybe in spite of the rough start, because viewers thrive on drama, is receiving positive feedback. We have been offered another run at *The American Baking Battle.* This one will be a wedding-themed show."

Kinzy, obviously still on the job, rushed over to Brenden with a champagne flute. He raised it and said, "To many more episodes of *The American Baking Battle.* I couldn't do it without you! Cheers!"

Rounds of "Hear, hear"s were hollered, then the noise died down to a manageable level.

"Well," Eric took the empty seat beside me, "anyone up for another toast?"

We nodded and lifted our glasses.

Eric cleared his throat. "To telling the truth and starting new ventures."

"What?" I set my glass on the table. "Does this mean . . . ?"

"Yes, it does." Eric smiled.

Shannon squealed. "Y'all, I'm so excited."

"About what?" Drake's deep voice came from behind me. He walked around the table and stood by an empty chair directly across from me.

"Courtney and I are developing a new cooking show for Eric to pitch to the network." Shannon waved her hand through the air. "Isn't that wonderful?"

"Wow." Drake rested his dark brown eyes, smoldering with interest, on me. "You'll be busy with three shows. How will you manage a social life? I believe you owe . . ."

"Drake, there you are." Kinzy pulled up beside him. "Brenden needs to speak with you."

For a moment, Drake held my gaze. The desire in his eyes sent a current of heat through me that warmed my skin.

Eric huffed.

I tried to control the emotion Drake's presence sparked in me. I'd promised him a dinner date before my eyes were opened to Eric's possible romantic interest in me. I planned to keep the date with Drake while I waited for Eric to make a move.

"Duty calls. I'll see you all next season, if not before." Drake winked my way, turned and followed Kinzy to the cocktail table, where Brenden stood.

"Where were we?" Shannon cut through the awkward silence left in Drake's wake.

"Talking about the future." I gave my full attention to Eric and hoped my eyes reflected my gratitude and interest. "The network agreed to let me confess my true background?"

He nodded.

All smiles, we clicked our flutes.

After taking a sip, Eric said, "The premiere episode of next season's *Cooking with the Farmer's Daughter* will start with your explanation. They are gearing up for a media frenzy. There is bad news, though. The company set to make your line of knives wants to wait until you have a program to showcase them."

The last news dampened some of my excitement, although from a business standpoint, it made sense, especially if the fallout from my admission tanked my ratings and popularity with viewers.

Shannon reached over and squeezed my hand. "Don't worry. With our individual shows' successes and the pick-up of another *American Baking Battle* competition, I'm sure the network will love our idea for a new show."

"Have you decided on a name and a premise?" Eric swallowed the last bit of his champagne.

"We have. You'll love it." Shannon beamed.

Eric looked to me.

"*City and Country Cooks.* We will prepare the same recipe with a twist on how it would work at an elegant dinner party or on a workday supper table."

Leaning back, Eric crossed his arms over his chest and drew his brows until a deep divot creased the skin above his nose; then his features relaxed. "I can sell that concept."

Shannon's and my cheers of excitement drew the attention of a waiter, who offered us each another flute of champagne that bubbled like the hope inside me.

Once we all held our fresh drinks, I tipped mine. Shannon and Eric followed suit and waited for my toast.

I smiled and looked at Shannon, who'd turned into a good friend in a short amount of time and now was a possible business partner. My eyes darted to Eric, an old friend with a new shine. Who knew what the future would bring? Right now, in this minute, I'd guess success and happiness. I clinked my glass to theirs. "To new beginnings."

# Grab These Cozy Mysteries
from
# Kensington Books